What can the Dowager L
finds herself in drastically reduced circumstances following the death of her husband? One solution is to find eligible husbands for both her daughters.

Verity, the elder strong-willed one, boldly suggests that Leo, Earl of Wonersh, the man who had once jilted her, would make an ideal husband for her younger sister, Eustacia.

But both the Earl and Eustacia have other partners in mind . . .

And can Verity herself emerge unscathed when her attempts to arrange other people's lives result in escapades which threaten to taint them all with the whiff of scandal?

By the same author in Masquerade:

JOANNA
SET TO PARTNERS
HEIR PRESUMPTIVE
THE ELUSIVE MARRIAGE
LYSANDER'S LADY
BRIDAL PATH

MILLS & BOON LIMITED
London · Sydney · Toronto

First published in Great Britain 1983
by Mills & Boon Limited, 15–16 Brook's Mews,
London W1A 1DR

ISBN 0 263 74273 3

Set in 10 on 10½ pt Times Roman
04/0583

Photoset by Rowland Phototypesetting Limited
Bury St Edmunds, Suffolk
Made and printed in Great Britain by
Cox & Wyman Limited, Reading

For Daphne Marshall,
the girls and, of course,
Mike.

CHAPTER ONE

THE removal of the Middleton household to their present residence in Cheltenham's Royal Crescent had never, in the time that had since elapsed, ceased to be a source of lamentation to the Dowager Lady Middleton.

While in no way to be compared with the spacious antiquity of Shurdington Hall, it had to be confessed that the lesser dimensions of the new house had considerable advantages over the old, not the least being the convenience of heating and lighting rooms of a reasonable size rather than shivering in vast dimly-illuminated chambers, with draughts whistling through from every point of the compass. So practical a consideration, however, could not be expected to appeal to her ladyship, reminding her as it did of her reduced circumstances, and it had taken the combined efforts of her exasperated family, friends and lawyers finally to convince her that such drastic retrenchment was necessary.

Seated in her drawing-room one particularly bright spring morning a few months after this momentous event, she was about to utter one of the faintly deprecating remarks that were all she permitted herself by way of protest against her changed situation when her elder daughter forestalled her by saying in the most off-hand manner imaginable, 'I understand Wonersh is expected back in England shortly.'

The Dowager turned quite pale and blinked as if she could not believe her ears. 'W—Wonersh? Verity, you cannot mean—no, no to be sure you cannot!'

'Why should I not?' Miss Middleton sounded a trifle amused at her parent's confusion. 'Because he once paid his addresses to me but thought better of the notion is no reason why he should not make Eustacia a perfectly conformable husband. No, I am not being callous or indifferent, I am merely trying to judge of my sister's situation with perfect impartiality. She is a sweetly pretty child but she is also inconstant and an outrageous flirt. I consider it to be of the first importance that she should be wed without delay to a gentleman who is capable of restraining her and showing her how she should go on.'

'But—but, Verity, Wonersh went off to Europe with that—that creature and—'

'Left her before too long, I understand, in favour of a French *belle-amie*,' nodded Miss Middleton, unperturbed.

'But—but, Verity!' wailed her ladyship, who was aware that she was repeating herself but was helpless to prevent it. 'He *jilted* you!'

'Not noticeably, mama. If you recall, the engagement was never announced because of dear papa's sudden illness so that, whatever the beau monde might have suspected, no one could know for certain how far things were in a way to be settled.'

The Dowager was a self-effacing faded lady, who still bore traces of considerable beauty but whose aspect generally was that of one who lived in constant expectation of receiving a sharp set-down from one or other of her strong-willed family. Now her soft brown eyes, like to those of a pleading spaniel, filled with ready tears.

'Yes, indeed, I had forgotten, but it was all such a harrowing time.'

'And is more than three years past.' Miss Middleton had no mind to be deflected from her purpose by lachrymose reminiscence. 'I daresay Wonersh has sown his wild oats by now and is prepared to settle down. He is an only son and there is the succession to be thought on.'

Lady Middleton dabbed at her tears with an ineffectual scrap of lace-edged lawn. 'He must be quite thirty now,' she supposed vaguely.

'Twenty-nine,' corrected her daughter. 'Nor will a wealthy wife be a prime object with him. The Percivals were never short of a penny.'

'But would not such a union be excessively distasteful to you?' asked her mother in simple wonderment. 'I mean—your younger sister to wed a gentleman who —who once—'

'So long as it is not excessively distasteful to Eustacia, mama, I shall be well content. He is a much better prospect than Nicholas Chisholm whom I have known since we were both in leading-reins. He was an odious little wretch then and he is no better now—a dandy, if you please. Eustacia is an uncommonly taking girl, and we should surely do better for her than a husband who thinks more of the cut of his coat than of the lady he is to marry?'

The Dowager rolled an apprehensive eye and waved her vinaigrette in feeble protest.

'But—but Godfrey and Annabelle would be so put out! They have quite set their hearts upon the match.'

Miss Middleton emitted what, in a less ladylike young woman, might have been described as a snort.

'No doubt it would greatly enlarge their consequence —an Earl is flying vastly higher than a prospective Viscount,' she said, dismissing the ambitions of her brother and his wife with withering contempt. 'Annabelle has become so top-lofty of late that I am out of all patience with her—nor, would I remind you, is it at all certain that Nicholas will succeed to the title. He is the heir for just so long as his uncle does not marry and produce a son.'

'Very true,' allowed her mother unhappily. 'But it must be remembered that Eustacia's portion will not be large and marriage to Nicholas, even should he not succeed to the title, is—well, rather more than might be hoped for.'

'My dear mama!' Miss Middleton shook her head with ill-concealed impatience. 'That has nothing to say to anything.'

'Oh, dear!' sighed the Dowager, giving up the unequal struggle. 'If only Annabelle was not in expectation of a Happy Event what a wonderful come-out she would have given Eustacia! But I must not be saying that, think what joy it will bring us to have a dear little baby in the family once more!'

Privately, Miss Middleton doubted that the prospect of her becoming an aunt was a cause for rejoicing, and could only be grateful that young Lady Middleton would not be pushing her sister off since the two could not be in the same room for minutes together without coming to cuffs. She did not, however, ravage her mama's sensibilities by expressing any such opinion but stood, as if lost in meditation, while the Dowager, eyeing her a little anxiously, felt a deep sense of unease, quite foreign to her gentle nature.

Because she was truly attached to her elder daughter her thoughts were centred less upon pleasing her son and his wife than upon any possible hurt or embarrassment to Verity. At the time of the disrupted engagement, her attention had been wholly taken up by her husband's illness, and it was not until some time after when, most unexpectedly, he had relinquished his hold on life just as the doctors were hailing his complete recovery, that her daughter had informed her she was not to be the next Countess of Wonersh.

Since Verity appeared to accept the whole unhappy matter without any outward show of distress, her mother readily concluded that her affections had not been seriously engaged. There were times, however, since then when she had found herself wondering if she had not been at fault in this comfortable assumption. Though lacking the spirited vivacity of her younger sister, Verity's gravely courteous manner and rare sweet smile were all of a piece with her classically regular features and elegant form. It was unfortunate that she should be fair, since dark locks were all the go, but her pale gold hair, wreathed becomingly about her small head, admirably set off her exquisite complexion. She was indisputably a beauty and, despite her lack of fortune, there had been several perfectly eligible gentlemen since Wonersh's defection who had wished to offer for her, but she would have none of them, declaring herself to be well content with her lot and very happy to remain with her mama. Further speculation on her ladyship's part as to the state of her daughter's affections was put an end to by the flinging open of the door and Eustacia's eruption into the room.

The younger Miss Middleton was, in contrast to her sister, small, dark, and impulsive. Her intensely blue eyes sparkled from under her deep-brimmed bonnet with a brilliance that was absent from Verity's steady grey-eyed gaze; her smile was warm and infectious, revealing even white teeth and deep dimples in either cheek. Her trim figure, modishly attired in jacket and petticoat with just the hint of a bustle, might be deemed by the over-censorious to be a shade on the plump side, but that could be put down to puppy-fat and need not give rise to immediate concern. In short, she resembled nothing so much as a cuddlesome kitten and was very well aware of it, but there was little that was kittenish about her understanding which was as acute as her sister's, giving her mama cause to lament that her girls had inherited their father's brains while her only son had the misfortune to take after her.

'Mama! Verity! I declare it to be the most diverting thing imaginable! Mr King is to issue invitations for a Grand Ball at the Assembly Rooms in July to mark the second anniversary of their opening! It is rumoured that the Duke himself may grace the event! I shall be past my eighteenth birthday—I may attend, may I not, mama?' Her ladyship beamed fondly upon her youngest child and was about to declare that nothing short of a catastrophe should prevent the young lady from attaining so desirable an object, but Eustacia hurried on without waiting for a reply. 'And Verity, for your especial pleasure, I am credibly informed that Mr Kean and a most talented company will celebrate the occasion by a performance at the Theatre Royal. Now, what have you to say to that?'

Miss Middleton, who had had the felicity of seeing Mr Kean display his talent some years previously at Drury Lane, was not visibly impressed by this intelligence. 'A posturing mountebank in a fur hat,' she remarked, thus disposing of London's monarch of the stage. 'But where did you learn all this, my dear? Surely not at the circulating library?'

'Oh, no.' Eustacia plumped down on the sofa beside her mother and peeled off her short Limerick gloves. 'I met Mr Warburton on my return and he escorted me home. He informs me that there is every hope that the new gas lamps will be installed all over the town in good time for the event—which will most likely be the case,' she added complacently, 'if it lies in his power to press for it.'

Over her head the Dowager's eyes met those of her elder daughter in anguished appeal, to which she received immediate response.

'Eustacia, my love,' expostulated Miss Middleton, all sisterly concern, 'unless I mistake the matter Mr Warburton is showing you marked attention. He has not, I believe, asked mama for permission to pay his addresses?'

Eustacia's soft mouth took on a mutinous pout. 'Well, I think it very likely he is going to!' she announced trenchantly. 'I told him that nothing would induce me to marry Nicholas Chisholm!'

'You—you what?' gasped her horrified mama.

'Everyone is taking it for granted that I shall jump at the chance of a title,' explained her youngest-born kindly. 'But, after all, it may never happen and Nicholas is such a quiz. The Warburtons are so delightfully rich, too,' she elaborated, darting a wary glance at her sister who had deserted her stance near the window and had moved to the fire, one hand resting on the mantelshelf, an expression of cold disdain on her face.

'The source of the Warburton fortune causes you no misgivings?'

'If by that you mean do I care a pin that grandfather Warburton was a coach-builder—well, I don't!' retorted Eustacia defiantly. 'And Theodore is not a—a man-milliner like Nicholas!'

'Theodore!' shrieked the Dowager faintly, finding her vinaigrette to be unequal to the situation and allowing it to fall to the floor. Miss Middleton was swift to retrieve it and restore it to her mother's nerveless hand.

'So unfortunate that you would be obliged to lead a very different sort of life did you contract such an alliance,' she sighed, with a nice show of regret.

Her sister thought this over. 'What do you mean—lead a very different sort of life?' she demanded to know.

'It may have escaped your notice that Mr Warburton's mother lives very retired,' enlarged Miss Middleton delicately.

'What of it? So does Mama live very retired. It is expected of widowed ladies.'

'The cases are totally dissimilar. Mama is obliged to observe economies, Mrs Warburton has no such need.'

'Mr Warburton presented me to his mother last week in the Pump Room at Montpellier,' countered Eustacia, on her mettle. 'I found her to be most agreeable, her dress very much *á la mode*, and her manner easy and unaffected.'

'Unhappily, the same could not have been said of her husband.' A gentle cough from her ladyship caused Miss Middleton to qualify this statement. 'Not, I understand, that he was not at all times perfectly genteel, but he had been brought up in his father's establishment and—' The slightest of shrugs completed her meaning. Eustacia's eyes narrowed.

'He still smelled of the stables? Is that what you would say? There are many nobly-born gentlemen who do that and no one thinks the worse of them for it! Why have you taken Mr Warburton in such aversion, Verity?'

'I cannot recall having expressed any sentiments whatsoever concerning him. I am only pointing out that his mother is not generally received.' Clearly Miss Middleton, having had her say, considered the subject to be closed, but her sister continued to pursue it with determination.

'When I suggested that you might put his name forward to Colonel Berkeley for membership of the Hunt, you did nothing about it.'

Miss Middleton declined to be drawn on that point. 'The season is over now, there is nothing to be done before the autumn.'

'I should have supposed,' murmured Eustacia with gentle malice, 'that, knowing my dislike of riding to hounds, it would have gratified you to see him thundering in pursuit of an unlucky fox rather than of your sister. Though it is a widely-held belief that foxes enjoy the chase,' she added musingly.

'And certainly one difficult to disprove since there are few people on regular speaking terms with foxes.'

The asperity of the reply did not daunt Eustacia. 'On the occasion of Godfrey and Annabelle's last visit, when we were making up a party for the theatre, you would not consider Mr Warburton either,' she persisted.

'My dear, you know how high in the instep Annabelle has become—I must have heard you remark upon it a dozen times. She would know very well who was his grandfather and would most likely have taken offence.'

Eustacia regarded her sister with smouldering resentment. 'Not only Annabelle has become very high in the instep!' she snapped. 'I suppose you are set upon my marrying Nicholas?'

'Not in the least,' returned Miss Middleton, quite unruffled. 'I am persuaded you would not deal at all well together.' She leaned forward to pat the girl's flushed cheek. 'Don't let us be at outs, my love. I have in mind that very soon we ought to give a small dress party to mark your come-out. We will talk of that later, but now I must be away if I am to have my ride this morning. You will accompany mama to the Pump Room in my stead?'

Upon receiving her sister's assent, she hastened from the room, humming a little tune under her breath. The door had scarcely closed behind her than Eustacia sprang to her feet and began to pace the floor.

'What I do not understand, mama, is why we all have to bow to Verity's judgment!' she burst out, her voice shaking with indignation.

'Well, she is so—so sensible, and she does have your best interests at heart,' the Dowager assured her. 'No one could be more concerned for you to make the best possible alliance.'

'Fiddle!' retorted Eustacia quite rudely, causing her long-suffering parent to have recourse once more to her smelling-salts. 'She would be better employed in arranging an alliance for herself! Mama, Verity is close on twenty-four! The next thing we know she will be an ape-leader, wearing a cap upon her head!'

Lady Middleton hastily straightened the dainty confection of lace and ribbon that had slipped somewhat askew on her greying hair, and endeavoured unsuccessfully to assume a reproving air.

'That is no way to be speaking of your elder sister,' she began, but her daughter was not taken in by this assumption of severity.

'Mama, why has Verity not married? She has had two seasons in London but all she gained was a reputation for being mighty hard to please. Is she, do you suppose, suffering from an Unrequited Passion?'

Her ladyship felt positively faint. Only the sure knowledge that such a course would serve no good purpose checked her from disclosing her own doubts on the subject. Eustacia could have no suspicion of the Wonersh affair, it had happened when she was still in the schoolroom and, in any event, as Verity herself had said, there was nothing to know. His lordship had paid Miss Middleton marked attention for a time but, at the first opportunity offered by an uneasy peace, he had flitted off to France to pursue a life of dalliance until the escape of the Corsican Ogre had plunged Europe back into war.

Involuntarily, she sighed. She had ever had a soft spot for dashing young bucks, and she had felt that Wonersh might have been just the one to counterbalance Verity's cool reasonableness. Becoming sharply aware that Eustacia was eyeing her in interested expectation of a reply, she plunged into speech.

'To be unwed at twenty-four is not to be quite at one's last prayers, dear child. I allow that after two seasons —well, your sister was never precisely a Toast, that would not have done for her at all, but her style was much admired, and I had high hopes—'

'High hopes of *who*, mama?' asked Eustacia with ungrammatical emphasis. Feeling herself to be driven into a corner, the Dowager edged away from the particular to the general.

'Oh, there were several very eligible gentlemen,' she declared airily, 'but—why it should be, I am sure I don't know—Verity found something to displease her in each one.'

'Perhaps she did not wish to be pleased.'

This shrewd summing-up of a situation that she had long suspected might exist had her ladyship at a stand, and she decided that it was time and enough the conversation took another turn.

'Great Heavens, it is close on eleven o'clock! I think I fancy the Cambray Spa this morning—how fortunate we are to have so diverse a choice of waters to hand, and another Pump Room building at Sherborne! Did I hear you say that it was likely the dear Duke would visit Cheltenham in July? Will he lodge with Colonel Riddell again, do you suppose? I must confess I think this notion of Verity's that we should hold a dress party to be a capital one, though how we are to fit everyone into these rooms, I am sure I don't know.'

Talking away volubly as she collected together her many scarves, her spectacles, her reticule and her vinaigrette, she managed to manoeuvre herself out of the room without having to contend with any more questions from her daughter. That needle-witted young lady, however, had learned enough to arouse her interest and her mama's peace of mind would have received a further jolt had she guessed at the speculation that was rife in Eustacia's lively imagination.

CHAPTER TWO

THE Earl of Wonersh wiped his blade carefully upon a convenient tussock of grass and replaced it in its scabbard.

'Gad, I did not think to blood my sword so soon upon returning to England,' he remarked in a considering way, 'and within a few miles of Cheltenham, too. D'you think they were footpads of the ordinary sort, Roger?'

His companion, who had been bending over the recumbent figure lying by the side of the road, straightened up and listened for a moment to the diminishing sound of retreating hoof-beats before replying.

'There was no demand to hand over our valuables or rolls of soft,' he said slowly.

'And why attack a light phaeton instead of a fat laden travelling chaise? And what do we do with this fellow? Is he dead?'

'Aye.' Mr Roger Percival resumed his perusal of the body. 'Nor, to judge from his appearance, will we learn much from inspecting his person.' His hands were busy as he spoke. 'Plainly dressed, nothing in his pockets of any value.'

'But a couple of barkers of the best sort,' pointed out the Earl, dropping to one knee beside him and picking up one of the pistols which lay by its late owner's side. 'This pair is by Boutet, I should guess, blue-barrelled with square-cut butts. Not to be looked for in the possession of a common footpad.'

'Doubtless acquired from some previous victim.'

Wonersh laughed shortly. 'I'll keep 'em, mine are less handsome.'

'They have a distinctive air,' allowed Mr Percival, getting to his feet and dusting off the knees of his buckskin breeches.

'And could lead me to a knowledge of their owner,' mused his lordship, nor did he observe the sharp glance his companion cast him. 'Leave him to lie there, Roger. We can report having seen the body when we pass through Cheltenham.'

'But not how he met his end?'

'No, there may be more to this than is at first apparent.' Wonersh laughed again as he rose, but there was a steely ring to the laughter. 'Though I believed I had settled that business before I left the Continent.'

'An *affair du coeur*?' enquired his cousin idly, but there was nothing idle about the look he directed at the Earl.

'You could call it that, I suppose, though not of my making.' Wonersh mounted nimbly into the waiting phaeton. 'Come, let us be on our way. I want to see Beauregard before nightfall.'

Mr Percival followed him without further comment, but the speculative gleam in his eye showed that his curiosity was unappeased. He was a well-set-up enough gentleman in his middle thirties, and dressed with the utmost propriety, but there was a singular lack of distinction about him as if he was perfectly content to blend into his surroundings and observe rather than be observed. In any event, his appearance was quite shone down by the tall figure of the Earl.

Though not generally held to be handsome, Leonard Mortimer Fitzroy Percival, fourth Earl of Wonersh, made up for his lack of regular good looks by an elegance of form and charm of address that was difficult to fault. Not, of course, that anyone was likely to attempt any such criticism for, despite his easy condescension, that indolent manner concealed a lively intelligence, nor did his lordship suffer the pretensions of less exalted persons with equanimity. His hair, as tawny as that of the beast for which he was named, curled crisply about his head. He was also the fortunate possessor of a remarkably winning smile, while his sleepy grey-green eyes could sparkle with animation when their owner's interest was engaged. These attributes apart, his features were unremarkable and betrayed as little of the man they masked as did his superbly-cut coats reveal the latent power of his compact frame.

His lordship appeared to be lost in his thoughts until Cheltenham was reached, nor did he leave the phaeton when Mr Percival stepped down briefly to report the finding of a cadaver on the London Road. On his return he found the Earl in conversation with a horsey-looking individual of indeterminate years who stepped back smartly, touching his hat, as Wonersh gave his pair the office to start.

'Parker. Used to be Sir Gervase Middleton's groom,' he offered in explanation to his cousin. 'In need of employment at the moment, the Middletons having, apparently, no further use for him.'

'Short of the ready, more likely.' Mr Percival looked knowing. 'Her ladyship has left the Hall, y'know, and moved into Cheltenham.'

'Very sensible of her. Devilish draughty place, as I recall.' There was a pause while the Earl manoeuvred the phateon out of the High Street and along the turnpike road to Gloucester. 'Does Miss Middleton still reside with her mother?' From his manner it might be supposed that the subject was one of supreme indifference to his lordship.

'Yes, both daughters are at home.'

'Both? Oh, there was a schoolroom chit, wasn't there?'

Mr Percival smiled waggishly. 'She'd not thank you

for that! She's by way of being a beauty, or will be when the curves subside a trifle.'

'Plump, is she?' mused the Earl. 'And Verity as slender as a wand—or is she not now?'

'In the considered opinion of many well-qualified judges,' pronounced Mr Percival, 'Miss Middleton is the finest-looking woman in Cheltenham and for many miles around.' Wonersh darted him a searching glance.

'But still unattached?'

'Aye, but not from lack of suitors, if rumour is to be believed. Could it be that your—ah, cavalier treatment of her has given her an aversion towards all our sex?'

The Earl's firm mouth hardened to a straight line. 'Be very sure, Roger, that if I wish for your animadversions upon my conduct I will ask for them,' he said pleasantly enough, but his companion made haste to assure him that nothing could have been further from his thoughts, and for the remainder of the journey little was said between the two gentlemen.

Beauregard, the family seat of the Percival family for generations before they were ennobled by a grateful monarch, was placed at no great distance from the town of Cheltenham. Successive heirs had added wings, thrown up towers, pulled down curtain-walls, and thereafter made commendable efforts to modernise the whole rambling fifteenth-century structure with varying degrees of success. At heart, Beauregard remained much as it had always been, a medieval stronghold that paid mere lip-service to the embellishments of a later age.

As he entered the great hall, Wonersh looked about him with a faint sigh of relief. Here, at least, nothing had changed. The spread of French tapestries upon the stark stone walls, the dim light filtering through the narrow windows, the suits of armour and weapons of war to be seen on every hand might not, to one less accustomed to such a setting, give an impression of homeliness, but for him they had all the comfort of familiarity. The servants, too, were greeting him with the ease of old retainers who had known him since he was breeched—indeed, to a casual observer, it might seem that he had stepped in after a brief visit to the Metropolis rather than returning to the place after an absence of more than three years.

'I have put your lordship in your old room.' Threadgold, his butler, gave his driving coat an admonishing shake as if requiring it to offer a satisfactory explanation for having left his care for so long a time. 'Miss Deborah is bent upon refurbishing his late lordship's apartments for your occupation.'

Wonersh's eyes gleamed amusement. 'And if I know my dear sister, I may not set foot in them until all is completed to her satisfaction.'

'Just so, my lord,' agreed Threadgold and was about to go into further detail when he was cut short by an imperious female voice ringing out from the head of the great staircase.

'Ah, there you are, Leo! A trifle sooner than I had looked for, to be sure, but nonetheless welcome for that.'

The speaker was a regal-looking lady past her first youth, who came sweeping down the stairs with a lively smile transforming her rather homely countenance. Daughter to the Earl's stepmother by an earlier marriage, the Honourable Deborah Liddell had, upon the death of her parent, taken over the duties of chatelaine to Beauregard as of right. This task she carried out with almost fanatical devotion and, being a lady of high principles and undoubted ability, neither the late Earl nor his son had felt the least uneasiness at placing their venerable home in her care.

'My dear Deb! What felicity to see you again—and in such looks!'

Her shrewd blue eyes twinkled at him as he bent to kiss her cheek. 'Spanish coin, Leo! My looks were never my greatest asset, as well you know! Roger!' She called over the Earl's shoulder to Mr Percival who stood contemplating this touching reunion with a quizzical air. 'There is an urgent message from Upper Croft, some flooding damage that Barton seemed to think worthy of your immediate attention.' Dismissing Mr Percival with a wave of the hand, she led the way into the morning-room and established herself in a deep-seated armchair by the fire from which vantage point she studied the Earl's appearance in detail. 'Hmm. You've gained in weight—no bad thing, though you will never be of full habit. Does your wound still trouble you?'

Wonersh, well-accustomed to her abrupt manner, smiled and busied himself with the varied assortment of decanters set out upon a side-table.

'Only with the changing weather. Do you still enjoy a glass of port—but I need not ask!'

'Indeed you need not!' she confirmed. 'It is the one extravagance I forgave your father, for his taste in wine was impeccable.'

'Then it is hardly to be called an extravagance,' he objected. 'You have too parsimonious a nature, Deb!' She chuckled.

'Maybe it is as well for you that I have.'

Still smiling, he set her glass beside her. 'What am I to infer from that, if you please?'

'That your father had become lax in the handling of his affairs and, but for Hazlett, our lawyer, and I, could well have reduced your inheritance.'

'Am I all to pieces, then?' enquired the Earl, sipping his port appreciatively and coming to seat himself opposite her.

'Of course not! You're as full of juice as a ripe medlar!' she assured him. 'And I can tell you that all the mamas with daughters of marriageable age are sharpening their claws in readiness to pounce when you appear upon the social scene!'

'In spite of my presumed predilection for straw damsels and their like?' murmured his lordship in a very self-deprecating way.

'Pooh!' Miss Liddell dismissed this objection as being of no account. 'Money speaks louder than morals and consequence before either. I saw Verity Middleton t'other day,' she added. 'Thought it only right to tell her that you were coming home before some other meddling busybody did. She said her mama would be happy for you to leave your card.'

'What?' The Earl stared at her over the rim of his glass.

'No accounting for it, is there?' she agreed. 'After the shabby way you behaved shouldn't have thought she would ever went to set eyes on you again. Why did you do that, Leo? Not at all in your style, I'd say.'

His lordship rose and, setting down his glass, stood looking into the fire, his hands thrust deep into his pockets.

'I had not intended her any discourtesy.' He spoke with constraint. 'Nor were the circumstances precisely what you suppose, but Bonaparte's escape from Elba quite put paid to any hopes of my returning to explain my behaviour.'

'Was there an explanation?' she asked.

'Yes,' he said shortly, 'but it doesn't signify now. I wrote to Verity—Miss Middleton. My letters were returned to me unopened. Being thus condemned without a chance to speak in my own defence makes it all the more strange that now she should be willing to receive me.'

'She's not at her last prayers, so you need not be thinking *that*,' Miss Liddell made haste to assure him.

'I would never have entertained such a notion,' he declared with such depth of feeling that she nodded as if confirmed in her opinion.

'Always suspected you were nutty on her,' she asserted cheerfully. 'Which made it the more remarkable when you went off with that woman. Who was she, Leo?'

The Earl hesitated, as if being obliged to come to a decision. 'Yes,' he said slowly, 'perhaps it is best you do know about it, but keep it to yourself, if you please, Deb. Briefly, one of our father's peccadilloes came home to roost—do peccadilloes roost? What an odd appearance they must give! Anyway, I thought it advisable to become fully cognisant of the facts before offering for Verity in case there should be more truth in the lady's claim than was quite comfortable.'

She said nothing but waited for him to continue which he did after a reflective pause.

'I got the bones of it from old Hazlett who, humming and hawing in his lawyer's dry-stick way, informed me that a pension had been paid from the estate since before I was born to a certain Person and did I wish to continue the practice. It had totalled up to quite a considerable amount over the years and I naturally wished to know more about the recipient. As it chanced, she was in London at that time and had communicated with Hazlett. Having heard of my father's death, she was doubtless wondering if his son was likely to be as accommodating. I found Mrs Ramsay at her hotel on the point of departure for Paris, where she was living. She prevailed upon me to accompany her, insisting that discussion of such a delicate nature lay within her son's province rather than hers. The mention of her son began to put the whole thing into perspective. I must confess to having been intensely curious about it all, so had it put about that I was coming down here for a short time and went off with her.'

'Your curiosity, Leo, has led you into scrapes in plenty,' Miss Liddell rebuked him severely. He made a wry grimace.

'Little did I suspect then that it would be more than three years before I set foot in England again.'

'Yes, that is something else,' she interrupted him. 'Why did you not—'

'You forget I was once again under the Duke's command. Nor was the wound I received at Waterloo quite such a trifling affair as you may have been led to believe. His Grace of Wellington then prevailed upon me to serve with the Army of Occupation, after which it seemed as good a time as any to embark upon a Grand Tour of Europe, which pleasure had been denied me previously.'

His manner was as indifferent as if he had been describing the activities of some slight acquaintance, but it was very plain to her that Miss Middleton's obduracy had played a great part in his decision to stay away from England for so long. After a slight pause she resumed the conversation.

'What sort of woman was this Mrs Ramsay? An ageing light-skirt or a practised courtesan of the stamp of Harriet Wilson?'

If the Earl considered the use of such terms to be inappropriate for a maiden lady of Miss Liddell's quality, he was too familiar with her starts to say so.

'Neither. I found her agreeable enough if a thought feather-witted, but certainly no dashing demi-rep. Her daughter was another pair of shoes,' he added reminiscently.

'Oh, there was a daughter, too?'

'Yes, but no sister of mine for which I was truly grateful!' He laughed softly. 'A pretty little pullet, that one!'

'But who,' enquired the bewildered Miss Liddell, 'was *her* father?'

'Legitimately, I collect, the convenient Mr Ramsay. If the lady is to be believed she went through some form of marriage service with my father. When later my parent discovered he had given her a slip on the shoulder he confessed that the ceremony had been all a hum and arranged for her to wed this man Ramsay.'

'But why should he do so much for her? He was not so considerate of his other convenients.'

'Maybe because he was very young and it had not—ah, become a habit with him?' She thought the cynicism ill became him but let it pass. 'Too, she was not a regular member of the muslin company, though what her precise station in life was I found it hard to define. The middling class, I should say, with probably enough standing to make things awkward for his lordship.'

'Seems to me she did handsomely out of breaking her leg,' sniffed Miss Liddell. 'Where is Ramsay now?'

'That was not made perfectly plain. The inference was that he was no longer with us.'

'Dead, d'you mean? And the daughter was the French *fille de joie* you were reputed to have gone off with later? Oh, what a piece of work you made of it, Leo!'

'I daresay.' He shrugged carelessly. 'But that was what you could term a *non-sequitur*.'

'Was it?' She took him up quickly. 'Did not Verity Middleton's returning your letters unopened—'

'Let be, Deb!' His voice was suddenly harsh. 'No good ever came of raking over dead embers.'

Unaffected by his gust of anger, she resumed her inquisition. 'What of the son—your half-brother?'

'Older than me by some six years, and as like to my father as he could stare. I'd not wish him to walk in here on you without warning.'

'Is that likely?'

'If he thought it would put me out of countenance, yes.'

'He would not attempt to claim your position?'

'No, he is honest enough to admit there is no hope without the proof his mother cannot supply, but he is fiercely resentful of my existence and would be happy to terminate it. Indeed, I am persuaded he has made the attempt on at least one occasion—possibly two, if one takes today's little episode into account.'

'Why, what happened today?' she asked, alarmed, but she had lost his attention for he was looking about the room with a puzzled air.

'Where—excuse me, Deb.' He went out into the hall and she heard him calling to Threadgold. Presently he returned, shaking his head ruefully. 'They've gone. I suppose Roger had a fancy for them, the sly fox!'

Then he told her about the pistols and how he had come by them. Despite his efforts to make light of it, she treated the matter with grave concern.

'You believe that your half-brother has attempted your life before now? But what can he hope to gain by that? If he succeeds in his object then his mother's pension will cease—I am right in presuming you are maintaining it?' He nodded and she continued. 'Roger is your heir until you marry and beget a son and he is not likely to put himself out to provide for your father's by-blow.' She stopped abruptly, plainly unwilling to express in words the turn her thoughts were taking.

'What is it, Deb?' asked the Earl quietly.

'Nothing—nothing that makes any sort of sense,' she averred. 'Save that, as I see it, the sooner you get yourself a wife and a quiverful of brats the better 'twill be for you.'

Wonersh chuckled. 'Meaning he can hardly do away with the whole family?'

'Just that. And don't forget I have a very particular iron in this fire. If anything should happen to you and Roger inherits, I'm out of Beauregard before the cat can lick its ear!'

That brought his eyebrows up in astonishment. 'Do you not deal together then, you and Roger? It did occur to me that you shuffled him off just now in a very high-handed fashion!'

'He manages the estate to perfection—why should he not when a French bullet or blade might have put a period to your life and left it to him? I cannot complain of his conduct in that respect.'

He frowned. 'Roger is my cousin, a rather bookish gentleman who has built his life around Beauregard for which I must be devoutly grateful.'

'His life *is* Beauregard,' she corrected him. 'It is Mr Roger this and Mr Roger that and he loves it all. He tolerates me only because I keep the interior of the place in prime condition, but I have no doubt he believes he could do it very much better.'

'He's jealous, d'you mean?' The Earl looked sceptical. 'It's possible, of course. I am forever confounded by the fact that so many people cannot bear not to be the first in everything they attempt.'

'While you,' said she, amused, '*are* the first in everything you attempt and care nothing for it. Excessively mortifying for your enemies, I do declare!'

'The devil, Deb!' he protested, half-laughing. 'You will have me seeing adversaries in every shadow! But you are quite out in one respect. There are certain spheres in which I do not excel.' She waited expectantly but his lordship did not choose to enlarge upon this theme. Instead he said: 'About this matter of marriage, do you think I should put my mind to it?'

'Yes, I do,' she replied at once. 'The business of the Ramsays makes it all the more imperative that you should establish the line of succession without loss of time.'

The Earl pinched the lobe of his ear between finger and thumb, a habit of his when forming a decision. 'Yes,' he sighed, 'you could be in the right of it.'

'This half-brother of yours, does he call himself a Percival?'

'No, James Ramsay. A stiff-rumped buck but no sapskull.'

'Why should he have taken you in such aversion?' she pondered. 'Envy, resentment, these are understandable, but to attempt your life is the outside of anything.'

'If you will have it without the bark on, he didn't care above half for my attentions to his sister—even took the view that I had despoiled her.'

'And had you?' she enquired with matter-of-fact interest.

He grinned. 'Any despoiling that had been done took place before my advent upon her particular scene. Unlike her mama, she was little better than a gazetted Cyprian. Who could Ramsay have been, d'you suppose?'

'If Hazlett cannot help you there I expect we shall never know the true answer,' she replied placidly.

The Earl regarded her with some amusement. 'You take it all mighty calmly, Deb.'

'Well, you don't need me to tell you, Leo, that your father's marriage to my mother was an affair of mutual convenience. He was all to pieces after the loss of his young wife, Beauregard lacked a mistress, and you a mother. My father and she had known each other for most of their lives so everything arranged itself very neatly. Such a union did not require fidelity to be one of its first conditions.'

'I'm sorry, Deb, I'd hoped you did not know about his fancy-pieces.'

She waved away his concern. 'How could I not? Why even here on the estate—but I never held him greatly to blame. I believe he was truly devoted to your mother, mine he treated with the deference due to her position and she asked for no more. But this Ramsay connection has me in a puzzle, happening as it did long before he knew your mother. He must have been a mere boy at the time.'

'He was, and all of a greenhead, too, I'd say,' said his lordship's son grimly. A discreet tap on the door interrupted any further criticism of his sire. 'Ah, here is Threadgold with the candles.'

The next few minutes were taken up with the Earl's enquiries after his butler's numerous progeny, the welfare of various members of the staff, the possibility of his lordship requiring the town house to be opened up for his use, and Miss Liddell's particular instructions about the preparation of one of the Earl's favourite dishes to be passed on to the kitchen.

'Good of you to remember I like eels stewed Wiggy's Way,' he complimented her when Threadgold had left them.

'I am not likely to forget!' she retorted, rising and going over to a tambour-topped writing table set between the windows. 'Since to offer you eels served in any other fashion was to invite you to cast up your accounts at the first mouthful!'

'What a tiresome small boy I must have been!' he quizzed her.

'Wayward, and a shade stubborn, but never tiresome,' she assured him, glancing over a sheet of paper taken from the writing-table. 'Perhaps you would care to peruse this and tell me what you think later.'

The Earl took it from her and was forced to bite his lip hard in order to prevent himself from laughing aloud. 'Tell you who I fancy is what you really mean! Good God, Deb, have you been preparing the ground in advance?'

'Only listing the possibles,' she replied equably. 'I felt it right that you should know the—ah, form.'

'You mean in case my choice fell upon some vapourish female who is not up to snuff?' hazarded the Earl, then his eye chanced upon a certain name on the paper in his hand and his expression sobered abruptly. 'No, I cannot —' He stopped, folded the paper and put it away in his pocket. 'Enough of that for the moment, I must go and attempt to make myself worthy of the superb meal you are planning to set before me.'

So saying, he took himself off to change his dress,

leaving Miss Liddell, wearing something of the air of an indulgent parent welcoming home the prodigal son, to finish what was left of her port.

CHAPTER THREE

It really was too provoking of Wilkes to have chosen that particular day to have fallen down the stairs and broken his collar-bone. But then, reflected Miss Middleton, one booted foot ominously tapping the ground, he was quite the most stupid groom she had ever had the misfortune to employ. When she compared him with Parker, her father's groom, she—but comparisons were odious and one got what one paid for which, in this case, was as much as she could afford.

After a week of almost incessant rain the sun shone from a clear sky and there was no more than a warm breath of wind. To be denied the opportunity of enjoying such unexceptionable weather went against the pluck. She came to a swift decision and despatched the terrified small boy who had come to apprise her of his father's misadventure to call up a hackney.

Her arrival at the livery stables which had charge of her mare might have occasioned comment had the owner been present for he had known Miss Middleton since childhood, but the stable-boy who saddled up the patient Marigold saw no reason to question the propriety of allowing a young lady to ride out unattended. In order to avoid meeting any of her acquaintance who might regard the escapade in a somewhat different light, she used little-known paths to take her away from the town's environs and presently found herself well on the way to Shurdington and her old home.

Upon later reflection, she was of the opinion that it

was the unaccustomed sense of freedom, not untinged with guilt at her indecorous behaviour, that had prompted her to indulge in further indiscretion. Certain it was that no sooner had the notion entered her head than it was acted upon.

'It is not as if the Cloudesley-Abbotts have not implored us to consider the Hall open for our inspection at any time,' she argued to herself. This was undeniably true. It was equally true that Lady Middleton had declared nothing would induce her to set foot over the threshold of the house again.

'To be obliged to see such jumped-up mushrooms ruling the roast there would quite put me out of curl,' she had moaned, and though her daughters had protested that to describe the new owners of the Hall as "jumped-up mushrooms" was something of a misnomer, her ladyship had refused to alter her decision.

'They are not a Gloucestershire family,' she had insisted. 'So why should they wish to establish themselves in a country seat in this locality? Depend upon it, they are here-and-thereians, suddenly raised to riches.' And no persuasion on the part of her family could change her in that opinion.

For her part, Miss Middleton had found Mrs Cloudesley-Abbott to be a lady of superior intelligence, who displayed an eager willingness to discuss possible alterations and improvements to the gardens and grounds, nor did she suspect the lady of toad-eating her in order to establish a friendship with one of the best-respected families in the district.

'I wonder if the lake has been re-fashioned as was proposed?' she mused as Marigold, feeling her hoofs to be on familiar ground, lengthened her stride towards where the tall chimneys of the Hall showed through the young green of the trees. It had been a matter of deep regret to Miss Middleton as much as to her mama that her brother Godfrey had been unable to take charge of the Hall, but his papa-in-law held the purse-strings and was well satisfied with his prestigious estate in Grove Hill, his town house in Albemarle Street, and his hunting-lodge in the Shires. Since Annabelle was his only child, it was to be presumed that she would inherit these desirable properties and her husband would be a sad nodcock not to realise on which side his bread was buttered.

Resolutely dismissing such lowering reflections from her mind, Miss Middleton directed the mare down a path that ran alongside the high walls enclosing the park. 'Oh, la!' she muttered crossly a moment later, reining the animal in, 'they've repaired the breach in the wall! Now how can I—'

She looked about her, but all the brushwood and overhanging branches had been cleared away along the length of the wall and she was about to resign herself to the fact that it was quite unscaleable when the mare, attracted by a particularly luscious piece of herbage, stepped in close to its base.

'But, of course!' she cried out in triumph and, calling upon Marigold to stand, with considerable difficulty she scrambled to her feet upon the saddle. 'Like some equestrienne at Astley's Amphitheatre!' she gasped, reaching up to grasp the top of the wall. But still she was short by several feet of being able to look over into the grounds of the Hall so, greatly daring, she placed a toe into a convenient cranny and hoisted herself free of Marigold's support. A further effort resulted in both her feet being securely lodged and she was enjoying as clear a view of her old home as could be wished for. The sight of figures moving about near the lake drew her attention at once.

'I do declare,' she breathed, 'they are making a cascade and a bridge! What I dreamed of above all things! And there—it must be a shrubbery planted to shield the formal gardens from the wind!'

Utterly absorbed in contemplation of what had been her particular interest at the Hall, she forgot the passing moments until one of the workmen by the lake turned to move in her direction. Having no wish to be caught playing the Peeping Tom, she lowered herself quickly and thrust out a foot to feel for the saddle. But Marigold, deciding that the grass grew greener on the farther side of the path, had moved away and no amount of pleas or exhortations from her mistress served to entice her back.

'Dear Heaven, what to do?' debated Miss Middleton, eyeing the drop beneath her and endeavouring to calculate her chances of coming off safe if she let herself fall to the ground. They were not, she concluded, very good, riding boots and habit not being the ideal apparel for climbing or dropping from high walls. Also the ground below, muddy from the recent rains, was littered with stones and broken pieces of brickwork so that, at best, a twisted ankle might be the reward for a sudden descent. 'And then you could well be in the basket,' she informed herself, 'because it is plain that this track is not used overmuch and you could lie here for—forever.'

With some vague idea of calling for help, she drew herself up again to peer over the wall, only to discover that the workmen had all disappeared, doubtless to enjoy their midday meal. By this time the strain of holding on by fingers and toes was beginning to tell and she looked about her desperately in search of assistance. To her relief she perceived the head of a horseman, bobbing up and down, approaching her along the track. Her pleasure at seeing him was promptly overshadowed by the realisation that for the elegant Miss Middleton to be discovered clinging to the wall like a fly to a window-pane would be a choice piece of tittle-tattle for the Cheltenham gossips to enjoy.

'Try for a little sense,' she adjured herself fiercely, 'better a passing humiliation than a broken limb, and the odds are on't that he'll not have the least notion of who you may be.'

In this comfortable assumption she soon found herself to be sadly at fault for the next moment she was gazing down upon the startled countenance of her sister's ineligible admirer, Mr Theodore Warburton.

'Good God, it's—it can't be—Miss Middleton!'

'I do assure you that it is, but if we might postpone discussion of my identity until I am on firmer ground, the better I shall be pleased!' she snapped with some acerbity. 'I cannot hold on—oh, help me, please!'

In a trice he was off his horse and running to her aid. Her numbed fingers relaxed their hold and, her feet refusing to sustain her full weight, she fell into his outstretched arms. The sudden acquisition of so beautiful a burden proved to be too much for his resolution and together they subsided in an undignified heap upon the ground. Hastily replacing her feathered tricorne hat at a rakish angle upon her disordered hair, Miss Middleton sat up and began cautiously to test her limbs for possible injury. Mr. Warburton, eyeing her warily, brushed himself off and got to his feet.

'I take it that is your mare, ma'am?'

'Yes, the wicked creature! If she had obeyed my command I should not have found myself in such an absurd pickle!' Ruefully she surveyed her York tan gloves which had been ripped and scored in her sudden descent.

'Your hands—forgive me, ma'am, I am a ramshackle fellow not to be thinking of your hurts. It was all—well, so unexpected.'

'Quite my own fault,' stated Miss Middleton firmly. 'And there is mercifully no great harm done. I could not resist the temptation to discover whether or not Mrs Cloudesley-Abbott had embarked upon the proposed alterations to the park.' She glanced at him sharply but his face expressed nothing other than concern for her predicament and, unbidden, a gurgle of laughter rose up inside her, witness to a lively and often inconvenient sense of humour. Suppressing this lamentable tendency, she went on as if it was the most natural thing in the world for him to have discovered her climbing up a wall. 'It was utterly bird-witted of me, to be sure, to have used Marigold for my stepping-off point, but as a general rule she is so tractable I had no notion of her not keeping the line.'

This reminded him to secure the mare who, having eaten her fill, was tending to think wistfully of her stable. Miss Middleton rose to rather unsteady feet and smoothed her habit with an air of concern but, behind her impassive countenance, her brain was whirling at an unprecedented rate.

It would be less than human of him if he did not turn this situation to his advantage. She could just imagine the sly snickers, the whispers behind the hands, the half-hidden smiles at the Assembly Rooms! A wave of disgust swept over her and she closed her eyes to shut out the awful picture conjured up of her sitting the evening through by her mother's side because no gentleman cared to ask such a social pariah to stand up with him!

His anxious voice cut through her disordered thoughts. 'Miss Middleton, I beg of you to rest here while I go and fetch help. You are in no case to be riding.'

But that she could not permit. Her only hope, she was persuaded, lay in cajoling him to keep a still tongue and to do that she would have to cast out lures and assume an amiability she could not feel.

'If you will bear me company, sir, I shall do very well. I am not, you must know, in the habit of riding without my groom, but he has suffered an unfortunate accident and I could not resist so glorious a day.' Collecting Marigold's reins into her hand, she allowed him to toss her up into the saddle and waited while he mounted his own horse and joined her. 'A good-looking youngster you have there,' she remarked affably, 'do you ride to hounds, Mr Warburton?'

'Only when staying with my uncle in Devonshire when I have an occasional day out with the "Let 'em Alones".'

'Ah, Mr Templer's pack.' She observed his excellent seat and light hands with increasing respect. 'But you are chiefly resident here in Cheltenham, are you not? Would not the Berkeley be the thing for you?'

'Were I acceptable for membership, ma'am.' The frankness of the reply had her at Point Non-Plus and she wondered what course she had best adopt.

'If I put forward your name to Colonel Berkeley,' she began tentatively. He raised a quizzical eyebrow.

'You mean he might be persuaded to overlook my unfortunate family connection?'

Really, this was not even wrapping it up in clean linen! She resolved to be equally blunt.

'Yes, Mr Warburton, I think it very likely he would.'

'And what of Miss Eustacia, ma'am? Would you also, of your kindness, agree to my paying her my addresses?'

Miss Middleton was as shocked as if he had landed her a facer. 'That is not for me to say, sir,' she managed at last. 'For that permission you must apply to my mother.'

'That won't fadge, ma'am,' he said quietly. 'All the world knows who calls the tune in your establishment.'

Unhappily by this time Miss Middleton's sorely-tried patience had run its course. 'How—how dare you!' she gasped, rounding on him, all flashing eyes and indignant bosom.

'My compliments, ma'am! Such a display of emotion vastly becomes you!' The admiration in his alert brown eyes was as unforced as his sudden smile. 'Be easy, I beg of you. I would not for the world embarrass you by mention of today's little mishap. So you really have no need to be civil to me, have you?'

Miss Middleton, rarely deflated, opened her mouth to rake him down and shut it again while she re-assessed the position. He watched her, still smiling.

'Your forbearance does you credit, sir,' she said stiffly. 'I would not wish to be behindhand in doing you any small service that lies in my power. I will speak to Colonel Berkeley.'

He bowed slightly. 'My thanks, ma'am.'

By this time they had arrived at the main Cheltenham road and were confronted by a small party of ladies and gentlemen upon horseback, among whom Miss Middleton was horrified to perceive her sister Eustacia.

'Verity! What's to do? Have you taken a toss?'

The alarm on her sister's face and on those of the other members of the party brought home to Miss Middleton what a very off appearance she must give, her gloves in tatters, the skirts of her riding habit muddied, and her hair in disorder. Before she could formulate some reasonable explanation, Mr Warburton had stepped smoothly into the breach.

'A toss, indeed!' he affirmed. 'And it was excessively fortunate that I met up with her mare heading for home and so discovered the lady.'

'Great Heaven!' exclaimed Eustacia unaffectedly amazed, 'I never dreamed that Marigold would display enough spirit to unseat anyone!'

'She was frightened by a—by a hare,' supplemented Miss Middleton. 'It rose up almost under her hoofs,' she added, feeling that if she had to tell a rapper, then it had better be a convincing one worthy of the standard set her by Mr Warburton. Then the others of the party were solicitously enquiring after her well-being and she was assuring them that, apart from scratches and bruises, she was tolerably comfortable when Eustacia voiced the inevitable question.

'But where was Wilkes?'

'I had sent him home with a message for mama

—something I quite forgot which required immediate attention.'

Miss Middleton, now fairly launched upon her mendacious career, was amazed to discover how glibly the words rolled off her tongue. Eustacia, however, looked totally unconvinced that there should be anything of sufficient urgency to cause Wilkes to desert his mistress and Mr Warburton had, once again, to come to her rescue.

'And home is where your sister should be, Miss Eustacia. Her fall may not have been damaging, but she has been severely shaken and is in need of rest.'

At once the penitent Eustacia offered to return with them but Miss Middleton would not hear of it.

'No, no, I collect you are engaged upon your long-promised expedition to Painswick. I would not for the world have you forgo that. Mr Warburton has kindly offered to escort me back to Royal Crescent.'

She fancied that Eustacia's glance rested overlong on Mr Warburton's suspiciously bland countenance, but she made no further protest and the two parties went their separate ways, Mr Warburton fully concurring in his charge's wish to avoid the more frequented roads. He continued to discourse amiably and without the least constraint in his manner, telling her about his recent voyage to the West India Islands.

'While there I made a study of the several qualities of mahogany produced in those parts, and also of other woods relative to the building of carriages such as lancewood and fustic.'

'Fustic?' she repeated, fascinated in spite of herself.

'A species of mulberry,' he elaborated kindly, 'also to be found in Brazil, which country I visited last year. It is a yellow hardwood, little employed over here, but occasionally used to form the naves of wheels which are intended for hot climates as it is not so subject to shrinkage as are our English woods.'

'Are you—have you still an interest in the carriage-building business?' she asked doubtfully.

'A holding interest only, but I cherish a secret desire to write a text-book on the manufacture and use of pleasure carriages, based upon my grandfather's extensive notes and my own observations.'

Miss Middleton, for the second time in as many hours, found herself at something of a loss. She was honest enough to admit that she had seriously misjudged her companion and was forced to revise her original estimate of his character. He was both intelligent and conversable, not a whit ashamed of his origins or his ambitions, one of which was clearly to marry Eustacia. He would be a sad come-down for a Middleton, nonetheless should she make a mull of her plans for her sister's future then perhaps his suit might be considered. Miss Middleton subscribed to the maxim that if a lady married into a lower order, she should do her possible to raise her spouse to her own consequence and, just so he did not use his finger-bowl for gargling or accompany her to the theatre in a set of dittos, be he sufficiently well-breeched, it might be hoped that, in time, only a very few would remember his beginnings. His father, unhappily, had not perfectly achieved this admirable transition but the thought of the well-mannered gentleman by her side indulging in either of the aforementioned solecisms aroused once more that sadly downtrodden virtue, her sense of the ridiculous, and she had much difficulty in repressing a giggle.

Catching his eye upon her, she made haste to urge him to further description of his travels. This comfortably filled the time until, arrived back at Royal Crescent, he lifted her down, enquiring courteously if he could do anything more for her.

'Yes, convey Marigold back to her stable, if you would be so kind.' Rather shyly, she held out her hand. 'I'm excessively obliged to you, sir. Your quickness of tongue quite saved the situation.'

'We must hope it did, ma'am,' said he gravely. 'And now, if you would be counselled by me, you will bathe your scratches and cuts and then lie down upon your bed with the drapes drawn for a few hours.'

'And my hartshorn, no doubt!' she quizzed him. 'What a poor thing you must think me, Mr Warburton!'

'On the contrary, ma'am,' said he, touching her hand to his lips. 'But were I the possessor of some exquisite masterpiece or *objet d'art* then I would not be easy until I was assured that it had the very best possible care.'

And that, mused Miss Middleton as she watched him ride off, leading the willing Marigold, was quite the prettiest compliment she had had paid to her in a long time. It was only after she had followed his excellent advice and was snugly tucked under the covers that it occurred to her to wonder just why he had been riding along that track which led only to the stable block at Shurdington Hall.

It became abundantly clear when the younger Miss Middleton returned from her outing later in the day and stormed into the bedroom where her sister sat, pensively repairing the damage to her fingers with pieces of court-plaster, that she had not been wholly deceived by Mr Warburton's facile explanation.

'Marigold threw you, indeed!' she scoffed. 'Do you expect me to believe that Banbury tale? And I suppose she then rolled over on Mr Warburton to make his dress as mud-stained as was yours?'

'No—o,' confessed Miss Middleton with quivering lip. '*I* rolled over on him!' Then laughter overcame her at sight of Eustacia's astonished face. 'Oh, I'd best tell you the whole, but you must promise not to breathe a word, in particular not to mama.'

'That's all very well,' objected Eustacia when the recital was completed, 'but I was not the only one to suspect you were cutting a sham! That horrid cat, Minerva Thistlethwaite, asked how I liked having my beau snatched from under my nose by my elder sister!'

'That has nothing to say to anything,' Miss Middleton soothed her, mentally registering the fact that Mr Warburton's intentions appeared to be generally accepted. 'She cannot forgive you for being so much prettier than she herself, so will go to any length to give you a set-down. Now, if you have a few moments after dinner, shall we go over the invitations for your party?'

'I take it you will be sending a card to Mr Warburton?' Eustacia's lower lip was thrust out in a very intimidating way.

'I can do no less after his gallant defence of my character,' Miss Middleton returned lightly. 'I daresay it will be a frightful squeeze, but I have added one or two more names to the number.'

Her sister came to look over her shoulder at the list lying upon the dressing-table. 'Lord Wonersh and Miss Liddell,' she read out, 'but I thought—has he returned to England then?'

'So I am given to understand.' Miss Middleton was carefully drawing on mittens to cover the repairs to her hands. 'And think what *cachet* it would give to your party to have a belted earl attend! Miss Thistlethwaite will be quite green with envy!'

'I seem to remember him running tame about Shurdington Hall at one time,' mused Eustacia. 'Was he one of your flirts?'

Miss Middleton shuddered delicately. 'Certainly not!' she replied. 'Now, if you please, the dinner gong will be sounding in a few minutes and you have not changed your dress.'

Thus adjured, Eustacia withdrew. However, upon entering her bedchamber, she made no immediate attempt to remove her habit but stood, the nail of one forefinger tapping her small white teeth, an expression of rare concentration upon her face, until the entry of her mama to beg her make haste put an end to her cogitations.

CHAPTER FOUR

WHILE there were several cogent reasons why Miss Middleton had decided to send a card to Lord Wonersh for Eustacia's début, the chief of them was her desire to make it plain that she had no quarrel with him and, at the same time, to ensure that her first encounter with his lordship would take place on her own ground and at a time of her own choosing. In this latter object, however, she was to be disappointed.

As she stood before her cheval-glass on the morning after the invitations had been despatched, judging the effect of an elegant cambric gown just received from the hands of her dressmaker, a slight frown marred the serenity of her classic features. Her meeting with Miss Liddell had led her to believe that Wonersh's affections were not engaged, but whether he could be induced to direct them upon Eustacia was quite another matter. For an instant her expression softened and a half-smile trembled on her lips, then the sound of carriage wheels drew her to the window and she perceived an excessively stylish cabriolet, with a crest emblazoned upon its shining panels, come to a stand before the street door.

The gentleman handling this spanking turn-out sprang lithely down, handing the reins to his groom, and directed a searching glance up at the house. Miss Middleton's heart, normally the most reliable of organs, seemed to turn over several times before resuming its regular beat, and she stepped back quickly into the shelter of the drapes.

The peal of the doorbell found her standing in the middle of the room, hands clasped to her throat, cheeks most becomingly flushed, in a state of extreme agitation, for which she promptly took herself to task.

'That the mere sight of him should throw you into the boughs is a great deal too bad!' she chided herself. 'You cannot hope to bring all off safely unless you have full control of your emotions!'

This severe admonition had its due effect for when Griffiths, her mother's elderly dresser, had laboured up the stairs to advise her that the Earl of Wonersh had called and, upon being informed that Lady Middleton was not receiving that day owing to a slight indisposition, had begged the favour of a few moments of Miss Middleton's company, she received the intelligence with an air of surprised resignation.

'Mama not feeling the thing? I had no notion of it.'

'Very sudden it was, miss, her headache.' Griffiths was wearing her most wooden expression and Verity drew her own conclusions. Lady Middleton, not knowing what course to adopt with his lordship, had cravenly deserted the field.

'I must receive him, I suppose. But—oh, this frock! I'd best change it. My sprigged muslin, Griffiths, if you please.'

'No call for that, miss. You'll do very well as you are.' Griffiths, after the way of old and trusted servants, knew as much and often more of the family's affairs than they themselves, and the Earl's appearance in her ladyship's salon had touched off a train of hopeful speculation. 'Such a nice gentleman as his lordship is, even thought to ask after my rheumatism.'

'Mmm.' Miss Middleton clearly was not impressed by this example of his lordship's goodheartedness. 'Where is Miss Eustacia?'

'Tucked up with some rubbishy novel, I shouldn't wonder.' Griffiths, picking up a soft white wool lace shawl from a chair to place around her young mistress's shoulders, expressed her contempt for the written word by an eloquent sniff.

'Then request her, if you please, to set it down and join me in the salon as soon as may be—and Griffiths! Her yellow jaconet, I think, would be most suitable.'

With a last approving pat to her shining hair, Miss Middleton swept from the room and downstairs with something of the air of one about to give battle. Her first reaction as she entered the salon was of gratification that she had arranged the flowers afresh that morning, for the room was bright with tumbling masses of wild cherry-blossom and the gold of belated daffodils. Then, as Wonersh stepped forward to make his bow, she was conscious only of how little he had changed in the years since they had met and, once again, her heart performed its odd convolutions. That much the same thought had occurred to him was evident from his greeting of her.

'I could scarce have believed you to be in greater beauty than my memory served to remind me, but so it is.'

The warmth in his voice shook her a little off balance, but she rallied quickly and, extending a languid hand, said lightly: 'You are too kind, my lord. Will you not be seated? Mama sends her regrets but she is not in plump currant this morning. When did you get back to England, my lord?'

Her cool reception of his spontaneous tribute had its predictable effect, and his expression changed to one of guarded watchfulness. Touching her wrist to his lips, he handed her to a chair where she arranged her skirts about her with meticulous care before raising her wide grey eyes to his.

'So we are to exchange civil whiskers, are we, ma'am?'

'What else, my lord?'

'It was not ever thus—Verity.'

'You refine too much upon old memories, my lord,'

said she, assuming a bantering tone, but he was not to be turned from his object.

'Why did you return my letters unopened?'

'What need to open them when all the world had told me of their content? At that time, also, my father was so gravely ill—' She stopped, unwilling to sound as if excusing her conduct, and he intervened quickly.

'Ah, that I did not know—could not know until very much later. Forgive me for my seeming lack of concern.'

'Quite understandable, my lord, there being so many other affairs to claim your interest.'

He, thinking back over the hundred days that had culminated in the battle of Waterloo, laughed shortly.

'You could say that, to be sure. Yet you condemned me unheard. Again I ask—why, Verity?'

'Condemned you, my lord?' There was a slight edge to her voice. 'I hope I accepted my *congé* with good grace and could only be grateful to have learned how excessively ill-suited we were before irrevocable ties had been forged.'

''Fore God, you could not have believed that!' he burst out, but she held up a hand in protest.

'It is all long past, my lord. Shall we agree to—ignore it?'

He stood silent, looking at her, wondering if the lovely laughing girl he had glimpsed years ago still lay hid beneath the exterior of this exquisite, composed creature, or had that been but a dream and was this the reality? She saw his face harden.

'If that is your wish, ma'am,' he returned indifferently and, womanlike, she felt unaccountably annoyed with him for having accepted her dictate so readily.

Further discussion was then put an end to by the entry of Eustacia, clad in a striking dark-blue riding costume, with a dashing beaver hat supporting a wealth of blue ostrich feathers and gold tassels surmounting her dark curls.

'Verity, I fear I cannot—oh, your pardon, sir!' She bobbed vaguely in Wonersh's direction. 'I am promised to go riding, you see.'

Miss Middleton, observing the effect of her sister's appearance upon the Earl, wondered that she should not feel more satisfaction at what was, after all, a most promising start to her designs.

'Why, of course, my love,' she cooed, 'but allow me to present to you my lord of Wonersh.'

'Wonersh? But I remember you!' exclaimed Eustacia ingenuously, laughing up at him. 'When I was a schoolroom miss and you paying court to Verity!'

The silence that fell after her words caused her to look from one to the other in dismay, but the Earl smoothed over the awkward moment by saying in his pleasant way: 'It is so many years ago after all, and you positively old-haggish now, I daresay!'

She gurgled with delight and allowed him to retain her hand for a shade longer than was quite necessary. 'Shall you find time to look in upon our little party next week, do you suppose, my lord?'

'I shall make it my business to do so, ma'am,' he assured her solemnly.

'It won't be a very *exciting* affair,' she warned him. 'Just a push to set me on my social feet!'

He looked down at her trim black half-boots, fringed with gold. 'And very pretty feet they are!' he complimented her.

'But so much happier dancing!' she whispered archly. 'Oh, do try to persuade Verity to let us roll back the carpets!'

'Eustacia, this is not intended to be a childish romp, but your first grown-up party!' Miss Middleton reproved her, but was interrupted by a small scream from her sister.

'The time! Pray forgive me, my lord, but my escort will have been looking for me these ten minutes past and he does not at all care for his horses to be kept standing, I can tell you!'

'I warrant he will think his cattle honoured when he sets eyes upon you, however long the wait,' the Earl assured her gallantly.

'Who is escorting you this morning?' Miss Middleton hoped she did not sound too much like a reproving governess.

'Why, Mr Warburton. He has just purchased a new mare—the prettiest thing, I do declare—and wishes me to try her paces. *Au revoir*, my lord—dear Verity!'

With a wave of her riding crop she was gone, the impact of her presence having had much the effect of a stone tossed into a still pool, its ever-widening ripples reaching out to the furthest corners of the room. The Earl glanced at Miss Middleton and did not fail to observe her troubled expression.

'I collect you do not approve your sister's choice of escort?' he hazarded.

'Oh, no doubt he is a perfectly estimable young man,' she said worriedly, 'but—'

'But?' he murmured, drawing his snuff-box from his fob and opening it with a practised flick.

'I hold to the opinion that it takes longer by far to acquire the bouquet of a gentleman than to mature a cellar of wine,' said she, rising in one swift graceful movement and beginning to pace about the room. The Earl, outwardly unmoved, took a pinch of snuff.

'So he is *that* Warburton,' he said pensively, tracing the delicate silver and mother-of-pearl inlay upon the surface of his tortoiseshell snuff-box with one long fore-finger.

'You know him?' she asked, surprised.

'Let us say I know of him,' agreed the Earl equably. 'And nothing, I assure you, to his discredit.'

Miss Middleton, once again, found herself to be at something of a loss. The last thing in the world she wished for was to have Wonersh approve Mr Warburton's attentions to Eustacia, almost as if he were an elder brother or—or brother-in-law, whispered a little voice. Immediately she whisked herself over to the window to conceal her heightened colour, just in time to see Mr Warburton throw her sister up into the saddle and the two set off, cosing away amicably like the best of friends, with an elderly and most respectable-looking groom in attendance.

'All perfectly proper, ma'am,' said the Earl's voice at her elbow, 'though I think I can appreciate your scruples.'

It was then that the outrageous notion occurred to Miss Middleton. 'My lord,' she begun, turning to face him, but finding herself forced to take a step back into the window embrasure because of his close propinquity. He gave no sign of moving, merely smiled upon her and looked mildly enquiring. 'My lord,' she said again, and then rushed on in a manner that quite shocked her when she recalled it afterwards. 'While, of course, there is no—no reason for you to consider yourself to have been in any way at fault in our previous con—association, yet such was the opinion of persons qualified to judge of the matter with impartial interest.'

'These—er, persons, in fact denounced me as a despicable scoundrel?'

'Yes,' said Miss Middleton in a very small voice, wishing that he would step back a little so that she did not have to crane her neck to look up at him.

'In which opinion, of course, you thoroughly concur?'

Miss Middleton drew a deep breath. 'I confess I did at the time, my lord. I am prepared to allow that I could have been mistaken, but your conduct was so—so inexplicable—'

She paused, tellingly, hoping she had not overplayed her hand.

'My letters would have explained it,' he reminded her.

'Are you asking me to believe that you have been wearing the willow for me these three years past, Verity?'

'Certainly not!' she snapped, then, controlling her tongue with an effort, continued on a calmer note. 'But I am persuaded that some small compensation is due to me for the abrupt departure of so hopeful a suitor!'

'What?' Now she was certainly assured of his attention. 'I—do I understand you correctly, ma'am?'

'I should be happy if I thought you did,' she informed him candidly. 'But I will be more precise. Not to put too fine a point on it, I need your help.'

'Anything I have is yours to command. If it is a question of money—' She shook her head.

'Nothing of that sort, my lord, though mama is not so well-heeled as she would like, which makes it all the more difficult because Mr Warburton is so—so plump in the pocket.'

'You'd best be plain with me, ma'am.' The curt authority in his voice set up her bristles. 'Do I understand this compensation you intend to extract from me for my alleged ill-conduct to be in some sort related to your sister?'

'Just so.' Miss Middleton was holding her temper on a tight rein. 'She is a dear girl, as good-hearted as she is beautiful but, as you have seen, a shade impulsive.'

'And, if crossed, liable to take her own line? So her careful sister wishes her to be weaned away from the notion of marrying Mr Warburton.' He looked over her head thoughtfully at the distant hills. 'Too obvious disapprobation might well drive her into his arms—or his carriage to Gretna Green.'

Miss Middleton recoiled at the mere suggestion. 'She would never be so rag-mannered as to do that!'

'The young are so incurably romantic, my dear Verity,' he quizzed her. 'Unlike us, who have long since cut our wisdom teeth.'

'She is not so far gone in fantasy as to forget her breeding,' she insisted. He shrugged and, to her relief, turned away to walk over to the fireplace.

'What other suitors are there in prospect?'

'Well, there's Nicholas Chisholm.' Her deprecating tone and faint moue of distaste brought a twinkle to his eye. 'A fop and not in her style.'

'Yes, I think we could do better than that for so engaging a young lady. I take it you are requiring me to run through my circle of acquaintance and select any suitable—er, candidates?'

'I doubt there is time for that, my lord.' Miss Middleton felt herself tremble all over at her own temerity. 'She has shown a decided *tendre* for Mr Warburton and mama—well, she will deny Eustacia nothing that seems to her within reason.' She hesitated and added, rather shamefacedly, 'It irks mama sorely to be so purse-pinched. She would not have my sister suffer the same indignity and might well approve the match.'

'So what would you have me do?' He watched her, plainly uncertain of her intentions.

'Offer yourself as—well, perhaps not as suitor but—if you could pay her some distinguishing notice, even indulge in a mild flirtation, she cannot but recognise how infinitely superior you are, she must be flattered by your attentions.'

'I never was very adept at flirtation,' said he in rather a stifled voice. Miss Middleton had a curious feeling that something violent was likely to happen to her, precisely what she did not know, but held her breath in fearful anticipation as he went on speaking. 'What if she takes my attentions to be serious?'

'Oh, depend upon it, she will not!' she assured him eagerly. 'But 'twill serve to distract her and gain us a little time.'

'You're scarcely flattering, ma'am!' he reproved her but so good-humouredly that it was plain the notion had not given offence and she breathed more easily. 'Meanwhile I have to seek out an eligible substitute for myself and, having lured the poor girl away from Warburton, leave my successor to play his part. Is that the ploy?'

'You'll do it, will you not, my lord?'

He looked down at the small hand, laid entreatingly upon his sleeve. 'If that is what you wish for, yes, I'll attempt it,' he said. 'But have you considered what food we are providing for the gossips?'

Miss Middleton had not and, for a moment, looked so adorably confused that it was only by an extreme effort of will-power that he restrained himself from taking her in his arms and kissing away her distress.

'No matter, Eustacia's happiness is my first concern,' she declared resolutely. 'Great Heavens! Whatever is that?' The room, which had darkened steadily unobserved by its occupants, was now sharply illuminated by a vivid flash of lightning on the heels of which sounded a mighty crash of thunder. 'Eustacia! She will be utterly drenched! And her new habit!'

He went to the window to observe that his groom had pulled up the hood of the cabriolet. 'Should I speed to her rescue? An unexceptionable way to establish myself in her regard, do you not agree?'

'Oh, yes, indeed, if you would!' she begged him, almost pushing him out of the room in her anxiety. 'I fancy they will have followed the course of the river westwards to cross the turnpike road and then on towards Tewkesbury. It is a favourite excursion with Eustacia and they set off as if intending to pursue it. They cannot have gone far as yet, my lord.'

A moment later he was hurrying down the path in the streaming rain and was into his carriage and away while she paced the salon, concerned for her sister's plight yet even more taken up with wondering if she had played her cards aright. Quite apart from his consequence, his personal attraction was such that she had little doubt of his being able to attach Eustacia's affections did he put himself out to do so. Once having achieved that object it would be impossible for him not to offer for her—or would it? A shiver ran down Miss Middleton's spine. He had evaded that issue once before, had he not? Her pretty mouth set in a mutinous line. Well, he was not going to do it again, she would see to that!

His lordship, handling the cabriolet in style, had not been entirely deceived by Miss Middleton's performance but, deciding to let things take their course, gave himself up to consideration of the matter in hand. Presently he perceived from some distance off a group of riders making use of the scant shelter provided by a clump of sparse pines and, a few moments later, he was being greeted by an exceedingly damp Eustacia.

'Quick ma'am, up you get and I'll have you home in no time!' He sprang down to lift her from her horse and into the cabriolet. 'Jevons,' he added to his groom, 'take the lady's mount and follow us. It will be no comfortable ride for you, I'm afraid, but better than walking.' Mr Warburton moved forward to protest at this high-handed removal of his charge and the Earl, with an eye on the broad band of blue sky now visible beyond the storm-clouds, made haste to reassure him. 'I am Wonersh, by the way, and am directed by Miss Middleton, who is in a rare taking, to get Miss Eustacia home without loss of time.'

At mention of the Earl's name, a shadow seemed to pass over Mr Warburton's frank open countenance, but he merely bowed his head in acquiescence as his lordship deftly turned his equipage and directed his willing steed on his homeward path.

'Dear goodness, but I am wet!' Eustacia, laughing as if it was the most natural thing in the world to be sitting in a pool of water beside a strange gentleman, took off her hat and carefully wrung out the sodden feathers.

'Best shake 'em before a fire, ma'am,' he counselled.

'Pull that rug about you, the air is chill enough. Miss Middleton'll not thank me if I let you take cold.'

She pooh-pooed the notion. 'I am in and out in all weathers,' she told him, 'though I warrant you Verity will have a hot bath prepared with enough mustard in it to boil me red as a lobster!'

His lordship, wishing he might be privileged to witness such an interesting spectacle, contented himself with saying: 'She shows a most sisterly concern for you, ma'am.'

'I wish,' returned Eustacia with startling candour, 'she would show more for herself. It would appear her prime objects in life are to be a chaperon to me and a companion to mama! Can you conceive of her becoming an old maid—Verity? It is beyond anything nonsensical!'

Wonersh, his eyes very steady on the road, appeared to be giving all his attention to his driving. 'I had supposed all young ladies cherished the hope of setting up their own establishments,' he said, choosing his words with care. 'After all, a complaisant husband might well be prepared to take Lady Middleton in charge, while in your case, ma'am, I do not see any prolonged difficulty.'

She dimpled at him. 'I knew you would understand,' she declared. 'But Verity—my lord, you are an old friend, are you not? Could you not persuade her of this?'

'I think I am the last person likely to persuade her of anything!'

The words were uttered with such unconscious bitterness that Eustacia judged it wise to turn the conversation to more general matters but, behind her sparkling flow of chatter, she was congratulating herself on her perspicacity. Her suspicions that something lay between her sister and the Earl appeared to have been well-founded. There was one person who could enlighten her more full and that, whether she cared for it or not, was Lady Middleton. However, there was no immediate opportunity to elaborate upon her plans for they had arrived back at Royal Crescent and Verity, who had been on the look for them, had herself hastened to open the door.

'My dear, you must be drenched! Quickly, upstairs —Griffiths is preparing a bath.'

With an amused 'I told you so' glance at the Earl who had accompanied her to the door, Eustacia ran up the stairs, pausing on the landing to look back and blow him an impertinent kiss before being hustled away by an outraged Griffiths.

'My lord, you are none too dry yourself!' Miss Middleton was all concern. 'Your coat—allow me to have it taken to the kitchen.'

His lordship stood, hands on hips, looking up after Eustacia, a speculative twinkle in his eye. 'A volatile young lady, your sister, is she not?' he remarked, then, recalling his circumstances, went on smoothly, 'I thank you, but I'll come to no harm. My duty to her ladyship, I trust she makes a good recovery.'

Sketching a bow, he left her staring after him, not a little put out. Closing the door behind him with an irritable bang, she went into the salon from whence she watched him exchange words with Mr Warburton, who had just ridden up with his groom. After which, to her surprise, the Earl's groom gave up his place in the cabriolet to Mr Warburton and the two gentlemen drove off together, apparently in perfect amity with each other.

Shaking her head in puzzlement, Miss Middleton went slowly upstairs to confront an exuberant Eustacia who plainly regarded the whole episode as a capital lark.

'Wonersh dashed up for all the world like—like Perseus coming to the rescue of Andromeda!' she chortled from the depths of her hip-bath.

'An unfortunate comparison, my dear,' Miss Middleton pointed out a shade acidly. 'If rumour speaks aright,

Andromeda was not wearing anything very much at the time.'

'Well, I am sure I was in little better case, so utterly soaked and clinging was my habit!' declared Eustacia, all cheerful unconcern. 'Which is, I suppose, why Th—Mr Warburton gave up his claim to me so readily!' Miss Middleton checked a gasp. Surely the Earl had not said anything of what they had discussed to her sister? Eustacia's next words, however, reassured her. 'What a very conversable gentleman his lordship is, to be sure. I don't doubt he has been a great breaker of hearts in his time.'

Miss Middleton forced a bright smile. 'You make him sound a very Methuselah, child!'

'And to judge from the way Mr Warburton refused to discuss him, I'll wager he was something of a rake,' went on Eustacia dreamily.

'It would have been excessively improper in Mr Warburton to have discussed his lordship's character with you,' Miss Middleton reproved her.

'Oh, fustian nonsense!' retorted her unimpressed sister. 'If not from Theodore, I shall get the *on-dit* about your Earl from someone else!'

'He's not my—Eustacia, do try for a little conduct, if you please!'

This lively discussion was terminated by the entry of Griffiths, holding a large bath towel. 'Come along now, miss! We don't want you to be quite done up!'

As Eustacia emerged like Venus from the waves, the sight of her rosy rounded limbs aroused sentiments of a markedly un-Christian nature in Miss Middleton's breast and, with a curt admonition to Griffiths to see that her charge was warmly wrapped, she retreated to the privacy of her own chamber to wrestle with her troubled thoughts.

The Earl, too, had much to occupy his mind as he drove back to Beauregard. The fresh green of the countryside was gently steaming in the warm sunshine that had succeeded the storm, but his lordship had no eyes for the beauties of nature. His conversation with Mr Warburton, before he had set that young gentleman down at the door of his mother's house in Cheltenham, had been enlightening and would certainly have astonished Miss Middleton had she been privileged to hear it.

So she was determined to give him his own again, was she? Well, two could play at that game, nor was he quite the chuckle-headed gudgeon she seemed to think him and so she would discover!

Jevons, who had feared his master to be riding rusty over something, was happy to see him grin broadly and settled back in his seat with an air of relief.

CHAPTER FIVE

Miss Liddell sat back in her chair and looked her visitor over with an appearance of dispassionate interest that gave no hint of her very real concern. There was no doubt of his parentage, one had but to glance at the portrait hanging upon the opposite wall to be convinced of that. The tall, rather loose-limbed figure, the aquiline profile, the heavy-lidded eyes, even the rather untidy russet-brown hair, all resembled the late Earl to a shade. His mode of address, too, had all his father's charm, a little hesitant, almost shy in its careful courtesy, and it counted for no more, she suspected, with the son as with the sire. Beneath her stepfather's seeming diffidence had lain an arrogance of immeasurable proportions and an unswerving belief in his right to do just as he chose. That some, at least, of this supreme self-confidence had been passed down to his son was apparent from the high carriage of the head, the faint curl of the thin lips as he uttered his softly-spoken sentences. Even the slight carelessness of his modish apparel hinted at a pride that took no heed of details that might trouble lesser mortals.

Hastily collecting her straying thoughts she forced herself to listen to what he had to say.

'So you see, ma'am, I have a very personal reason for asking if I may be conducted around Beauregard. But for the absence of a scrap of paper—' He raised his shoulders and spread his hands in a would-be humorous gesture of resignation, but there was little of humour in the dark eyes fixed upon her.

'You would be in authority here? Is that what you would say, Mr Ramsay?' She felt a sudden urge to prick the bubble of his complacency, to shatter that smoothly-smiling façade. 'Well, as to that, I have never taken the head cowman's first-born over the place and his claim, I have no doubt, is as good as yours.'

James Ramsay's face reddened ominously and his eyes smouldered with anger. 'I had not expected—' he began stiffly, but she cut him short.

'The truth is often unpalatable, sir. Nonetheless, I shall accede to your request because, in one respect, you have preference over all other claimants. Since you are, I imagine, all of thirty-five years of age, you must be his late lordship's eldest son.'

'Thirty-six, to be precise, ma'am.'

He was so simmering with rage she could almost feel the heat of his fury beating at her from across the room.

'Indeed?' She pursed her lips consideringly. 'Were he alive your father would be scarce—' She paused a moment to consider. 'Fifty-five? Precocity is much to be admired, but not in all things.'

The cool contempt in her level tones stung him to retort. 'You spoke of other claimants, ma'am. Are there, then more—unfortunates of his begetting?'

'To my knowledge at least six, and I don't doubt the tally is far greater,' Miss Liddell informed him cheerfully.

'Perhaps you had best take 'em round the house in parties!' He was trying to pass things off with a show of humour, but the grim set of his mouth betrayed him.

Miss Liddell rose from her chair. 'I myself will conduct you.' She moved towards the door, then stopped to look at him enquiringly. 'What would you have done, I wonder, if Lord Wonersh had been at home this morning?'

'Played least in sight,' he returned promptly. 'His lordship and I are not precisely bosom-bows.'

'So he tells me.' Her lips twitched and she said no more on that head as she led the way from the room. Her quick brain had registered the fact that he had assured himself of the Earl's absence before presenting himself at Beauregard which seemed to postulate a confederate or, at least, someone in the household willing to impart information if suitably recompensed.

The tour took a considerable time for the visitor was deeply interested in every detail and she, loving the great house as she did, found herself to have a store of sympathetic patience in answering his many questions. They had arrived at the book-room which she had left until the last because it had just been re-decorated and the painters had but removed their pots and ladders the previous day, leaving the room in a state of disarray, when they were joined by Mr Roger Percival.

'Your pardon, Deborah, but if I might have a word with you.' He glanced indifferently at the visitor, then blinked and looked again more closely.

'Pray excuse me, Mr Ramsay.'

Taking Mr Percival by the elbow, she thrust him before her into the hall and shut the door firmly behind them.

'In God's name, who is that?' he demanded to know.

'Who do you imagine?' she hissed, drawing him away from the door. 'One of his late lordship's little slips, and bent on making mischief, I'll be bound.'

His fingers pulled at his neatly-tied cravat as if it offered some constriction to his breathing. 'What is he doing here?'

She told him briefly. 'What is your business with me, Roger?'

'Oh, it don't signify, not now.' Mr Percival was plainly disturbed. 'That fellow—he's of an age, Deborah! He's a deal older than Leo. All the others—forgive me, I have no right to be speaking to you in such fashion.'

'All the others came about when my mother was Countess here, you would say?' she finished for him. 'While this one you might term a boyish indiscretion?'

He smirked. 'What a young cockerel his lordship must have been!'

'Aye, and what a dunghill he built for himself to crow upon!' she rapped out, effectively wiping the smile from his face. 'Good-day to you, Roger, I must return to our cousin. Do you dine with us tonight?'

He bowed his thanks. 'I would be glad to, there are one or two matters of which I would speak to Leo.'

'You know he does not care to be troubled with business affairs at the table,' she warned him. He shrugged.

'I must risk that, he's so devilish hard to pin down else. Where is he this morning, by the way?'

'In Cheltenham, paying a social call.'

He looking knowing. 'On the Middletons, d'you suppose?'

'I daresay.' She was being carefully non-committal.

'Surely he does not hope to have that handkerchief picked up where he dropped it?'

'I am not in Leo's confidence,' said Miss Liddell grandly, and returned to the book-room.

Here she found Mr Ramsay standing by the library steps in the attitude of one who might have just come down off them. Seeing her raised eyebrows, he explained that he had been greatly taken by the fine equine painting that hung above the fireplace and had presumed to inspect it more closely.

'My stepfather commissioned Mr Clifton Tomson to do several of his horses some years ago. They are, I think remarkably fine studies. Now, unless there is anything more you particularly wish to see—'

He disclaimed any such requirement and she pulled the bell-rope for Threadgold to show him out. He thanked her for her courtesy in a perfectly civil, if not over-effusive manner, as if anything that had been done to oblige him was no more than his due, and took his leave rather in the style of an honoured guest assured of a warm welcome on his return which did nothing to lessen her dislike of him.

She was still in the book-room, searching for a misplaced volume, when the Earl returned an hour later.

'I hear we have had a visitor,' he said without preamble, perching himself on the corner of the library table. 'And that you took him on an extensive tour of the house.'

'How—oh, Threadgold, I suppose. He cannot have failed to notice the likeness. No, don't be at daggers-drawing with me, Leo. I wished to discover just what sort of man was your half-brother.'

'And did you?'

'Yes, to a point. While outwardly he is your father's very self, I am not satisfied that he resembles him so closely in character. Oh, he's top-lofty enough, but not so self-indulgent, I'd say.'

'He's not had the chance for it.' The Earl flicked a speck of mud from the skirts of his riding-coat. 'What more did you discover?'

'That he showed an uncommon interest in that painting over the fireplace, having passed by most of our fine collection with no more than a cursory glance, not being, he informed me, any great judge of such things.'

The Earl followed the direction of her eyes. 'My father, too, took small interest in paintings other than those of his horses,' he reminded her. 'Another family trait?'

Miss Liddell, noting his faintly sardonic expression, forbore to comment on this suggestion. 'Roger called this morning with some grumble or other,' she told him. 'But he did not even mention it so taken aback was he at sight of Mr Ramsay. Did you find Lady Middleton in good spirits?'

'I did not find her at all. I found her daughters, though. In fact, I rescued Miss Eustacia from the storm in true knight-errant fashion.'

'Did you, indeed? That must have pleased Miss Middleton.'

'I can only presume that it did since she wishes me to engage her sister's affections.'

Miss Liddell's mouth opened and shut several times before she could frame a reply. 'You're bamming me, Leo!'

He smiled lazily at her. 'Odd, ain't it? No arduous task, mark you, she's a taking little chit. But I have a rival, a Mr Theodore Warburton.'

Miss Liddell, wearing the expression of one who knows none of this could possibly be happening, merely said: 'Oh!' and waited.

'Verity don't approve of him, thinks I could cut him out with Eustacia,' volunteered the Earl.

'Oh!' said Miss Liddell again. 'But why should you?'

'Penance for my past misdemeanours. I have a suspicion that Verity intends me to proceed so far in my advances to her sister that, once Warburton is—er, eliminated, I cannot, in all honour, turn back.'

'As she believes you did once before?' He made no reply but sat, gently swinging a leg, staring into the fire. 'What shall you do, Leo?'

'Why, oblige the lady, to be sure.'

'But—Eustacia?'

'I take to be no fool. I shall call tomorrow to enquire after her health and invite her to drive with me, if she is so disposed.'

'To enlist her aid against her sister? Have a care, Leo!'

He laughed. 'Ostensibly I am merely the bait to entice her away from Warburton. That done I then give way with reluctant grace to some as yet unnamed candidate—you could help me there, Deb, you are good at compiling such lists!' He stood up and stretched hugely.

'The devil but I'm hungry! Is there aught to eat?'

Being thus reminded of her housewifely duties served to distract Miss Liddell's attention as he had intended it should and, during an excellent luncheon of pickled mackerel and a florentine of veal supported by a Welsh rarebit and apple fritters, no further mention was made of Miss Middleton's devious designs.

At the dinner-table that evening Mr Percival gave full vent to his apprehensions regarding Mr Ramsay's visit.

'It's beyond anything, Leo, to encourage the fellow to come here! The servants must be relishing their chatter-broth! I thought you more up to the rig, Deborah, than to be letting him set his foot inside Beauregard!'

Seeing her bridle indignantly, the Earl intervened. 'She could hardly show him the door,' he said mildly. 'And, in any case, what harm's done?' Mr Percival shuffled uneasily on his chair but, as Threadgold then entered to remove the covers and set out the port, no more was said of Mr Ramsay. 'You'll take a glass with us, Deb?' The Earl's hand rested on the decanter while he looked enquiringly at her.

Miss Liddell, however, thoroughly incensed at Mr Percival's cirticism of her behaviour, declined the invitation, saying she had letters to write, and quitted the room leaving a strong atmosphere of disapproval in her wake. Her excuse having been born of her irritation, she was at a loss to know how to occupy herself and turned her steps in the direction of the book-room in search of something to read. Here, as she had given orders for the fire to be allowed to die down, the candles had not been lit nor the drapes drawn, and the room was shrouded in the dusky light from the tall windows.

Feeling her way to the table, her fingers soon located a branch of candles and, once she had them burning steadily, she ascended the library steps. Perched upon the very top, she was leaning forward, candles held aloft in one hand, to pick out the volume she was seeking, when she was aware of a stealthy movement in the shadowy room and the next moment the steps rocked violently. Before she could save herself she was pitched sideways, the candles fell from her hand and she followed them to the floor, striking her head against a nearby standing-desk with such force as to become momentarily insensible.

At first, when she regained consciousness, she found herself unable to move and feared she had suffered a serious injury. Then she realised that the steps had fallen across her legs, pinning her down. As she began slowly to extricate herself a smell of burning assailed her nostrils and small flickers of light relieved the near darkness. It was a full minute before her befuddled senses grasped the fact that the candles had set light to a pile of papers that had fallen off the top of the standing-desk. They, in their turn, had scattered against the drapes which, being of old worn silk, were now blazing away merrily.

'How fortunate the new curtains have not been hung,' Miss Liddell congratulated herself in a very bemused way then, as the flames leaped higher, she was brought to full understanding of her own imminent danger and gave vent to her alarm to the considerable extent of her healthy lungs.

In no time at all the room seemed full to overflowing with all manner of people in varying stages of agitation. The steps were lifted off her lower limbs and she was picked up to be carried from the now smoke-filled room into the salon where she was deposited upon an excessively uncomfortable couch, fashioned after the Egyptian style favoured by the Prince Regent in his seaside pavilion at Brighton.

'In God's name, Deb, what happened?' His lordship was on one knee beside her. 'You have a lump coming up the size of a pigeon's egg on your foreheard.'

'I—I fell over—at least, the steps fell over and I

dropped the candles,' she explained, not very coherently.

'But those steps are as solid as any!' It was Mr Percival's voice coming from somewhere behind her head. ''Gad, Deborah, had I not seen for myself that you scarce sipped your wine tonight, I'd have said you were bosky!'

'Roger, if you would be so good, please supervise the quenching of the flames.' The Earl's voice was uncommonly curt. 'I will join you when I am satisfied that Deborah has taken no lasting hurt.' He waited until Mr Percival had left them, then said in a more gentle way: 'Now, Deb, how did this come about? I can understand your losing your balance and falling off the steps, but not your overturning them for, as Roger says, they are undeniably solid.'

She caught at his hand. 'Leo, I was pushed! There was someone in the room!'

He regarded her with some concern. 'You're not feeling quite the thing, are you, Deb? Lie still, I'll fetch you some brandy.'

'I'm not all about in my head, if that's what you mean,' she assured him, wriggling on the cold, slippery couch. 'Oh, I do think this is a perfectly odious piece of furniture! How—how long have I been unconscious?'

'Not above a couple of minutes. It's no time since you left the dining-table.'

She struggled to a sitting position. 'Then he may be in the house still—whoever pushed me.'

'If he was a thief he would have made good his escape—yes, Threadgold, what is it?'

'Your pardon, my lord, but I thought it best to inform you that I summoned help from the stables to subdue the flames and Jevons, who came running at once, was all but knocked flying when entering from the Green Court by a man unknown to him, who at once made off into the woods.'

'There, you see!' began Miss Liddell triumphantly, but the Earl silenced her with a motion of his hand.

'Did Jevons catch sight of the man's face?'

Threadgold cleared his throat significantly. 'A glimpse only, my lord, the light being very bad. He said it gave him a fair turn, he not being the sort of man to believe in ghosts, but the resemblance to your lordship's late lamented father was very marked.'

'I see.' The Earl stood up, giving a sharp tug to his striped satin waistcoat. 'Fleeting impressions are notoriously unreliable, Threadgold.'

'Yes, my lord. I am of the opinion that Jevons will understand that also, my lord.'

The butler bowed and withdrew, leaving a slightly stunned silence behind him.

'But why, Leo?' Miss Liddell sounded almost plaintive. 'However much I may have provoked him this morning he cannot have taken me in such dislike as to return this evening in order to do me an injury!'

'What is most likely is that he came this morning to spy out the land—which you obligingly revealed to him—and came back this evening for some purpose which you interrupted.'

'But he didn't have to near kill me!' she objected. 'He had only to slip out of the door when I was upon the steps and, even if I had heard him, he would have been gone before I could do aught about it.'

'True.' The Earl was plucking at the lobe of his ear and she waited for the outcome of his deliberations. 'You said you thought he had mounted the steps when you left him alone this morning?'

'Yes, to inspect a painting—or so he said.'

'Supposing that were not so, supposing his interest was quite other?'

'I did not have to move the steps this evening, they were in the same position as—Leo! Do you remember that old story of there being a secret hiding-place behind the panelling in the book-room?'

'Which we never found, search as we might.'

She chuckled. 'I well remember the day your father caught us pulling out all the books and throwing them on the floor!'

'So do I,' said the Earl with feeling. 'Since he considered it unsuitable to chastise a female child, I suffered for us both! But how should Ramsay know of any secret cupboard, and what interest could it hold for him?'

'I don't know,' she confessed. 'But the only reason I can think of for his assault upon me would be that he feared I was near to discovering something he needed to know like—well, proof of his mother's marriage to your father or—or another will, leaving him the bulk of your fortune.'

'Don't let your taste for the romantic quite overpower your good sense, Deb,' advised his lordship. 'If my father had wished so to dispose of his fortune there was nothing to prevent him doing so openly. As to the other, if he did indeed go through a legal form of marriage with Mrs Ramsay or whatever her name was then, and did not wish to acknowledge it, why keep the proof? She makes no such claim and my father has been dead these four years. Time and enough for any rival claimant to put forward his case against me. Come,' he held out a hand to her, 'upstairs with you. It's plain to see you've got a thundering headache.'

Miss Liddell clutched at him with sudden urgency. 'Give me your word, Leo, you will not discuss what we have spoken of here with any other.'

'Apart from Hazlett and Roger,' said he, assisting her to stand, 'I cannot think of anyone with whom I might be tempted to share such a promising crim. con.'

'Not Roger,' she interposed quickly. 'Hazlett, perhaps, might be able to throw some light on this whole unsavoury business.'

'Why not Roger?' he asked, humouring her. 'Do you

fear he will spread abroad the tale of my possible illegitimacy? It won't further his case, you know. If I'm a bastard then Ramsay is not!'

He heard her sharp intake of breath. 'Don't talk like that, Leo! What are you smiling at?'

'I wonder how Verity would reconcile her plans to such a comeabout!'

'Marry Eustacia off to Ramsay, I daresay!' she countered. 'Is the fire quite extinguished in the book-room now? May I see the damage?'

'Tomorrow morning you may,' said the Earl firmly, leading her out of the room to the foot of the staircase where her maid was awaiting her. 'Good-night, dear Deb, take a James's Powder and keep your feet on the ground until I see you again.'

He found Mr Percival in the book-room, lamenting over the confusion caused by the fire. 'These books all lying about—as Deborah's not in prime twig, if you wish for it, Leo, I'll come in tomorrow and put the place to rights.'

'Thank you, Roger, but I have arranged for a librarian, a young gentleman who has worked in the library at Chatsworth and is recommended to me by His Grace of Devonshire, to present himself here next week to start upon the task of cataloguing the whole so there is little point in sorting it out now. It is more than twenty years since it was last done and much has been added in that time to the collection.'

'Oh, if that is the case, of course there is no more to be said.' Mr Percival sounded quite miffy. 'How is Deborah?'

'Much as you might expect after such a heavy fall.'

'She—ah, she can tell you no more of how it happened?'

To the Earl's keen ear the question sounded deliberately casual. The devil! Deborah's suspicions were beginning to colour his outlook, too!

'Apart from the fact that she overreached, dropped the branch of candles and, in attempting to save them, turned the steps over, there is little more to tell,' he said dismissively. 'Come, Threadgold will see to all this, we have two glasses of port awaiting us.' He led the way back to the dining-room, remarking over his shoulder: 'By-the-by, are those pistols we—er, acquired t'other day still in your possession?'

'Pistols? Why—no, you took them in charge, did you not?'

'And left them upon a table in the hall, since when I have not seen them. I presumed you had removed them for safe-keeping.'

'Likely Threadgold did, or one of the footmen. Uncommon fine port this, Leo, I could endure any amount of it.'

Despite this protestation, his lordship had not the pleasure of his cousin's company for very long for Mr Percival soon declared that all this disturbance had brought on an irritation of his nerves and he would be the better for his bed.

The Earl sat for a time afterwards by the dying embers of the fire, so absorbed in meditation that he started when Threadgold came to enquire if he needed anything more that evening.

'I fear I have not done justice to this excellent wine,' he remarked, pushing forward his empty glass. Threadgold re-filled it and then held up the still more than half-full decanter.

'Nor did Miss Deborah, by the looks on't,' he remarked drily.

'She drank none of it,' said the Earl.

'You would think differently to judge by Mr Roger's remarks, my lord.'

The Earl hesitated, greatly tempted to ask a question, but contented himself with saying: 'Thank you, Threadgold. Good-night.'

'Good-night, my lord.'

The old man went quietly out of the room, leaving his master to savour his port, but the Earl's enjoyment of the wine was soured by the knowledge that Mr Percival apparently was determined to spread the impression that Miss Liddell's accident should be put down to an over-indulgence in her favourite drink. Why? So that no other reason might be suspected? If that was so then Roger must be aware that her fall was not an accident.

Shaking his head wearily, he collected his candle from the hall and made his way upstairs to his bedchamber where he soon dismissed his valet and was snug between the sheets as quickly as he might. But he lay wakeful long that night, tossing beneath the handsome brocade hangings depending from the canopy of his great bed, turning over the events of the day without coming to any satisfactory conclusion about any of them save one, and the hopeful contemplation of that particular circumstance finally sent him to sleep with an anticipatory smile upon his lips.

CHAPTER SIX

WHILE the dimensions of the rooms at Royal Crescent denied the possibility of a gathering of such proportions as could have been accommodated at Shurdington Hall, Miss Middleton had resolved that only the best of everything would do for her carefully chosen guests.

Her brother, Godfrey, had handsomely offered to supply the champagne and while it was, of course, unfortunate that he and Annabelle could not be present, she being now very close to her time, Miss Middleton could not help experiencing a profound sense of relief in the knowledge that her sister-in-law's critical eyes would not be peering about, seeking to find some fault in the arrangements.

Although steadfast in her refusal to concede to Eustacia's plea for dancing, she proposed to set up a few card tables in the hope of luring a number of unattached gentlemen to attend who otherwise might have found the evening to be a sad bore. Despite having planned the entertainment with such meticulous care she had, however, no great expectation of all her invitations being taken up and was pleasurably surprised when, by ten o'clock, the rooms were as full as they could hold and Lady Middleton beginning to complain she could not stand another moment to receive any late-comers. It was then that my lord of Wonersh and Miss Liddell arrived and only her daughter's hand, pressed firmly into her tightly corsetted back, gave her ladyship strength to remain on her feet and greet them with tolerable composure.

In the week that had elapsed since the Earl's gallant rescue of Eustacia from the storm, he had called very properly to enquire after her well-being, and had followed this up by taking her driving on two occasions. While Miss Middleton had to allow that, outwardly at least, her plans seemed to be going forward with admirable smoothness, yet she could not quite rid herself of the suspicion that she had not carried off the situation just as she would have liked and that his lordship was very well aware of the trap she had set for him.

Nor did the fact that Mr Warburton appeared to have accepted the Earl's intrusion into his affairs with phlegmatic resignation do anything to soothe her ruffled sensibilities. Not that she had been expecting him to be so cucumberish as to ring a peal over Eustacia for her inconstancy but, secretly, she had hoped for a confrontation between the two gentlemen that would inevitably commit the Earl to go his length in his pursuit of the young lady.

She was recalled to the present by the touch of his hand upon hers and his voice speaking low under cover of Miss Liddell's congratulations to Lady Middleton on the profusion of flowers, everywhere displayed to perfection.

'For which, I am persuaded, you are wholly responsible. Yet, for all that, ma'am, there is no blossom here tonight of greater beauty than she who set it there.'

Miss Middleton, resolved that no one should accuse her of trying to shine down her sister, had chosen to wear a demure dove-coloured crape grown, opening from the waist to show an oyster satin petticoat, with only a single row of pearls for adornment. That the soft colours vastly enhanced her delicate colouring and gave her a look of almost ethereal loveliness had not in the least occurred to her, and she was momentarily thrown into confusion by his lordship's forthright compliment.

'Indeed, my lord, you put me to the blush,' she protested, as well she might for her cheeks were glowing. 'Save your pretty speeches for Eustacia, this is her evening.' He stood, still holding her hand, looking down upon her, an inscrutable expression in his eyes. What strange eyes they were, she thought irrelevantly. A moment before they had been the grey of sun-warmed cloud, yet now she was put in mind of cold water washing over jagged rocks. She experienced a curious pang, akin to a sense of loss, and quickly turned from him to greet Miss Liddell. 'But what has befallen you, dear Deborah? As cruel a bruise as ever I saw!'

'No one but myself to blame,' declared that lady stoically. 'Overstretched myself on the library steps and took a toss.'

'Set the place on fire, too,' supplemented the Earl, reluctantly releasing Miss Middleton's hand. 'And the painters scarce out of it, so all's to do again.'

Discussing this misfortune in more detail took up some little time, then Wonersh led his stepsister to join the other guests in the crowded reception rooms. Presently Miss Middleton, yielding to her mother's pleas, followed them. As she moved through the press, increasingly she became aware that Wonersh's presence was largely responsible for so prestigious a squeeze though curiosity, as she well knew, was the prime incentive. For an instant, a passage cleared across the room direct to where the Earl stood in conversation with Eustacia and her friend, Miss Thistlethwaite. Her sister had plainly been deploring the excessive heat for Wonersh, as easily as if there had been none but their two selves in the room, led her to a nearby vacant sofa and, taking her fan from her hand, proceeded to employ it to good effect, talking away animatedly the while and obliging Miss Thistlethwaite to remove herself, which she did with a very ill grace. The Earl, as if conscious of Miss Middleton's regard, turned his head to look directly at her, and his left eyelid flickered in an unmistakable wink.

Lady Gower, the doyenne of Cheltenham society to whom Miss Middleton had been speaking at that moment, missed nothing of this exchange nor of her young hostess's abstraction.

'Clever of you to have got Wonersh here tonight,' she remarked in her supercilious drawl. 'This is the first time since his return that he has bestirred himself to do the pretty socially. Engaging young buck when he chooses, better make sure of him this time, m'dear.'

Miss Middleton experienced an overwhelming urge to put the impertinent old woman in her place. 'Yes, indeed, he has been most kind in offering to help push Eustacia off. He remembers her only as a schoolroom miss and was quite astonished to discover she had grown into so captivating a young lady.'

'Hmm!' came the uncompromising reply. 'She's all of that, and there are many other young ladies coming into season who'll set their caps at him. You'd do well to remember that men of his age like 'em young and malleable.'

Lady Gower was of the generation that called a spade a spade and made no bones about it.

'I?' Miss Middleton was all wide-eyed innocence. 'Why, what can you mean, ma'am?'

'Don't try to cozen me, my girl! Nor try to be too clever for your own good! Wonersh is no small catch and you would make him a better countess than any of these baby-faced chits.'

Miss Middleton conceded defeat and, murmuring that she saw her mama beckoning to her, made her escape. A glance towards the sofa informed her that the Earl appeared to be fairly embarked upon a flirtation with Eustacia, holding her fan so as partially to screen their faces as he whispered outrageous compliments into her delighted ears. That fan! She stopped short in the middle of a sentence and resumed it a moment later so much at random that the lady and gentleman to whom she was speaking exchanged a wondering look from beneath raised eyebrows. She had laid the fan aside with other small gifts of his, since to return them at the time seemed to be making too great an issue of his desertion. They were, after all, no more than any gentleman might give as Christmas or anniversary presents to a lady of his acquaintance. The fan was a delicate brisé affair in ivory, decorated after the manner of Angelica Kauffman, and she had been turning it over in her hands when Eustacia had entered the room and exclaimed at its elegance.

'What, this old thing? You can have it if it pleases you,' Miss Middleton had replied carelessly, nor had she set eyes upon it again from that day some six months before. Now to see his long fingers playing with the sticks as he used it to a nicety in his dalliance with her sister went quite against the pluck.

Of a sudden as she looked about the congested rooms, the taste of success turned to dust in her mouth, the fashionable throng became the dullest, most insipid collection of persons that ever she had encountered, and Eustacia a tiresome little brat who ought to be in her bed upstairs instead of playing at grown-ups with her elders and betters. Somehow, she got through the remainder of the evening, looking to her guests' comfort and discussing such diverse subjects as, if medicine be ranked among those arts which dignify their professors, to judge by the popular demand for Dr William Kitchiner's book of recipes might not cookery lay claim to an equal if not a superior distinction? Or whether the style of wearing one's hair *á la Chinoise* was not most unfair to golden-haired beauties, since who had ever heard of a blonde Chinese? Upon these, and other pressing topics of the day, she discoursed with ready fluency, but if any gentleman seemed disposed to single her out and make her the particular object of his attentions she slid away, as elusive as quicksilver, though with never a hint of rebuff to offend his sensibilities.

Later, the house at last quiet and empty of guests, she stood in her night attire by the window of her bedchamber, looking down upon the now deserted arc of the Crescent. Not quite deserted, she perceived, for a man was pacing slowly along the pavement, looking up at the houses as he passed. When he came opposite her window he stopped and, the errant moon making a brief appearance from behind the clouds, a silvery beam flickered across his upturned countenance.

Something in the pose of his head as he stood there. bare-headed, the night breeze ruffling his hair, his cloak flung back over one shoulder to display his well-made person, was fleetingly familiar, so that she at first supposed him to be one of the party who had, perhaps, forgotten or mislaid something and had returned in the hope of finding the household still astir. Then a bank of cloud swept over the moon again and when it had cleared away he had gone.

Shivering, as if touched with the cold finger of premonition, she got into bed and, finding sleep to be elusive, determinedly began to count sheep jumping through gaps in hedges until one of them looked over its shoulder and winked at her. This, despite her unaccountable depression, induced in her a strong desire to laugh, for anything less sheep-like than my lord of Wonersh could not be imagined, but before she finally fell asleep all laughter had left her and her pillow was damp with the tears she no longer felt the need to hold in check.

The following morning was a bright blustery one, the brisk wind slamming doors and bustling through windows flung wide to air the stuffy rooms as if bidding the lethargic inhabitants to be up and about their business. Lady Middleton, sitting up in bed drinking her chocolate and going through her post, was in a rarely congratulatory mood.

'Our first entertainment here and the greatest success that ever I saw,' she enthused. 'All credit to you, my dear Verity, for making it so. Depend upon it, there will not be room upon our mantelshelf for the invitations that will come pouring in after this!' Her elder daughter made no reply and her ladyship eyed her uneasily. 'You are not perfectly satisfied? My love, you are quite worn down, so much as you have had upon your shoulders. You'll come about in a day or two, take my word for it. Eustacia is up and out riding already.'

'Already?' echoed Miss Middleton.

Her ladyship beamed. 'I suspect an assignation with—well, one should not hazard a guess, of course, and I was insistent that Wilkes accompanied her—but Lord Wonersh was most marked in his attentions last night, was he not?'

'Most marked,' agreed her daughter hollowly. Lady Middleton's latent maternal sense could well have been aroused by this apathetic response had not her attention been arrested by the handwriting upon one of the letters strewn over her coverlet.

'Why, I do declare it is from your Aunt Susan—and posted in London! She and your uncle will be returned from Portugal then!'

Miss Middleton moved away to look over some library books set upon a side-table while her mother unfolded the single sheet of hot-pressed paper and rapidly skimmed through its contents. Lady Susan Daventry was her father's sister and had been her own kind hostess and chaperon during her two seasons in London. No one could have been more assiduous in launching her upon the social scene—vouchers for Almacks, invitations to the most elegant establishments, introductions to every gentleman of breeding and fortune who might conceivably be on the look for a wife—and no one was more disappointed when all these inducements failed and her niece declined to profit by any of them.

'Oh, but this could not have fallen out better!' Lady Middleton's voice cut across her gloomy reflections. 'Your aunt finds herself to be quite blue-devilled with no young people around her and begs that I "lend her one of mine"—such a quaint turn of phrase, but what an opportunity for Eustacia—though, to be sure, Susan makes no mention of a season.'

'She cannot be aware that Eustacia is out yet.' Miss Middleton spoke as if weighing up the prospects. 'As for me, she must assume that I am safely lodged upon the shelf.'

'What nonsense, Verity!' protested her mother. 'When I know not how many gentlemen last evening complimented me upon your appearance. Your aunt mentions you particularly and with great kindness. You were ever a prime favourite with her.'

Miss Middleton smiled faintly. 'Aunt Susan hardly knows Eustacia, mama, or thinks of her as still a child. That is all the reason for her preference.'

Her ladyship brightened visibly. 'Then do you think—' she began hopefully.

'No,' said Miss Middleton. 'To send Eustacia away now would be to lose every advantage gained last night.' She held out a hand for her aunt's letter and perused it swiftly. 'As you say, there is no mention of any social expectations. My uncle is much concerned with his affairs, Aunt Susan is lonely and would like a conversable companion until she settles back into her old ways, there is no more to it than that. Besides, we are in the last days of April, the London season is already launched. For Eustacia to enter upon it at this stage would serve no good purpose.'

Lady Middleton at once saw the sense of this reasoning. 'Better far that she should build upon her successes here,' she agreed. 'But what am I to say to Susan? I would not wish to be disobliging in any way for—who can tell? If, by the autumn, things are not in a way to being settled—'

'Quite so. And should my aunt take a house in Brighton this summer—you know how you love to be at Brighton, mama! So,' ended Miss Middleton, on a note of conscious virtue, 'I shall go to London and bear her company for a time.'

Lady Middleton looked her alarm. 'Yes, but Verity, if you are not here—'

'That has nothing to say to anything. You will, of course, chaperon Eustacia,' pursued her daughter relentlessly, 'and see that she knows what's what.' Her ladyship plainly was not in entire agreement with these sentiments, but found herself unable to fault them. 'That is settled then.' Miss Middleton folded her aunt's letter and tucked it away in her reticule. 'I will reply to this and inform Aunt Susan that I hope to join her in Park Place as soon as I may.'

'And—of course! You will be in London and at hand for dear Annabelle's lying-in!'

However much Lady Middleton might feel elated at this prospect her daughter could not feel it to be a matter for congratulation, but she devoutly hoped that, as her sister-in-law had secured the attendance of two eminent accoucheurs for the Great Event, her services would not be required.

'Yes, everything appears to be falling out very neatly,' she agreed. 'Now, I have one or two calls to make this morning and, if I am to be off to London within the week, they had best not be postponed.'

The calls, being of a business nature, were soon dealt with and, revelling in the fresh breeze, she decided to extend her excursion and take a walk while she considered the advantages of her aunt's hospitable offer.

Apart from the pleasure of seeing Lady Daventry again, to whom she was deeply attached, there was all the attraction of once more enjoying the varied delights of the Metropolis. For her, London was a constant entertainment, an ever-changing pageant that never failed to hold her interest. There were even times when she regretted not having been born one of the opposite sex so that she might savour the enjoyment natural to every young buck of visiting Cribb's Parlour, playing maçao at Watier's, sporting one's buff at Mr Jackson's Boxing Academy, looking in at Tattersall's, or blowing a cloud at the Daffy Club. She was forced to smile at thought of how her circle of acquaintance would regard such an admission from the proper and highly-regarded Miss Middleton and, once more, her fancy flew to one whose sense of the ridiculous would lead him readily to understand so indecorous an ambition.

That this visit to London would also remove her from Cheltenham and close association with my lord of Wonersh was, she was persuaded, a very good thing. While in no way allowing that her affections had been at all re-animated towards him, she was obliged to confess that she was not entirely unaffected by his easy address and elegant person. If her departure smacked somewhat of flight, she could defend her position by pointing out that, once her plans were fairly launched, there was nothing more for her to do in Cheltenham and, like every good general, she knew when to abdicate her authority and leave her subordinates to carry out her orders.

So absorbed was she in these various considerations as she walked along Lower Well Walk that she had no eyes for anything around her until, as she was passing the entrance to Mr Gardner's brewery, a warning shout brought her head up with a jerk. To her alarm she perceived a dray with a team of strengthy horses advancing upon her. For a moment she stood, unable to move, then, as full comprehension of her danger dawned upon her, she tried to fling herself out of the path of the approaching peril. At the same time a strong arm caught her about the waist and whisked her to safety.

'I—I must have been day-dreaming,' she gasped. 'Th—thank you, sir, I am much obliged to you.'

'That you were, ma'am,' said a pleasant well-bred voice. 'It was fortunate that I was walking close behind you and was at once aware of your situation.'

He was standing, hat in hand, still holding her elbow as he smiled down upon her, a tall gentleman with reddish-brown hair and slumbrous dark eyes. Miss Middleton, a trifle put out by her narrow escape, regarded him doubtfully.

'But surely, sir, we have met, have we not?'

He bowed. 'I have not had that pleasure, ma'am. If I may introduce myself, my name is Ramsay, James Ramsay.'

'Ramsay?' she repeated in rather a dazed way. 'No, I don't think—well, I am Miss Middleton.'

He bowed again. 'Now that the proprieties have been observed, may I offer you my arm to wherever you were bound? If you will forgive me, so narrow an escape is most likely to affect the sensibilities, particularly in the aftermath of recollection.'

She managed a tremulous smile but had to acknowledge the good sense of his reasoning. 'It is only a step to Royal Crescent, sir, but I am persuaded my mama will wish to thank you for your good offices.'

Mr Ramsay, who had been dogging Miss Middleton's footsteps since she had left home in the hope of a chance encounter, could hardly believe his good fortune and put himself out to be agreeable. He was, she discovered, lodged at the Plough and was in the course of a tour of the better known English spas. His first enthusiasm was for Bath, but he was much inclined to favour Cheltenham above any other by reason of the diversity of its waters, and lent an eager ear to what she had to tell him about Captain Henry Skillicorne who had built the first spa there, and Their Majesties' visit that had given the final accolade to the town. Soon they were cosing together like old friends and were in a fair way to establishing the first trenches of an acquaintance by the time they reached Royal Crescent. Then Mr Ramsay's flow of conversation came to an abrupt halt as he perceived the Earl's phaeton standing before Lady Middleton's door.

'I believe, ma'am, that I must leave you here.'

'No, no,' she protested. 'Why will you not—oh, we have a caller. But it is only Lord Wonersh, an old freind, who doubtless, will wish to add his thanks to mine.'

'Doubtless, ma'am.' There was a sardonic twist to his lips as he echoed the word and stopped to remove his beaver and take her hand in farewell. Why, she could not be certain, but the movement put her in mind of the man she had seen the previous night, walking alone in the Crescent. It was he, of that she was convinced, and that, of course, would explain the sense of familiarity she had experienced when seeing him again to-day. It would also explain how he had known which house was her mama's if he had been on the look for it last night. But why should he be interested in where she lived? He was no ardent young blood, but an assured man-of-the-world, and most unlikely to be wasting his time gazing up at an unknown lady's window. Except that she was not now unknown to him.

His voice broke in on this troubled sequence of ideas. 'I shall hope to have the pleasure of seeing you again if, as you tell me, you visit the Pump Rooms regularly with your mother,' he was saying, 'and, with your permission, will dare to presume upon so irregular an introduction. Your servant, ma'am.'

She murmured something conventional and, with a slight pressure of her hand, he was gone, moving swiftly round the corner and out of sight. Feeling not a little bewildered by this sudden departure, she walked on to be greeted by Wonersh, who had come out of the house and was standing by his carriage.

'Your cavalier took his leave somewhat precipitately,' said he with less than his usual urbanity.

'Yes, he—I—I don't think he wanted to meet you,' she heard herself saying without much surprise, as if she had known it all along.

His eyes flashed. 'Indeed? Am I then so undesirable a character? It's best you tell me, ma'am, one does not realise these things of oneself, I believe.'

'Of course not!' Still further confused by his hostility, she tried to pour oil on these inexplicably troubled waters. 'He—he has just saved me from a particularly nasty accident.'

His expression changed to one of concern and, in a moment, he had the whole story from her.

'James Ramsay, eh?' He nodded as if having his suspicions confirmed. 'Yes, I know him.'

Something in the way he said it led her to a swift conclusion. 'And are no friend of his? I am sorry for that, my lord, but I have cause to be grateful to him and—and I confess I found him to be a very agreeable gentleman.'

'A very fortunate gentleman, at all events, to have so fair a defender!' he quizzed her. 'But I will say no more on that head. I learn from Lady Middleton that you are to leave us for the greater joys of the Metropolis.'

'Yes, my aunt has need of me.' She flung the statement at him like a gauntlet, and he was quick to pick it up.

'Running away, Verity?' he murmured sweetly.

Her hands itched to box his ears but, suppressing so ignoble an impulse, she bade him a curt good-day and marched into the house past the startled butler who still stood, holding the door for his lordship's departure, and upstairs to her bedchamber. There it took all of five minutes to compose herself sufficiently to allow of her calling upon her mother and recounting the events of the morning.

The Earl, although perfectly composed, wore a constrained expression as he drove back to Beauregard. At the dinner table that evening he surprised Miss Liddell by informing her that he proposed to open up his town house for a time.

'Perhaps you would be so kind, my dear Deb, as to take whosoever of the staff you may need with you and set them to taking off the covers and putting the place to rights?'

'If that is what you wish, Leo, I will see to it at once,' she responded readily. 'Had you in mind to go up for the remainder of the season?'

'I am not perfectly sure.' He appeared to be giving his whole attention to making a choice between roast veal with a cream sauce or stuffed chicken quenelles. 'I understand the Daventrys are back in town.'

Miss Liddell thought that over before making a pronouncement. 'I daresay Lady Daventry will be wishful of asking one or both of her nieces to spend some time with her.'

'I believe she has already done so and Miss Middleton will be joining her aunt very soon.'

'Oh, then perhaps I can take her up with me when I go to Berkeley Square. I shall be delighted to renew my acquaintanceship with Lady Daventry, such a well-informed, lively mind as she has. But, Leo—'

'I must felicitate you, Deb.' His lordship had come down in favour of the chicken quenelles and was devouring them with evident relish. 'This dish is worthy of Carême himself.'

'It is borrowed from one of his menus,' she confessed, 'though I was not at all certain that François could carry it off.'

'Pray send him my congratulations and a glass of port. I think it admirably done.'

The Earl then turned the conversation to topics of the day, and however much his stepsister tried to steer it back to the subject of Miss Middleton's visit to her aunt she found herself being gently but inflexibly fobbed off until she was forced to give up the attempt.

CHAPTER SEVEN

Miss Liddell's amiable plan of conveying Miss Middleton with her to London met with general approbation, except perhaps from that young lady herself. Though acknowledging them to be quite unattainable, she had secretly been cherishing dreams of dashing through the night in the Royal Mail or, at the very least, enjoying a daytime journey on the Regulator or the Retaliator, if one could be said to enjoy eleven or twelve hours at a stretch in a stage-coach. That such a method of progression would be highly unsuitable for a Middleton she was left in no doubt on hearing her mama's strictures upon the subject, but as the alternative meant depriving the Dowager of her carriage and groom for several days, to say nothing of Griffiths being obliged to sit beside her in grim disapproval of the whole project—for that inflexible damsel considered London to be a frippery place and altogether beneath the touch of any decent-thinking female—Miss Middleton accepted Miss Liddell's offer with a nice show of grateful complaisance.

The day was a warm and brilliant one when they set out, being speeded on their way by a slightly lachrymose Lady Middleton and a frankly envious Eustacia. The carriages bearing the baggage and the staff necessary for opening up the Earl's house in Berkeley Square had proceeded directly from Beauregard and would be in London before them as Miss Liddell, never one for getting over the ground to break her neck if it threatened to inconvenience her, had decreed that she and Miss Middleton should halt their journey near Oxford and continue to the Metropolis at their leisure on the following day.

'I have written to bespeak rooms for us at the Spread Eagle at Thame,' she said in her comfortable way. 'I know it to be somewhat off our road, but the service there is of an excellence unequalled in my experience and Oxford has become so excessively restless and overcrowded.'

Miss Middleton murmured a suitable reply though, if the truth be told, her mind was on other things. The two days preceding her departure had been as full as they could hold with last minute preparations and purchases, since to be going to London in whatever capacity called for a sartorial effort of no mean degree.

Due to a combination of fine weather and a race-meeting being held at that time, the press of visitors in Cheltenham was beyond the ordinary, the greater part idling about at their ease, admiring the fine buildings and well-stocked shops. Miss Middleton, discarding her carriage in favour of an excursion on foot, had been surprised to see Mr Roger Percival sauntering along the Promenade, and was about to raise a hand in greeting when a group of young women, as bright as parakeets in their gay silks and twice as noisy, had intervened and obscured him momentarily from her view.

When they had passed she perceived that he was no longer alone, a taller more commanding figure had taken his arm and was leading him into an adjacent coffee-house. As she could obtain no more than a glimpse of their retreating backs, Miss Middleton was willing to allow that she could have been mistaken, but she was persuaded that the second gentleman had been none other than her gallant rescuer, Mr James Ramsay.

There was, of course, no reason why the two gentlemen should not be acquainted though, as Mr Ramsay was clearly no friend of the Earl's, it seemed an unlikely chance that he should be on terms of apparent affability with Mr Percival. She was debating how best to bring the matter to Miss Liddell's attention when that lady solved her problem for her.

'I hear from Leo that Mr Ramsay's intervention t'other day saved you from serious injury.'

'Indeed, yes.' Miss Middleton gave her companion full details of the near-disaster and went on to add, 'I must confess to having been favourably impressed by Mr Ramsay. A most gentlemanlike sort of man and not one to put himself forward in any way.'

Miss Liddell, who held a less charitable opinion of the Earl's half-brother, pursed her lips and chose her words with care.

'Oh, he's prime and bang up to the mark, no doubt, and has a pronounced air of fashion, but as to the rest, I cannot say.'

Miss Middleton looked her surprise. 'Why, do you suspect him of being a—a Queernabs?'

Mindful of the Earl's injunction to convey some sort of warning to Miss Middleton not to permit too great a familiarity to develop between the gentleman in question and herself, Miss Liddell found herself in something of a quandary and decided that only the truth would serve.

'Not to wrap it up in clean linen, he is the late Earl's eldest by-blow,' she said bluntly. 'Who was his mother and what his upbringing we cannot be perfectly certain. All we do know is that the lady was married off to a Mr Ramsay to give her son a name.'

Miss Middleton, no missish young lady, was not visibly affected by this distressing disclosure. 'But such misfortune should command sympathy rather than censure,' she declared roundly. 'Yet Leo made his aversion very plain when we spoke of—of Mr Ramsay.'

Miss Liddell took comfort from the uttered 'Leo', but decided to turn the conversation to safer issues. 'There's no accounting for it to be sure. But here we are at Burford. I suggest we take a cup of coffee at the Lamb while the horses are being baited. I intend to keep my own team for the whole journey so it will be well to cossett them a little over the initial stages. By-the-by,' she added, gathering up her reticule and jewel-case as the chaise drew to a halt outside the Lamb, 'I know I can rely upon your discretion in that other matter. I would not wish to make Mr Ramsay's stay at Cheltenham uncomfortable in any way.'

Miss Middleton gave the required assurance, adding as the groom sprang down to open the door and let down the steps, 'He appears to be on easy terms with Mr Percival.'

'What?' Miss Liddell sat back heavily on the cushions and stared at her.

'Yes, I believe I saw them cosing amicably together in Cheltenham yesterday.'

Miss Liddell said no more on the subject, but her brain was working furiously behind the flow of pleasant banalities which served as a defensive façade for her thoughts.

'With the continuing good weather in mind, I had the chef pack us a picnic hamper and suggest we broach it at Minster Lovel. I do so dote upon the place and the tale of how the skeleton of the last Lord Lovel was found, seated at a table in a secret room, where he had been inadvertently locked in and forgotten, never fails to chill my blood.'

If Miss Middleton considered that to be an unlikely sort of recommendation for a picnic place, she kept her scruples to herself and assented readily to her friend's suggestion. Later, reclining in the shade of the grey ruins with no witnesses other than a few wide-eyed sheep, she was obliged to confess that the choice of location could scarce have been bettered. As was to be expected, the Beauregard kitchens had produced a repast fit for the most discerning palate. Cold salmon and cucumbers, potted prawns and finely-sliced beef with green salad and pickled walnuts were supported by a pistachio cream, buttered oranges, and a variety of cheeses, all washed down by a pleasing light hock and coffee made by Miss Liddell on a small spirit stove. This, being both hot and strong, was designed to offset the pleasant somnolence induced by partaking of a generous meal on so warm a day. Curiously, however, Miss Middleton found it to have quite the contrary effect.

From under heavy lids, she noted drowsily that the carriage had been drawn well into the shade. Doubtless the groom and coachman were enjoying their own meal near to where the horses stood, freed from the traces, contentedly munching the thick close grass. A slight snore informed her that Miss Liddell had succumbed to the prevailing circumstances and was fast in the arms of Morpheus. A moment later her own head began to nod and, when the groom presented himself beside her to enquire when the ladies would be pleased to resume their journey, she experienced the greatest difficulty in focussing her gaze upon him.

'I think, perhapsh—perhaps, not for h—half—an —hour?'

Great Heavens, she sounded to be quite castaway! Her speech was slurred and the man's dark visage bent over her swayed and receded in the strangest manner. He seemed content with her reply, however, and walked away, but her visual memory, struggling against an increasing desire for sleep, kept urging her that something was not as it should be. Admittedly, she had seen him only when stepping in and out of the chaise and had paid him scant attention, but was not the groom a large, fair young man, whereas this other was slim and saturnine?

'Probably the coachman,' she reassured herself. 'C—can't remember what he looks like. Can't remember anything very much. Never mind, I shall come about presently.' After which profound reflection she promptly fell asleep.

When she awoke she felt as if she was struggling up from the bottom of a deep pit and slipping back two feet for every foot gained in the ascent. Her first clear understanding came with the realisation that, instead of reposing upon a rug spread upon lush greensward in the full midday warmth of a summer's day, she was lying upon a hard stone floor and there was little warmth or sunshine discernible in her immediate surroundings. As she stirred and made an effort to sit up, Miss Liddell's voice spoke in her ear.

'Ah, you are with me again. Thank Heaven for that at least!'

Miss Middleton blinked at her. 'Why should I not be?' she asked, rather peevishly. 'What is this place? Why is it so dark?'

'It is dark,' explained Miss Liddell, answering her questions in reverse order, 'because it is close on eight o'clock. You have been insensible for over six hours. This place I believe to be an old tower or folly not very far from Beauregard. For the rest, we have been kidnapped.'

'K—kidnapped!' echoed Miss Middleton, shocked into sitting up too abruptly and finding the experience an unpleasant one. 'But—who would do such a thing? And why?'

'If this missive is anything to go by,' Miss Liddell held up a single sheet of paper between finger and thumb as if it had been some poisonous reptile, 'Mr James Ramsay is our captor. We are to persuade Leo, if you please, to relinquish the earldom in favour of one who has a better claim to it, else my near lifeless and no doubt ravished form will be deposited upon his doorstep. Should he not accede to this demand then yours will follow in due course, or so I take to be the meaning of this quite extraordinary epistle.'

Such an astonishing revelation about one for whom she had cause to feel gratitude had less effect than might have been expected upon its recipient. 'May I see—I—oh!' Miss Middleton put a hand to her head and groaned faintly.

'Have a care!' Miss Liddell steadied her. 'It will take you a little time to recover from the effects of whatever sleeping potion was introduced into our coffee. I have been awake this hour and more and am only just beginning to think clearly.'

'Why was I insensible for so long?' Miss Middleton, experiencing a wave of acute nausea, wondered if she was going to be ill and set her mind resolutely against such a humiliating course.

'You had a second cup of coffee. Now, if you will be advised by me, you will lie back and allow your sensibilities to recover gradually. The disorder of the stomach will soon pass.'

Having no choice in the matter, Miss Middleton obeyed this injunction, and within twenty minutes or so was rewarded by being able to rise to her feet, albeit shakily, and take proper stock of her surroundings. These afforded her little comfort.

The small room in which the ladies were confined was starkly circular and beyond doubt, as Miss Liddell had observed, the topmost storey of a tower. A pointed roof loomed high overhead while the only source of light was provided by a narrow slit window. One corner of the floor sloped down to a drainhole, placed there for whatsoever purpose Miss Middleton could not immediately conceive, and the only entrance to the room appeared to be an aperture some three feet square and two feet from the ground which was closed by a massive-looking metal door. This fitted smoothly into the wall with no sign of bolts or hinges, all of which were clearly set on the outer side. A small panel in this formidable obstacle hinted at a spy-hole, though as this also was operated from the other side she could see no advantage that might be derived from it by anyone within the room.

'This tower,' Miss Liddell informed her, 'I believe to be one just outside the confines of Leo's estates. There are hardly likely to be two such in the neighbourhood. It was built into the rock face of a small cliff or cutting by some medieval ancestor of his, for what purpose no one can be sure. Some said to confine his enemies, while others asserted it was used to entertain his lights of love, though I should have thought it deucedly uncomfortable for the latter purpose. It was once part of the Beauregard lands, but I cannot say who owns it now. All I can tell you is that it is a desolate and little-frequented spot.'

'So that any cries for help are most unlikely to bring a horde of rescuers to our aid?'

'On the contrary,' said Miss Liddell grimly, 'the place has such an unsavoury reputation that anyone hearing our cries would, in all probability, remove themselves from the vicinity without troubling to enquire into their source.'

'But why so near to Beauregard?' puzzled Miss Middleton, endeavouring to shake off the mists that clouded her normally percipient brain.

'For convenience, perhaps? Or because it is the last place anyone would think to look for us?' Miss Middleton nodded her acceptance of this simple logic and resumed her inspection of the room. The only furniture was a stool and a rough wooden bench on which one of them might lie at a time. On it, she was pleased to see, reposed the picnic hamper, and on the floor nearby stood two stone jars. 'Fresh water in one of them,' supplied Miss Liddell, following the direction of her gaze. 'The other appears to have contained spermacetti oil, there is still some in it. If only I had had the forethought to bring my Argand lamp we would be well provided with light.'

Disregarding this satirical witticism, Miss Middleton was inspecting the inward-sloping wall that was the rock-face of the cutting. A little above the level of her head was set a round metal cover, fitting flush into the surface of the rock. This, unlike the door, had a handle which gave it all the appearance of a large cooking-pot lid.

'I have tried pushing and pulling it, but it doesn't move,' said Miss Liddell in a slightly despairing way. 'Would you care to read this—er, demand?'

Miss Middleton took the letter from her and, with some difficulty, managed to decipher the ill-written script in the indifferent light that prevailed. It was, as Miss Liddell had informed her, a brief ultimatum. Either the Earl accepted an unnamed claimant, presumably Mr Ramsay, as the legitimate heir to the title and to Beauregard, or the two ladies would remain imprisoned. Should he continue obdurate beyond a certain time then the prisoners would be obliged to suffer starvation, beatings, and other unpleasant refinements not specifically detailed. The Earl would be informed of the situation without delay, but if they wished to add a plea on their own behalf, writing materials and ink would be found in the hamper. A messenger would call in the evening of the following day when a letter could be passed out through the spy-hole.

Miss Middleton sat down on the stool and looked at her companion. 'I cannot believe it,' she said flatly.

Miss Liddell shrugged and opened the hamper. 'Writing-paper—the best—ink, and quills,' she said with a gesture of the hand, 'and none of the food has been touched. I daresay you don't feel very sharp-set but it will be dark soon and we had best eat while we can. We have enough for at least two meals but I don't suppose it will remain fresh for more than another day. May I pour you some wine?' Then, seeing the troubled expression on the girl's face, she went on briskly. 'We cannot be too nice in our notions, my dear Verity, and the dictates of nature are quite beyond our power to control.' She thereupon turned her back while Miss Middleton thankfully explored the possibilities of the sloping floor and the drainhole.

When they had finished their meal Miss Liddell consulted her watch. 'It is past nine o'clock,' she pronounced. 'They will have given up all hope of us at the Spread Eagle, I have no doubt, but as everyone else will presume us to be there our absence will not be remarked upon as yet. I wonder what has happened to the coachman and groom? I pray they have not met with harm.'

Miss Middleton could only devoutly echo this hope and, for a time, the two ladies sat disconsolate in the ever darkening room. At last Miss Liddell, whose ebullient spirit would not permit her to remain inactive, rose and began to pace the confines of their prison.

'What will Wonersh do?' she pondered.

'What can he do?' returned Miss Middleton. 'For your sake, if for no other, he will not permit us to languish here a moment longer than needs be, so he must yield to Mr Ramsay's demands.'

'Who will, of course, produce proof of his mother's marriage for the world to see. But where could it have lain all these years and why should it come to light?' She caught her breath suddenly. 'The book-room! Leo thought Ramsay might have been seeking something there—perhaps, on the contrary, he might have been wishful of finding a place to hide something, something that could be "found" later.'

'Like a marriage certificate, legally witnessed? There is no possibility that such a thing does truly exist—is there?'

Miss Liddell shook her head emphatically. 'Not a chance in the world,' she declared. 'Oh, I'll not deny his late lordship had many an odd kick in his gallop, but he had a fondness for Leo, he'd not serve him so ill a trick.'

'Then, once we are freed, Wonersh can declare it all to be false!' burst out Miss Middleton, then she caught her friend's eye and her face fell, 'but not—not, I suppose, if he had given his word to let it stand. Oh, these gentlemen and their points of honour! I am out of all patience with them!'

'My dear, there is no sort of use worrying yourself into a frenzy,' soothed Miss Liddell, 'and I can assure you my honour is not as nice as that when dealing with a scoundrel, which is doubtless why I am to be disposed of the first! What are you about, Verity?'

Miss Middleton was dragging the heavy bench over to the wall provided by the quarry face. 'I am resolved to see what lies behind that cover or whatever it is!' she announced, placing the picnic hamper on the bench and, tucking up her skirts, climbing on top of it. From this elevation she was comfortably placed to seize hold of the handle of the round lid and tug at it fiercely. At first, she had no more success than had had Miss Liddell then, by chance, the picnic hamper yielded under her weight. She was thrown sideways and forced to alter her grip on the handle which moved slightly under the additional pressure. 'Why, I do believe it doesn't pull, it twists!' she gasped, suiting actions to words. The next moment she was flat on her back on the floor, the metal lid on top of her, while an accumulation of dried leaves and dust spilled out of the round aperture revealed above her head.

Miss Liddell, having first assured herself that her companion was unhurt and the contents of the picnic hamper undamaged, was quick to assess this new development.

'It is a small tunnel or passage, cut upwards through the rock and into the ground beyond,' she decreed, standing on the bench to peer into the dark opening. 'And there must be an exit t'other end, because I can feel fresh air blowing upon my face.'

'Do you suppose Leo's ancestor used to thrust his enemies down it so they came hurtling into the room?' enquired Miss Middleton whimsically. Miss Liddell, however, took the suggestion quite seriously.

'They would have to have been very slightly built folk,' she pointed out. 'Verity, this hamper cannot support our weight, let us try the stool.' But the stool was not sufficiently tall to further her purpose and, for an instant, she stood irresolute. 'Help me turn this bench over,' she then commanded. 'It will give us another foot or two of height.'

'What do you hope to do?' asked Miss Middleton when this task had been accomplished.

'See if—I can—fit—' Miss Liddell's voice was muffled as she endeavoured to insert her head and shoulders into the cavity. 'Not possible!' she gulped, emerging red-faced from her efforts. 'Even if I could wriggle my bosom through, my lower extremities would undoubtedly stick fast! But the actual opening is the narrowest part, the tunnel is wider inside, and there are rough protuberances in the rock surface that would be of assistance in drawing oneself upwards.' She dropped to the floor and eyed her companion. 'You are a deal more slender than I, Verity. Would you care to attempt it?'

Miss Middleton needed no urging and was already climbing on to the bench. While she endeavoured to insert her person into the tunnel Miss Liddell stood anxiously by, ready to thrust or pull as necessity required. Unhappily, however, even that slight form stuck firmly below the waist and no amount of writhing or twisting would ease it through the unyielding circle. Finally, disheartened and not a little fearful of becoming inextricably wedged, Miss Middleton gave up the attempt and slid back into the room where she ruefully surveyed the damage done to the skirts of her jacket and petticoat.

'It needed but an inch or so and you would have been

through!' lamented Miss Liddell. 'Your skirts—'

'Yes, my skirts!'

Without hesitation, Miss Middleton began to divest herself of her outer garments and presently stood, dimly revealed, in bodice and pantalettes.

'But you have no notion of where you may arrive at the other end or who you may encounter!' Miss Liddell glanced up at the slit window. 'There is still some daylight left, wait until it is fully dark, when none may observe your state of undress.'

'If I am successful in getting through, you can tie my petticoats in a bundle and secure them to my ankle with this scarf,' instructed Miss Middleton. 'But first, let us see if it will answer.'

Five minutes later, with not only the pantalettes but the tender flesh beneath them scratched and lacerated by her unavailing struggles, she was forced to concede defeat.

'Almost was I convinced at one moment that I was through, but this cambric is an unyielding stuff. I vow had my wretched garments been of satin—' She stopped suddenly, lost in thought, while Miss Liddell sat on the stool, head bowed on her hands in weary resignation. 'Deborah,' went on Miss Middleton slowly. 'Very soon it will be quite dark. If I divested myself of these tiresome pantalettes—'

'My dear, it is not to be thought of! You would be ripped to pieces on that rough surface.'

'Did you not tell me there is still some spermacetti oil in that jar?' Miss Middleton continued speaking in the same deliberate way.

'You mean—apply it to your person so that you might slide through the entrance?' There was a long pause while they both considered the suggestion, then Miss Liddell shivered. 'It grows chill, these early May evenings are very treacherous. You'd best keep on your jacket.'

'Yes, being short it need not hinder me.' Acknowledging the unspoken acceptance of her plan, Miss Middleton went over to inspect the contents of the jar. 'There is not a deal of oil here, but I need only apply it from waist to knee.'

'Verity,' said Miss Liddell, a tremor in her firm tones, 'have you considered that, even if you do get into the tunnel that you may meet with a further obstacle or it may decrease in size as you advance along it? Only a small amount of débris fell out when we uncovered it which seems to postulate there well may be some sort of guard or covering at the other end.'

'And I, caught like a fly in amber, unable to get up or down? I imagine our captor would find a way of releasing me,' returned Miss Middleton coolly.

'It—it quite puts me in a taking even to think on't,' shuddered Miss Liddell.

Nonetheless, both ladies thought of it until Miss Middleton said stoutly: 'Neither does the thought of Wonersh sacrificing his good name and possessions on our behalf bear thinking of. I must make the effort, Deborah.'

'Very well.' Miss Liddell accepted her decision, albeit reluctantly. 'Then we had best prepare you for the light will soon be gone.'

It was full dark when Miss Middleton once more climbed upon the bench and proceeded to insert herself into the tunnel. Miss Liddell, eyes averted, was making a tight bundle of the discarded garments, and was quite taken by surprise when, with a joyful shriek, her friend disappeared from view, leaving only her feet waving out of the opening. Sliding back a little, she waited for the bundle to be secured about her ankle and then was gone on her hazardous journey upward towards that faint breath of fresh air.

To her vast relief, the tunnel widened considerably but, although the roughness and irregularity of the surface assisted her progress, it added greatly to her discomfort. When, at length, her groping hands dug into earth, she realised she had passed through the rock-face and was advancing into the hill behind it. Here the tunnel took an acute curve and levelled out. Having laboriously rounded this, she perceived ahead of her a dim circle of lesser darkness than that about her. For a moment she lay, gasping from her exertions, before gathering herself for the final effort. The earthen walls of the tunnel, though supported at intervals by wooden stakes, had crumbled in places and her progress was slow but, at last, the cool outside air was blowing upon her face and she stretched out an exploratory hand to find her passage blocked by some form of grill.

'Now don't be a chuckle-head,' she adjured herself severely. 'You guessed this might be the case so do not let it put you all aground.'

An inspection of the grill showed it to be no more than very strong wire, twisted and deeply embedded in the soil about the opening. Desperately she strained at it until her probing fingers found a place at the top of the obstruction where the wire had come away from its protecting earth. For a full ten minutes she worried away at this point, her hopes sinking even lower then, just as she was about to give her aching fingers a rest, the whole affair gave way and tilted outwards. Not troubling to disengage the lower extremities of the wire, she crawled painfully out over it and collapsed in a trembling, exhausted heap upon the grass beyond.

It was a clear but dark night and, for a time, she lay breathing a silent prayer of gratitude and watching the stars twinkle in the great arc of the skies above her. Then the coolness of the air playing upon her heated body reminded her of her unclothed state, and she hastily undid the bundle attached to her ankle and donned her nether garments.

Recalling her arrangement with Miss Liddell, she

thrust her head back into the opening and halloed three times. After a pause the answering signal came back faintly to her ears and, satisfied that she had allayed her fellow-prisoner's fears, she pushed the grill back roughly into the mouth of the tunnel whereupon some low-growing branches of gorse sprang up into their former position, effectively concealing it.

It had been agreed between them that she should make no attempt to release Miss Liddell. To be plunging about in the dark, trying to find a way down to the base of the tower, could well result in disaster, nor was it likely that their captor had left keys ready to hand for any chance passer-by to set them free. Resolutely Miss Middleton wrapped the scarf which had secured her clothes about her head and shoulders and set off in what she hoped was the general direction of Beauregard.

CHAPTER EIGHT

WHILE Miss Liddell had been explicit in her directions, claiming that the outer perimeter of the Earl's estates could not be above a mile from their place of imprisonment, nonetheless it was a full hour before Miss Middleton stumbled upon a high ivy-covered wall that appeared to extend endlessly on either hand.

Reminding herself with somewhat acerbic humour of her proven skill in scaling walls, she unhesitatingly essayed the ascent only to find herself hampered, as ever, by her petticoats. Without an instant's hesitation, so fast was it becoming an accepted practice with her, she removed them, tied them in a roll across her shoulders and, greatly aided by the strong-growing ivy, was presently sitting on top of the wall, looking down upon the Beauregard lands.

Miss Liddell's recommendation to her had been to rest until daylight once she had achieved the relative security of the Earl's demesne, since to be moving about at night in unfamiliar country could lead to her losing all sense of direction. Miss Middleton, however, chose to disregard this sapient advice and felt her decision to be justified when, after what seemed to her to be endless struggling through dense woodland, she came upon a bridle path, sufficiently wide and firm underfoot to give all the appearance of regular usage.

Praying that it might not be leading her away from the house, for she had no very clear idea of where it stood in relation to her own position, she hurried along it for a mile or more until, overcome by exhaustion, she was obliged to rest. Making a pillow of her petticoats which she had not troubled to put on since movement was so much easier without them, she made herself as comfortable as was possible under the shelter of some brushwood and in two minutes was lost to the world.

When she awoke the stars were paling and dawn was streaking the sky. She was troubled but not surprised to find her limbs to be sore and stiff after such a night's exertion and the doubtful benefit of a very hard couch. Getting cautiously to her feet, she inspected her bedraggled person in detail.

'Oh, la!' she muttered. ''Twas as well it was a dark night, these pantalettes are so torn as to be scarce decent! Petticoats on, my girl! People will soon be stirring abroad and there's no saying who you may encounter.'

This done, and a comb with which she had the foresight to provide herself pulled through her tangled locks, she set off once more, her prime object being to discover a stream at which she might slake her thirst. It was not long before she heard the welcome sound of water bubbling and gurgling at no very great distance and plunged into the woods in search of it. Having drunk her fill, she sat down to unlace her soft kid half-boots, which had suffered sadly from the rough treatment meted out to them, and dabble her aching feet in the icy water.

By this time it was full daylight and she reminded herself that she had still some miles to go while poor Deborah must be counting the minutes to her release. Drying her feet with her scarf, she was easing them back into her boots when a sound other than the twittering of newly-awakened birds or the stirring of small animals in the undergrowth caught her attention, the thud of a horse's hoofs upon grass and then, more sharply, upon the stony surface of the bridle path.

Clutching a boot in one hand, she endeavoured to hop

up the bank from the stream to be rewarded by the sight of a horseman going by at a brisk canter. She opened her mouth to call out to him but the cry was stifled in her throat when she perceived the rider to be Mr Roger Percival whom she had last seen in the company of Mr James Ramsay.

'Now you really are being foolish beyond permission!' she reproved herself. 'How can you possibly imagine that Mr Roger would have a hand in this villainy?'

Yet what was he about on so remote a track so early in the morning if not going to satisfy himself as to the security of the prisoners? Admittedly he lived in a house on the estate, the exact whereabouts of which she could not be certain, but it well might be close at hand and he in the habit of taking exercise at dawn. Somehow, she felt that this was not the case and prayed that Miss Liddell had had the good sense to replace the cover to the tunnel. Even so, would not someone peering through the spyhole see every corner of the room and at once discover that one prisoner was missing? The very thought added wings to her feet and she was soon hastening along the track, eyes and ears alert for any sound of Mr Percival's return.

The first sound, however, to reach her ears was the creaking of a farm cart, proceeding in the same direction as she herself. The stolid cob which was drawing this vehicle was being guided by a lumpish youth seated upon a board placed across the cart, who was so startled by her sudden appearance at his side that it was clear he had been making up for lost sleep. Pulling the cob almost back upon its haunches, he stared down at her, open-mounted and blinking.

'I have met with an accident,' explained Miss Middleton succinctly. 'My horse bolted and threw me. As you can see, I am far from being up to snuff and would be grateful if you could carry me to Lord Wonersh's house.'

Her deliverer took a moment to absorb this intelligence before removing the straw from his mouth. 'Where was you then when this 'appened?' he required to be told.

Realising that, despite all appearances to the contrary, he was not the gullible chawbacon she had taken him to be, Miss Middleton elaborated upon her hastily-contrived story.

'I was just beyond the confines of the estate, near the old tower, and thought my best course was to try to find my way to Beauregard.'

''Tis all along o' five miles from 'ere,' the yokel informed her with the triumphant air of one putting forward an irrefutable argument.

'Yes, and unless you will be so obliging as to take me up beside you and convey me there I shall be quite at a stand,' reiterated Miss Middleton, experiencing a strong desire to shake sense into him. He looked doubtful.

'I b'aint a-goin' that way.' The remark was a statement rather than a protest.

'I can claim some small acquaintance with his lordship,' she pressed on smoothly. 'I think he would be pleased for you to render me such assistance.'

A look of alarm crossed his face and she feared that this disclosure might put him in a fright. She was forced to allow, too, that she must present a very off appearance, looking more like a slattern than the lady of quality she proclaimed herself to be. At last, he spat out the straw and thrust down a hand to assist her.

'You'd best come up, then.'

In a trice Miss Middleton was installed beside him on the plank and wondering how she could play least in sight if Mr Percival should ride up behind them. Happily no such disaster occurred but, an hour later with a third of their journey yet to cover, she observed a gig bowling briskly along a grassy track on a converging course with their own. In this vehicle were seated two gentlemen, one of whom she thankfully recognised to be the Earl.

'Why, there is my lord! Please—can you arrest him?'

The youth looked as if she had taken leave of her senses in suggesting such a course, so, throwing off the scarf which she had tied over her hair, she stood up in the jolting cart and waved it enthusiastically to attract the Earl's attention.

Wonersh, who was accompanied by his steward, might have ignored this gesture from an unknown and unkempt-looking young woman as not being any possible concern of his, had not the sun, choosing that moment to burst forth in full splendour, directed its rays upon her pale gold hair, lighting it up like a nimbus about her head.

'Verity!' Wheeling the gig about, he was at her side in a moment. 'What has passed? Why are you here?'

'I took a fearsome toss—oh, the most infamous ill-luck, I assure you!' she interrupted him quickly, very aware of the steward's attentive ears and feeling that, until his lordship knew the full facts of the case, the less said about it the better. 'But it is a long story. May I claim your hospitality while I tell it?' He looked at her beneath frowning brows, a dozen questions trembling on his lips. 'Deborah is in prime order,' she forestalled him, hoping she would be proved to be right, 'But I had to return and had it not been for this good fellow,' she laid a hand on the yokel's sleeve, causing him to shy away nervously as if she had struck him, 'I should still be trudging through your woods, getting wearier by the moment.'

The Earl was no slowtop and it was becoming increasingly clear to him that, whatever misfortune had befallen the lady, she had no wish to discuss it in a general way.

'Ah, you'll be one of Jem Hawksley's boys?' he said pleasantly to her charioteer. 'Your father'll not be best pleased at your taking time off to rescue distressed damsels!' The youth was understood to foretell that his papa would most like dust his breeches to some effect did not my lord speak up for him. 'Aye, that I'll do, never fear.' The Earl put a hand in his pocket and passed over something of solid worth. 'That for your trouble, my lad, with my thanks.' He turned to his steward. 'Blakeney, assist the lady to descend from her—er, carriage, if you please. If you will wait here, I'll send the gig back for you.'

Once established by his lordship's side, Miss Middleton allowed a blissful sense of security to take possession of her, but they were no sooner out of earshot of the others than his voice, harsh with anxiety, aroused her.

'In God's name, Verity, what has happened? I thought you to be in Thame with Deborah! And don't spin me any havy-cavy story of a fall from a horse —regard your hands, your clothes, you look beat to a standstill!'

Nobly repressing a desire to inform him that he would cut an equally sorry figure had he enjoyed her recent experiences, Miss Middleton told her story in admirably few words.

'My lord, we must act promptly,' she concluded. 'My absence may already have been discovered. If—if your cousin is hand-in-glove with James Ramsay—'

'That I cannot believe.' He was almost talking to himself as he urged the mettlesome mare to lengthen her stride. 'Roger cannot profit by supporting Ramsay's claim.'

'Might he not name his price for such support?' she ventured, her heart aching a little for the hurt her words might cause him. His mouth hardened to a thin line.

'Beauregard for him, the title for Ramsay? Is that what you would say? Casting lots for my possessions like—'

'Oh, no!' The half-choked gasp checked his bitter outburst and he glanced at her, surprising the glisten of tears in her eyes. At once his expression softened.

'Forgive me. Our first object must be to have your hurts attended to and—the devil! Deborah's despatched most of the female staff to Berkeley Square! It seems that I shall have to be your nurse!'

'Oh, no!' gasped Miss Middleton again, mindful of the intimate nature of her injuries. 'I can perfectly well look to myself! You must waste no time in rescuing Deborah.'

'I wonder you have any clothes left if that tunnel is as rough and narrow as you say,' he remarked.

'I wonder I have any skin left—' she began then, realising the least said about the manner of her escape the better, she fell silent.

'So?' said his lordship, observing the bright colour mantling her cheeks and drawing his own conclusions therefrom, 'you—ah, you were obliged to dispense with some clothing?'

'With my skirts, yes,' said she firmly, staring straight ahead of her and thus failing to notice the twinkle in the Earl's eye as he allowed his imagination to conjure up the most delightfully improper fancies. Then his glance fell upon her hands, clasped tightly in her lap, the nails broken, the knuckles bruised and bleeding, and his amusement faded.

'I doubt not that Deborah will give me a truer tale of your courage,' he said gently.

That being precisely what Miss Middleton feared, she formed an instant resolve to be the first to speak to Miss Liddell upon her release and beg her discretion. This wish she found to be not as easy of attainment as she had supposed, for the Earl had conceived the capital notion of depositing her at his steward's house where his wife, a capable sort of woman, could attend to her, while he went on to Beauregard to muster aid for his assualt upon the tower.

Before she could think up any reasonable objection to this arrangement, they were drawing up before a neat dwelling, set in a garden bright with flowers.

'But—Deborah! May I not be with you when you go to free her?'

As she spoke she stood up but, in attempting to step down from the gig, found her knees quite unprepared to bear her weight and would have fallen to the ground had he not gathered her up in his arms and swept her into the house.

'No, you are not coming with me! I'll not have you utterly done-up. Mrs Blakeney, here is a lady in need of your care. Pay no heed to any protest but keep her here until I return for her.'

With that he was gone and she had to submit to being stripped and bathed while an incredulous Mrs Blakeney exclaimed in horror at her numerous cuts and contusions. As it seemed pointless to hold to her story of being thrown from a horse, she conjured up a tale of how she and Miss Liddell had gone exploring in the tower and the door had closed upon them. Whether or not the good woman believed it she could not tell, nor did she greatly care, for all her mind was filled with fears for Deborah and whether the Earl would be in time to save her.

'There, miss!' Mrs Blakeney straightened up and wiped her hands on a clean towel. 'I've used my own infusion of marigolds on the worst of your scratches, having found it to be generally beneficial in such cases, but if you'll take my advice, you'll rest there as you are until his lordship comes back for you.'

'I can hardly receive him like this!' objected Miss Middleton, looking down upon her lacerated but shapely person.

Mrs Blakeney said nothing but privately held to the opinion that if the expression on the Earl's face as he had carried Miss Middleton into the house had anything to say to anything, then such a confrontation would afford him the utmost gratification. Which was as it should be, she considered, the young lady being as pretty as a picture, while it was time and enough that his lordship thought about getting himself a wife and setting up his nursery.

Her kind attendant being much of the same height as herself, Miss Middleton gratefully accepted the loan of a blue gingham gown, not in the first stare of fashion to be sure, but fresh and smelling of the lavender in which it had been laid away.

''Tis an old thing, miss, but more like to fit you than anything else I can offer, me not being as slender as when I was a girl.'

Regarding herself in the mirror, Miss Middleton found the simple frock to suit her admirably, and Mrs Blakeney bore away her stained and tattered petticoats to the wash-tub, leaving her guest to rest quietly in the shaded room. A short time later, hearing the murmur of voices below and presuming them to be those of the Earl and, hopefully, Miss Liddell, she bestirred herself and hurried downstairs. She entered the kitchen to find Mrs Blakeney up to her elbows in suds, talking to Mr Percival, who at once turned to greet her with his customary courtesy.

'But what a tale of misadventure! You must be worn to the bone, my dear lady! And Deborah, too! But Leo will soon have her out of that.'

Repressing the urge to inform him that she was not his dear lady, she accepted the chair he set for her. She could not but feel, also, that there was less of surprise in his greeting than might be expected. Admittedly, he had had time to compose himself after hearing Mrs Blakeney's version of her story, but could it be that he was well aware of her escape? Should she not have stressed more strongly her doubts of his cousin to the Earl? Then, listening to Mr Percival's gravely concerned voice and meeting the steady regard of his limpid blue eyes, she began to question her own misgivings and to wonder if she had not, after all, mistaken the matter.

All these apprehensions were forgotten as a certain

commotion outside heralded the Earl's return, but she looked in vain for Miss Liddell.

'There's no broaching that door at all.' Wonersh drew off his gloves and slapped them down on the kitchen table in testy impatience. 'Even a pistol ball in the lock might not answer but only wedge it more fast. Since the demand note says that someone will be presenting himself at the tower this evening, I have agreed with Deborah that we do nothing until then. I have left two of my fellows hidden nearby to keep watch and will myself return at dusk.'

'Demand note? What are you saying, Leo?' Mr Percival looked to be quite bewildered, and Miss Middleton's doubts receded still further into the background of her mind. The Earl directed a swift glance at his steward's wife.

'Your husband and the other men have had to know the truth of this, Mrs Blakeney, but I'd as lief it did not go beyond them and we four until I have got Miss Liddell off safe.' He then briefly related the events leading up to the existing unhappy situation. 'The ladies were confined in the tower by intent, as part of a set design of holding them to ransom.'

Miss Middleton chanced to be looking directly at Mr Percival at that moment and fancied she glimpsed the hint of a smile touch his mouth before he burst into dismayed exclamation.

'But this is preposterous! What can the fellow hope to gain by such infamy? Oh, money, I suppose! You'll not pay it him, Leo?' The Earl cut him short.

'Preposterous or not, it is true. And money is not his object but, thanks to Miss Middleton, the whys and wherefores of that need not trouble us. I am hopeful that whoever comes to the tower tonight will have a key on his person, or can be persuaded to tell me where one is to be found. Failing this, I will endeavour to shoot off the lock. The last course left to us is to use gunpowder and blow the door apart. This I am reluctant to attempt since it carries with it the risk of injury to Deborah and, indeed, destruction of the tower itself which is an old and uncertain structure.'

'So—so Deborah must stay confined for all of today? May I not go and speak to her, be near her for at least part of the time?' implored Miss Middleton.

'And be observed by your captor who will then know the game is up and hedge off?' Seeing her disappointed face, he relented slightly. 'Perhaps tonight, if you so wish, you may accompany me. If no one comes before first light, then we must presume our movements around the tower this morning have not passed unnoticed and we must resort to our final measure. I am sending a messenger to Berkeley Square to explain that Miss Liddell has been delayed. Would you wish him to convey a message to your aunt?'

'What? Oh, yes, yes, please!' Miss Middleton had almost forgotten that she had ever been on her way to London to visit Lady Daventry.

'My chaise, groom and coachman—together with your necessities for a night's lodging at Thame, and even Deborah's jewel-case—are come back safe. Apart from sore heads, they are none the worse for their experience. And now, Roger, might I request you to call for your phaeton and drive Miss Middleton to Beauregard?'

Of a sudden, Verity was very sure she had no wish to be driven anywhere by Mr Percival. 'Oh, surely—it is no great distance, I would not dream of putting Mr Percival out in such a way.'

Wonersh regarded her in lively astonishment. 'What, had you thought to walk? Now that is pitching it a bit too strong, ma'am. I know you to be as game as a pebble, but—'

'If you are going back to the house, can you not take me up before you?' She rose as she spoke, turning to the Earl so that her face was hidden from his cousin, her lips framing the word 'please'. As ever, his lordship was quick to take her point.

'Well, if you will have it so,' he said easily. ''Tis but a few minutes after all.'

Mr Percival emitted a small titter of disapproval. 'If I may not be of service to the lady, perhaps I can offer to help free Deborah? Though I warn you I am no authority on the uses of gunpowder.'

'Nor I,' admitted Wonersh ruefully. 'But let us hope it will not come to that. Now, ma'am, if you please.'

Adding her thanks to his lordship's for Mrs Blakeney's kind offices, Miss Middleton submitted to being set up in front of the Earl and held in the crook of his arm. As the big chestnut, unperturbed by her extra weight, swung into an easy canter, she asked herself why she had preferred this uncomfortable and excessively intimate mode of travel to a brief and surely innocuous drive in Mr Percival's phaeton. The Earl, clearly, was thinking along the same lines.

'You cannot be imagining that Roger would do you any harm? What maggot has got into you that you should so distrust him?' His faintly scornful tone stung her to retort.

'Since the blame for any mishap I might suffer must be put to his account, I don't doubt I should be safe enough,' she snapped.

'Then why would you not ride with him?'

Miss Middleton's answer surprised even herself.

'Because I could not be easy in his company if he is helping to set up a usurper in your place!' His arm tightened about her.

'So your distaste for his company is not solely on your own account?'

She knew her colour to be rising and endeavoured to answer him in a very offhand way. 'How should it be? When I think of poor Deborah's predicament and—and those wicked threats—' Her voice tailed off indecisively.

'You know, there is one very good thing that has come out of all this unsavoury business,' he remarked in so innocent-seeming a way that she suspected he was laughing at her.

'Wh—what is that, my lord?'

'I am going to allow you to find that out for yourself, ma'am!'

She lifted her face to his in question and, bending his head, he kissed her gently on the mouth.

'Ooooh!' gasped Miss Middleton. 'My—my lord!' She knew she ought to cut him down for such presumption but found herself quite unable to formulate any such reproof.

'My poor tired gallant girl,' he whispered, pressing her head back on to his shoulder. 'But now is not the time to tell you, you are too worn.'

As he spoke they entered upon the drive to Beauregard and he set the chestnut at a gallop along the grass verge so that she was obliged to cling to him to retain her precarious seat, and had neither time nor breath to ask him what it was he wished to tell her.

While a bedchamber was being prepared for her by a couple of flustered kitchenmaids, who comprised the entire female staff left to the household by Miss Liddell, she sat down to a welcome breakfast at which she was joined by the Earl. Her enjoyment of the trout fried in parsley butter, the featherlight omelette and crisp broiled bacon, was tempered by consideration of Miss Liddell's plight. Seeing her preoccupation, he gently teased her out of it.

'Deborah is no vapourish female but, on the contrary, blessed with uncommon good sense. She'll come about, depend upon it.'

'But if Mr Ramsay should not present himself tonight —suppose, after all, it should not be Mr Ramsay?'

The Earl, whose appetite appeared to have been unimpaired by events, helped himself liberally from a succession of chafing-dishes. 'We have no proof that it is,' he agreed. 'That is why I need to lay hands upon him or whoever else comes to the tower.'

Miss Middleton sipped her coffee, marvelling that she should feel so at ease at his table, but decided it was unwise to examine her feelings too closely in that respect. Then she visualised Eustacia sitting in her place as his countess and all but choked. His lordship eyed her enquiringly.

'Is the coffee not to your taste, ma'am? I'll send to the kitchens for a fresh pot.'

'No, no, it is just that—that my last experience of the beverage was not a happy one.' How readily, she reflected, does one fall into an equivocal way of speech!

'I can assure you, ma'am, that this contains nothing to induce sleep,' he assured her solemnly. 'Nor, I think, would it be necessary, for you can scarce keep your eyes open! Come, bed for you if you are to accompany me this evening.' His hand under her elbow, he assisted her to rise and led her from the breakfast parlour through the Great Hall. At the foot of the Grand Staircase, wide enough as the guide-books were wont to assert, to take six horsemen abreast, she faltered, doubting her ability to make the ascent, but playfully chiding her for her lack of resolution, he steadied her to the door of her bedchamber. There he hesitated, holding the door for her. 'Can you manage? I doubt either of those chits of girls would be of much assistance.'

'Would you play the lady's maid, my lord?' she murmured archly.

'If you will allow me, ma'am.'

She directed a startled glance at him and encountered such a look in return that her eyes fell and she made haste to reply.

'I—I shall do very well, my lord. Th—thank you for your kindness.'

'The kindness is all on your part, my—lady.' He

raised her bandaged hands to his lips. 'Sleep well.'

Left alone, she set about the painful business of disrobing, regretting her refusal to accept his aid with hooks and buttons. And why had he called her 'my lady'? It was as if he had been about to say something else but had changed his mind at the moment of utterance.

The small valise she had prepared for her night's lodging at Thame had been unpacked, her nightrobe laid upon the bed, and her toilet lotions and perfumes set out for her use. As one in a dream, she hung up Mrs Blakeney's blue gown in a closet and, sitting before the dressing-table mirror, soothed her fine skin with a touch of honey-water.

'Perhaps I ought to drink some of it!'

The notion was not so absurd as it might seem for the essence, being based upon a spirituous liquor, was known to be a restorative in cases such as hers. Shaking a few drops on to a finger, she moistened her lips, and found the subtle flavour of cloves, vanilla and orange-flower water so agreeable to her taste that she was encouraged to put the flask to her mouth and take a deep draught. This having no immediate effect beyond inducing a pleasant sense of well-being, she struggled into her nightrobe. Finding the tying of the ribbons too fiddlesome a task for her sore fingers to perform, she left them loose so that the robe slipped low about her shoulders and applied herself to brushing out her hair. Inexplicably, her movements became slower and slower until, at last, she could scarce raise her arms above her head.

'Must—must go to bed,' she told herself and made her uncertain way to the four-poster, hung with crimson and gold drapes, the tester surmounted by the Percival crest of a falcon transfixing a serpent. With her last waking effort she ascended the dais which supported this imposing structure and fell prone upon the richly-embroidered covers.

CHAPTER NINE

Mr Percival had also been partaking of a substantial breakfast, but it was doubtful whether he derived quite the same enjoyment from it as had the Earl and Miss Middleton.

To a stranger, meeting him at the Earl's table, he was a quiet, well-mannered gentleman, neither too wise nor too simple, content with his undeniably comfortable lot, but a worker for all that, seeking no praise for performing the duties that clearly gave him much pleasure. Had anyone enquired of him whether he found fulfilment in administering his cousin's estate, he would have unhesitatingly replied in the affirmative and would have been sincere in the assertion.

He was inordinately fond of quoting Sir Thomas Browne: ' "The greater part must be content to be as though they had not been, to be found in the Register of God, not in the record of man." '

Quoting him, perhaps, but not necessarily agreeing with him, for Mr Percival was not quite the unworldly country gentleman he would have others believe him to be, nor was he devoid of ambition.

His prime aim in life was to be undisputed master of Beauregard. There were two obstacles standing in the way of this achievement. The first was, of course, the Earl, the second and lesser of the two, was Miss Liddell. Yet her knowledge of Beauregard, its history, its functions, and its maintenance, were no more easy to brush aside than was the Earl's undoubted ownership of that venerable pile. And now there was Mr James Ramsay who, while useful as an accessory when attempting to overcome the first two obstacles, might well of himself constitute a third.

Pushing aside his empty plate, Mr Percival stretched out in his chair and considered Mr Ramsay. He had believed it to be a capital notion on his part to make that gentleman's acquaintance in the most innocent-seeming way, implanting the seeds of the plot against Wonersh in his ready brain, but the silly gudgeon had made a mull of the business in the book-room. Overturning Deborah was well enough, but a little thought would have rendered her insensible until the flames had done their work. Then there was the attack upon the curricle when Wonersh had killed that wretched fellow. Fortunately his companions had had the good sense to come back and remove the corpse before the minions of the law had found it—but to use those pistols that had once belonged to Mr Percival's father was an idiocy beyond compare!

Now everything had been put at risk once more by allowing Miss Middleton to escape from the tower. A faint frown marred the smoothness of Mr Percival's brow. Perhaps, after all, he had been at fault in allying himself to Mr Ramsay, and would do well to cut the connection.

He rose, pulling down his cassimere waistcoat over a comfortably distended stomach, and strolled to the window. The vista before him was a fair one, being an open expanse of greensward fringed by woodland sweeping down to a small lake, beyond which lay the trim hedges and formal gardens of the great house, its roofs just visible through the trees. For once, however, Mr Percival's thoughts were not centred upon Beauregard.

Did he not fulfil his part of the bargain and warn Ramsay to stay away from the tower, then the Earl would have the culprit and the key in his hands, Miss

Liddell would be freed and Ramsay obliged to leave the country. It was unlikely that Wonersh would wish to make the matter generally known by an open denunciation of his half-brother. On the other hand Ramsay, in his own defence, might well implicate him, Roger Percival. Easy enough to deny such accusation, but mud had a way of sticking wherever thrown and, as he well knew, his standing was none too high in Miss Liddell's eyes. Miss Middleton, too, appeared to have taken him in aversion for whatever reason was not immediately plain —doubtless the malice dripping from dear Deborah's tongue had done its work. It remained to be seen whether the Earl's opinion of him had been equally affected.

His housekeeper, entering to clear away the breakfast dishes, disturbed his cogitations and was dismissed with an impatient wave of the hand which sent her scuttling off in high alarm.

'Best stay out of his way,' she advised her husband, who performed for Mr Percival those offices not within her scope. 'He's in a bad skin over something.'

He nodded his understanding. Unlike the greater part of his acquaintance, Mr Percival's staff were under no illusions as to their employer's capability for vindictiveness. Had they been privileged to see the smile stealing over his face at that moment they would have been doubly convinced that his deliberations boded no good for someone.

'That's the ticket!' He snapped his fingers in triumph. 'I shall warn Ramsay—tell him all has come to nothing and he must begone before Wonersh sets the Runners on his trail. That way I will ensure his silence and his dismissal. Then Leo will be obliged to open the door by force and—who knows? I may even be rid of Deborah by the same stroke while none could question my part in the business!'

He flung back his head and laughed, a chilly mirthless

sound that sent a shiver down his housekeeper's spine as she hurried past his door in pursuit of her duties. Then he sobered abruptly as his thoughts dwelt upon another aspect of the affair. Though rumour had it that the Earl was paying his addresses to the younger Miss Middleton, Mr Percival was of the opinion that this might be a ploy on his lordship's part to insinuate himself into the Middleton household and establish his credit with the elder sister. The lady's feelings were more difficult to assess. Did she still hold the Earl's previous desertion of her against him or would the prospect of becoming the Countess of Wonersh outweigh any such fault? Having heard Mr Ramsay's account of what had passed at that time, Mr Percival could not but feel that Wonersh had only to tell her the true story to be forgiven. But not all of the story—no, surely not all! What of Ramsay's lovely sister?

This time Mr Percival's laugh had the ring of pure enjoyment. It would not suit his book at all if the Earl took a wife and set about establishing a direct line of succession, so Miss Middleton must be led to believe that her noble admirer was a sad rake and seemingly unrepentant for his previous misdemeanours. That, unless he had much misjudged the lady's character, would cook the Earl's goose for him. Indeed, if all fell out as he hoped, the obstacles in his path would be reduced to one, Wonersh himself.

Greatly cheered by this conclusion, Mr Percival ordered his phaeton to be put to, informing his groom that he would have no need of his services, since for the man to catch a glimpse of Ramsay's face might well queer the whole business.

It was late afternoon before Miss Middleton opened her eyes again and looked wonderingly about her. For a time she could not recollect where she was or what circumstances had lodged her in this vast bedchamber. Then the sight of her toilet possessions on the dressing-table and her clothes folded neatly upon a chair brought memory rushing back so fast that she was obliged to clasp her aching head in her hands in an instinctive effort to steady her racing thoughts.

Never should she have drunk that honey-water! She could not even recall getting into bed, yet here she was, comfortably disposed and supported by a mound of pillows. Somewhere in the back of her mind she retained the oddest impression that the falcon had descended from his crest to gather her up in his mighty talons and slide her between the sheets! Which was beyond anything absurd, for how should the creature do such a thing? Yet so strongly was this image fixed in her mind that she crawled to the end of the bed in order to look up and assure herself that the bird was still there.

A soft knocking on the door sent her scurrying back beneath the covers, but her visitor was only one of the kitchen maids, desirous of informing her that his lordship had set the dinner hour forward to six o'clock and would miss be wishful of joining him at the table?

'Why, yes, but—but what is the time now?' asked the bemused Miss Middleton.

' 'Tis gone five, miss. His lordship said as how I was to help you did you need me.'

Miss Middleton, proclaiming herself to be greatly rested, declined the proffered assistance and, strongly resisting the temptation to ask who had put her to bed, dismissed the much relieved maid with a word of thanks. To be truthful, she did not dare have anyone by her while such strange phantasies were uppermost in her mind lest she should say or do something quite out of line.

The longcase regulator clock was striking the hour as she entered the Great Hall to discover the Earl deep in converse with Mr Percival. He broke off immediately to enquire if she had slept well.

'Indeed, yes, I thank you. Apart from an odd dream, that is.'

'Tell us about this dream,' encouraged the Earl, 'or was it too true to life to be spoken of?'

'It was perfectly idiotish, I assure you! Just imagine the Percival falcon descending from on high and tucking me up in bed!'

'Quite remarkable!' agreed his lordship gravely. 'I would not have believed it to be so benevolent a bird. Ah, Threadgold, are you ready for us?'

'If it suits your lordship's convenience.' The old butler bowed to Miss Middleton. 'I have presumed to set the meal in the breakfast parlour, my lord, there being so small a company.'

'Capital!' The Earl offered his arm to the lady. 'We will be a deal more snug there than in the dining-hall.'

'Snug', in Miss Middleton's opinion, was hardly the most apt adjective to apply to any of the rooms in Beauregard, but then her host murmured a few words in her ear that cast her into such confusion she had no thought for any other thing.

'In the clutches of a falcon, eh? Undiluted honey-water, ma'am?'

How could he possibly have known unless—dear God, could it have been he who had put her to bed? She trembled so violently at the very notion that, but for his firm clasp of her arm, she must surely have sunk to the ground. As he handed her to her chair, she raised her eyes in anguished appeal, but he only smiled tantalisingly in response before taking his place at the head of the table. Mr Percival, seating himself opposite her, missed nothing of this by-play, which went far to confirm his suspicions regarding the Earl's intentions towards the lady.

Miss Middleton never quite knew how she got through the meal, nor had she the least recollection of what dishes were set before her. She could only be thankful when it was over and she stood on the front steps of the great house, shivering a little despite being warmly wrapped in a cloak belonging to Miss Liddell, and listening to the Earl's instructions.

'You will remain in the chaise, if you please, with Jevons and the coachman to guard you, while Roger and I go on to join the two fellows on watch at the tower.'

Still faintly rebellious at not being allowed to give active succour to Miss Liddell, she was obliged to appear satisfied with this arrangement and suffered him to hand her up into the chaise. Then he and Mr Percival mounted their horses and took up position on either side of the carriage. As they moved off the moon, hitherto obscured by fleeting cloud, bathed them in so clear a light as to make the Earl express a devout hope that it would not continue to do so else their hopes of arriving unobserved at the tower would surely be dashed.

Although the journey took less than an hour, the minutes passed with agonising slowness for Miss Middleton before a halt was called to their progress and the chaise pulled discreetly off the track, away from prying eyes.

'It may well be a long time before you hear anything,' the Earl warned her, 'nor do I propose to send you any account of how things are going on since to be moving about unduly is to invite attention.'

Miss Middleton quite understood this precaution and watched the two gentlemen merge into the darkness of the woods surrounding the tower. Then, making a mental resolve to stay alert, she wrapped herself closely in her cloak and resigned herself to a lengthy vigil. After a time, the steady ticking of the carriage clock proved so soporific that, despite her very real concern for Miss Liddell, she found herself nodding off and, in order to stay awake, began to recite nursery rhymes in a soft undertone.

In the midst of this commendable exercise Miss Muffet became inexplicably involved in riding a cockhorse to Banbury Cross, and when she fixed her eyes again upon the timepiece she was astonished to discover that the hands stood at half-past three.

Outside, everything was still and dark, the sky now heavy with rainclouds, while of Jevons and John Coachman there was no sign. Miss Middleton formed the decision that she had remained inactive for long enough. She was preparing to descend from the chaise, a slightly hazardous feat because of the angle at which it rested, the horses being freed from the traces, when her glance rested on the pistol holster by her hand. Her father having held to the opinion that every lady ought to know how to prime and aim a weapon in her own defence, she had no hesitation in removing the pistol and satisfying herself that it was loaded. Tucking it into the pocket of her cloak, she lowered herself to the ground.

Stertorous breathing from nearby informed her that neither of her guards was taking an interest in her activities and, reminding herself that they would deserve no less if they got the rough edge of the Earl's tongue for their negligence, she slipped away into the darkness.

Mr Percival's hopes of a disastrous climax to the night's work were not destined to be fulfilled. Once the Earl had given up all hope of Mr Ramsay putting in an appearance, he instructed Miss Liddell to lie on the floor of her prison, well away from the door, while he put his pistol to work on the lock.

'We'll be no worse off if it fails,' he said cheerfully, 'and it's a deal less dangerous than gunpowder. Don't raise your hopes too high, Deb, and put your fingers in your ears.'

Miss Liddell was understood to retort with some feeling that it seemed very probable both she and her hopes could be blown sky-high at one and the same time.

'Oh, never in the world, my dear,' he assured her. 'We'll have you safe out of there in no time.'

'Well, I hope you may be right,' said the lady irritably, since to be lying on a cold stone floor at that hour of morning was not at all to her liking. 'Now, do make haste—please, Leo!'

The sound of the pistol shot reverberated through the building but, upon examination, the door still remained fast.

'Another shot might do it,' mused Wonersh. 'Let me have one of your barkers, Roger. I left the second of my pair in the chaise.'

'Here it is, my lord.'

Miss Middleton's timely intervention brought a flood of condemnation upon her. What was she doing there, his lordship thundered, and why had she disobeyed his orders and left the security of the chaise to wander through the woods alone in the dark? The fact that she seemed to be quite unharmed and totally unrepentant for her folly merely added fuel to his anger and fluency to his tirade.

When he paused to draw breath, she reminded him coldly that Miss Liddell was still awaiting release, or would he prefer that she discharged the pistol? Snatching the weapon from her, he thrust her behind him with marked lack of ceremony.

'Be pleased to be quiet, ma'am,' he snapped. 'This is no situation for ladies to be concerning themselves with.'

Miss Middleton bristled. When she thought of the discomfort and inconvenience, to say nothing of actual bodily harm, which she had been forced to endure during the past twenty-four hours, she could not hold that to be a fair comment, and it required a very great effort of will to ignore the ill-concealed male amusement in evidence around her and stand meekly aside while the Earl took aim at the damaged lock.

The violence of the explosion in so confined a space quite startled her, but a moment later she cried out in relief as the door swung slowly open. Then she was running to clasp Miss Liddell in her arms and exclaim over her distraught appearance.

'I really felt that if I had to spend another night alone there, I should be a candidate for Bedlam!' confessed that lady. 'Towers creak and whistle—did you know?'

'And your ordeal was quite unnecessary after all!'

Miss Middleton darted a malevolent glance at the Earl who had removed the cover to the tunnel and was inspecting it with what she considered to be unwarranted interest.

'I'm truly sorry, Deb, for having prolonged your misery.' He stood back and surveyed the opening. ' 'Pon my word, this must have been a very tight squeeze. It seems scarce large enough to admit a child.'

'Yes, had not dear Verity had the presence of mind to—'

Miss Liddell got no further for Miss Middleton was hustling her downstairs, protesting that she must be beyond anything tired and the sooner they were back at Beauregard the better for all concerned.

The groom and coachman, having had the benefit of their master's opinion of watchmen who go to sleep and allow their charge slip their care, were in a suitably chastened mood, and the homeward journey was accomplished without mishap. Miss Liddell, in a sort of frenzy of relief, was disposed to discuss her experience at length and Miss Middleton, profiting by their being alone in the carriage, the gentlemen riding alongside as before, took the first opportunity that offered to put in a plea for discretion.

'I am aware that such action was—was necessary if we were to escape, but the very notion of all the circumstances being made known must offend every instinct of propriety.'

Miss Liddell allowed that to be so. 'Did you suffer greatly from the roughness of the passage?' she enquired.

'Yes,' said Miss Middleton with feeling. 'I'm as sore as if a whip had been laid about my sides.'

This admission called for a spate of commiseration from her friend who, nonetheless, pointed out with strong common-sense that so unusual an incident could not be kept entirely under wraps since so many people knew something of it already, and they must formulate a story to satisfy the curious.

'Well, if you must, say I removed my petticoats. I have admitted as much to his lordship and I daresay he has told Mr Percival,' conceded Miss Middleton, assuming an off-hand manner. 'No one who has not seen the tunnel is likely to speculate further.'

Miss Liddell was about to say that the Earl had seen it but, as she was feeling a little fatigued, she deemed it wiser to let the matter rest.

Their entry into Beauregard was as unobtrusive as was possible, Threadgold being the only member of the staff who had been apprised of the expedition. Miss Middleton assisted her friend upstairs to bed and was preparing a tisane for her in the housemaid's closet when Wonersh's voice at her elbow all but caused her to drop the kettle.

'I'll carry it in to Deborah. You, I suggest, ma'am, have had enough activity to satisfy even you for one night.'

He still sounded angry, she noted wonderingly but, too tired to dispute his authority, she surrendered the cup into his hands. 'Thank you, my lord.'

'Why did you not obey me and stay in the chaise? Had you thought of the possible consequences if Ramsay had been lurking nearby and discovered you?'

She gave a tinkle of rather shaky laughter. 'Then all would be to do again. How very tiresome that would have been for you, my lord!'

With a muttered exclamation he set down the hot cup. 'Tiresome indeed!' he said curtly. 'May I ask what are your plans now, ma'am? Do you propose to continue your journey to London or will you return to Cheltenham to recover from your exertions?'

Miss Middleton thought this over, frowning deeply in concentration. 'To return to Cheltenham would call for a full explanation of all that has taken place,' she reasoned, 'and would arouse the sort of gossip that is least wanted. Some unexceptionable tale of accident or what you will would suffice to account for our belated arrival in London, and no one at home need know the truth of it.'

'If that is your wish, ma'am, but it is your well-being that is my first concern.' She was glad to hear that the anger had gone from his voice. 'Your hurts, your fatigue —oh, don't try to cozen me! That tunnel must have acted like an abrasive upon your person.'

Miss Middleton drew herself up very erect. 'If you please, my lord,' she said, icily reproving, 'have I your permission to retire?'

She swayed as she spoke and his hands, outthrust to steady her, touched a rawly-sore spot on her arm. In spite of her determination to show no weakness before him, she winced.

'Verity, you cannot—'

'Please let me go, my lord!'

The imperious command took him by surprise and he released her at once, then stood watching her as she made her way to her bedchamber in a fury of frustration that was beyond her understanding.

Miss Liddell, knowing him as she did, was better able to judge his mood.

'Being confined together in such circumstances tends to give one a very fair insight into the character of one's companion,' she pronounced, sipping her tisane appreciatively. 'Verity's understanding is of the highest order, her sensibilities refined and her resolution undoubted. She has a lively wit and a well-ordered mind. In fact—'

'In fact all she lacks is a heart!' he interrupted ironically.

'A heart?' she repeated in astonished accents. 'Leo, you know better than that! You know her concern for her mother and sister—you have told her about the Warburton connection?'

'No, why should I? Let her discover for herself what she is denying her sister when it is too late.'

He was wearing his mulish look, she observed, and wondered what Verity had done to re-animate his enmity.

'You prefer to go on with this absurd charade of pretending to engage Miss Eustatcia's affections?'

He turned away to lean an elbow on the mantleshelf and look down into the fire. 'Maybe I will play it out in earnest.' He spoke so low she could scarce hear him. 'That should teach her a lesson.'

Miss Liddell, over whose countenance a look of hope had begun to creep, quickly schooled her expression to suit the circumstances.

'Marry Miss Eustacia, you mean? No, that will not answer, not if she is truly attached to Mr Warburton.'

The Earl appeared to be much struck by this observation. 'I'd not wish her unhappy. Shall I thrust them into each other's arms?'

'And prove to Verity beyond all question what a despicable scoundrel you are?' Miss Liddell set down her cup. 'In fact, pay her out for ever having doubted you by showing her to have been perfectly right in doing so? Not in your best style, Leo.'

'Did she really strip to the buff to get out of that place?' he asked suddenly. 'She wouldn't confess it to me.'

'To be sure she wouldn't,' agreed his sister placidly. 'And there's no need to talk in that vulgar way. She rubbed herself down with oil, too,' she added, shamelessly betraying her friend's confidence.

The Earl seemed to experience some difficulty in speaking but at last managed to say: 'She—what?'

'There was a little spermacetti oil left in a jar. It seemed a pity not to put it to good use.'

He grinned. 'So—slippery as an eel—'

'Don't be letting your imagination run away with you!' she chided him. 'We thought it best to wait until dark, not knowing what she might encounter at the other end.'

'Popping like a rabbit out of a hole—no, more like a mermaiden from a pool!' He caught her eye and they both burst out laughing. Miss Liddell's mirth, however, was short-lived.

'She seemed to think it a small price to pay for your peace of mind,' she stressed. 'It is my belief she still has a fondness for you, Leo.'

'Then she is going to have to admit to it,' he retorted.

Miss Liddell gave an exasperated snort. 'You men and your conceits! So your mind is made up?'

'Not yet.' The Earl's face was suddenly grim. 'Once again, there's Ramsay to be thought on.'

'I doubt we'll hear more from him,' she said confidently. 'He must know himself to be quite discredited. Roger, however, is still with us.'

'If I believed he'd had a hand in this, I'd horsewhip him,' said his lordship savagely.

Miss Liddell said nothing in defence of her opinion, but she retained a visual memory of Mr Percival's expression when the door of her prison had swung open and his was the first face her glance fell upon. In her opinion, he had looked to be far from gratified at her happy release.

'What tale do we concoct to offer to Lady Daventry?' she asked.

'Something plausible and the nearest to the truth the better,' he advised. 'You were set upon by footpads who, on hearing another coach approaching, took fright and made off.'

'But as either the coachman or the groom had received some injury, we thought it advisable to return to Beauregard.'

'And I have held you here until I was able to accompany you—tomorrow, if you so wish?'

'That will do very well. I will discuss the details with Verity later.'

The Earl bade her good-night, or rather good-morning, for it was now past six o'clock, and left her to her thoughts which, to judge from her contented smile, afforded her considerable satisfaction.

CHAPTER TEN

LADY Daventry held her tambour at arm's length and inspected her needlework with a look of distaste.

'I cannot conceive why the design saw fit to recommend blue roses,' she complained. 'Of all flowers, surely the colours of the rose are established generally as other than blue!' She darted a glance at her niece sitting beside her, apparently absorbed in *The Ladies' Monthly Museum*. 'Sally Jersey called this afternoon while you were visiting your sister-in-law. She left us vouchers for Almack's.'

Miss Middleton looked up in surprise. 'But, dear aunt, I am not here for the season but to be a companion to you.'

'Fustian nonsense!' retorted her ladyship bracingly. 'You were ever a favourite with all the patronesses of Almack's—no mean achievement, let me tell you! They are as delighted as I am to welcome you back to the London scene. Oh, I must reply to that letter from your mama,' she ran on in the same breath. 'I take it I say nothing of your mishap on the journey?'

'No, no, if you please. The slightest hint of such a thing and she will be up in the boughs and blaming herself for ever having allowed me leave her side.'

Lady Daventry sniffed. 'You could not have been in better company than that of Deborah Liddell, and in Wonersh's travelling chaise, too.' She paused, her nimble fingers busily sorting out her silks. 'Though, as it happened, you were excessively fortunate to be rescued by the arrival of another carriage. Who were your saviours?'

'I don't know,' said Miss Middleton truthfully. 'We warned them to be on their guard against similar attack, then seeing how it was with our coachman we turned and made all haste back to Beauregard. But they were two stout young gentlemen with their grooms, all perfectly capable of giving a good account of themselves.'

Have a care, she warned herself, lest you trip yourself up in unnecessary detail! It was over a week since she had arrived in Park Place and the trials and excitements that had gone before had assumed the quality of some Gothic nightmare.

'Tomorrow is Wednesday,' mused Lady Daventry. 'Shall you care to visit the scene of your former triumphs, I wonder? If so, I shall be happy to accompany you.'

Miss Middleton, knowing full well that her volatile aunt was as eager to visit Mr Almack's establishment in King Street and pick up the threads of her acquaintance as any young lady aspiring to see and be seen, had not the heart to deny her that pleasure and could only demur on the score of not having a thing to wear.

'You are excessively fortunate,' her ladyship informed her, 'in that the simplest of get-outs best becomes you. I do not hesitate to tell you, my dear Verity, for you are not so bird-witted as not to be well aware of it, that you are blessed with looks above the ordinary. Your lilac tiffany needs but a length of silver net draped about the shoulders and—yes, my small diamond set, I think. You are of an age to carry it off.'

'I am of an age to be wearing a lace cap and sitting with the matrons!' said Miss Middleton bitterly.

'Fiddle!' Lady Daventry put down her tambour and, rising, began to pace about the elegant salon. She was a small plump personage, just past her fortieth birthday, and it was plain to see from whom Eustacia had inherited her boundless enthusiasm and brilliant blue eyes. 'It will be time and enough to be putting yourself on the shelf when others do so, and I see no evidence of that as yet. Just because all these ambitious mamas try to marry off their daughters out of the schoolroom is no reason for you to wear such a Friday face. Has Wonersh returned to Berkeley Square, do you know?'

'I understand that Deborah is in daily expectation of his arrival,' replied Miss Middleton stiffly.

'Hmm. It is always pleasing to have a gentleman in attendance and you know how your uncle abhors dancing or any such social activity, he had a surfeit of it while we were in the Peninsula.' She stood, preoccupied, one small foot tapping the floor. 'I understand that Nicholas Chisholm is in town. Would he do for an escort, d'you think?'

'Oh, no.' Her niece was quite adamant. 'He would be most likely to ask me what I thought of his chances as a suitor for Eustacia and I should be obliged to tell him.'

Lady Daventry pursed her lips consideringly. 'He is not wholly ineligible,' she observed, 'but now I think on't, your mother mentioned a Mr Warburton in her letter whose attentions to Eustacia appear to be causing her some disquiet.'

'Oh, dear, I had hoped that Wonersh would have put a stop to that!' ejaculated Miss Middleton without taking thought. Her aunt pounced.

'You were not hoping to catch Wonersh for Eustacia? Oh, no, Verity, that's pitching it a bit too strong! After all, it was you who took his interest at the first!'

'But failed to hold it.' Miss Middleton's tone was very dry. 'Eustacia is grown to be a beauty, ma'am. As like to you as she can stare,' she added pensively.

'I don't care if she is Aphrodite's self,' returned her ladyship, 'and that's least likely if she favours me. Such a connection would be downright indecent!'

Accustomed as she was to her aunt's impulsive outbursts, Miss Middleton was quite shaken off balance by this judgment.

'I beg of you, ma'am, not to be saying such things,' she implored. 'There was nothing between his lordship and I that could lead anyone to suppose he—he was dangling after me.'

'That,' said Lady Daventry in the tone of one who has now heard it all and can expect no further surprises, 'is all my eye and Dick's hatband, but have it so if it eases your pride. So now you wish to fob him off on your sister? Be warned, my dear, Wonersh is no tame bull to be led by a ring through his nose! But this Mr Warburton, can he be Fanny Warburton's son?'

'I know nothing of his mother, she married into trade.' Miss Middleton's tone was less than encouraging, but her aunt took scant notice.

'That's right—a carriage-builder, was he not? And then she dropped out of sight, more's the pity. She was at one time a close friend of my sister-in-law. I remember her well as Fanny Percival.'

'Percival?' Miss Middleton all but dropped her magazine. 'You can't mean—'

'But I do!' nodded her ladyship emphatically. 'First cousin to the last Earl and utterly cast off by him after her tragic *mesalliance*. Does the present Earl maintain this stiff-necked attitude?'

'I—I don't know,' admitted Miss Middleton, understandably floored by this development. 'He—oh, he might have told me!'

Lady Daventry resumed her seat and bent her head over her tambour to conceal her amusement. 'You can hardly blame him for being less forthright with you than you have been with him,' she pointed out.

'I have been perfectly candid with him,' snapped Miss Middleton, her temper very much on the fret. 'I asked him to make a show of attracting Eustacia so as to—to draw her attention away from Mr Warburton.'

Lady Daventry regarded her niece in lively astonishment. 'And what if he prove to be as sure a hand at that as—Verity, are you quite astray in the head? If Wonersh agreed to such a course then, depend upon it, he has his own reasons for so doing. What if he does, indeed, engage Eustacia's affections?'

'Then he must offer her marriage.'

'Of all the totty-headed schemes—to ask him to supplant his own cousin!' deplored Lady Daventry.

'I did not know Mr Warburton was his cousin!' Miss Middleton cut in irascibly. 'Nor do I think that will make any odds either way. My lord is odiously puffed-up—so abominably arrogant—that the relationship will count for nothing with him.'

'Well,' sighed her ladyship, 'if Wonersh escapes your trap—as, being prime and bang up to the mark, I make no doubt he will—and Mr Warburton is frightened off—which would be a pity because I have heard on good authority that his father was a very warm man indeed—there is always Nicholas Chisholm, I suppose.'

Miss Middleton made no reply to this sally for this was a possible eventuality which had caused her much heart-searching. On the other hand, had the Earl agreed to her plan because he, too, could not approve of Mr Warburton as an eligible parti for her sister? Somehow she felt this was not the case, Mr Warburton was, after all, half a Percival. Could it be that his lordship was indeed taken with Eustacia and intended to woo her for himself?

The likelihood of so successful an outcome to her designs did not afford her the satisfaction that might have been expected, and though she was presently immersed once more in *The Ladies Monthly Museum* the printed word blurred before her eyes in the oddest way, and her aunt might be forgiven for wondering whether Verity's understanding was not a trifle slow since she never once turned over the page.

She was still in the same perturbed frame of mind on

the following evening when she accompanied Lady Daventry to Almack's. The extreme youthfulness of most of the other ladies present was enough to cast her into the dismals, and not even the cordial welcome extended to her by the redoubtable patronesses and the constant flow of attentive partners helped assuage her feeling of being quite out of place in such an assembly.

'I am as outmoded as last year's fashions,' she told herself, even as she smiled and made suitable reply to the elaborately-turned compliments being paid her by young gentlemen in satin knee-breeches and wondrous neckcloths reaching to their ears. Then her amusement faded to be replaced by something like panic as she perceived the Princess Lieven approaching with Wonersh by her side.

'My lord of Wonersh is, I believe, no stranger to you, Miss Middleton,' Mme. de Lieven was saying, her eyes sharp with interest, 'nor, indeed, can I recommend him as a partner for the waltz since he informs me he has no aptitude for the dance. Perhaps you being so notable a performer would care to instruct him?'

With that she was gone, leaving them facing each other and, as the musicians in the basket balcony struck up a lilting air, Miss Middleton had no choice but to allow the Earl lead her on to the floor. Then, his arm lightly but firmly clasping her waist, he whirled her away, giving no sign of any lack of proficiency but, on the contrary, playing his part with easy confidence. He granted her a few moments to regain her composure before saying softly:

'So very silent, ma'am? I don't have to tell you that a modicum of conversation is desirable—nay, obligatory, in these circumstances!'

'My attention is supposed to be centred upon directing your steps!' she reminded him tartly. 'Though I cannot conceive of your needing any such instruction for, as I recall—'

She shut her lips firmly against further reminiscence but he was quick to seize upon the opening.

'We have danced together here many times before,' he finished for her. 'Our steps suited perfectly then, why should they not now. Was that your meaning?'

It was but she had no intention of telling him so. 'Nothing stands still, my lord, neither time nor our experience nor—' She struggled for the right word and again he provided it.

'Our sentiments, would you say, ma'am?'

The laughter in his voice made her long to give him a set-down, but she forced herself to go on talking lightly, as if their conversation was of the least importance.

'You are looking very grand tonight, my lord. I must count myself vastly honoured to be standing up with you.'

His amusement deepened. 'Quite beneath my touch, is that what you would say? And you the brightest diamond here tonight.'

She looked at him in genuine amazement and then around her to meet the envious stares of numerous young women sitting on the red velvet sofas with their mamas. The envy she could understand for Wonersh, in his superb coat and silver-embroidered waistcoat, a single fine pearl glowing discreetly in the folds of his perfectly-tied neckcloth, made every other man in the room look either dowdy or over-dressed, but the frowns of ill-concealed annoyance on the faces of the matrons had her in a puzzle, for how should she provide any sort of threat to the aspirations of their nubile daughters?

He, watching the play of emotion on her expressive countenance, reflected that one of her most admirable attributes had ever been an inability to recognise her own perfections, and he was about to elaborate upon her superiority to any other lady present when she responded with an assumed archness that set his teeth on edge.

'Oh, as to that, my lord, as you must know, the diamond is adamant, a stone of impenetrable hardness that reflects the brilliance all about it.'

His eye travelled from the slender pendant about her neck to the subdued glitter amid the lace of her bosom. She had discarded the silver net about her shoulders, rightly judging that Lady Daventry's diamonds would show up better without it, and her throat rose pure as alabaster above the delicate lilac of her gown.

'Why have you not wed, Verity?'

The outrageous question quite put her out of countenance. 'Really, my lord,' she began, bridling in protest, 'our acquaintance may be of long standing but—'

'And don't trouble to tell me it is for lack of offers or any such whisker,' he went on as if she had not spoken. 'I know of at least two gentlemen who make no secret of their chagrin that you will not consider their proposals. And one a Duke's son,' he added wonderingly. 'How much higher can you aspire, ma'am? A Royal Duke, perhaps? But you are behind the fair there. I doubt there's one of 'em has not snatched up his German princess already. Besides there are all the little Fitzes to be thought on!'

Her cheeks flamed but she was determined not to let him tease her into losing her temper. 'I do not aspire to anything, my lord, save to be allowed to live my own life peaceably with my dear parent and sister.'

'And to secure for your sister the sort of establishment you should be enjoying now! Is that what she wants, too?'

'Of course!' Miss Middleton paused, struck by a lowering thought. Did Eustacia really wish for social advancement, a title, a fortune? Her preference might be quite other—indeed, knowing her wayward ways, Miss Middleton suspected that an arranged marriage could drive her to the extremes of imprudence. Dismissing her doubts, she rallied to the attack. 'Why did you not tell me about Mr Warburton?' she asked flatly.

He raised his eyebrows in feigned astonishment. 'You mean his—ah, connection with my family? Now how did you learn about that, I wonder?'

'My aunt, of course!' she snapped. 'It would appear that her sister-in-law and Mr Warburton's mother were at one time bosom-bows. Well?'

'My dear Verity, I could not flatter myself that such a relationship would further the poor young man's cause in your eyes.'

'But you—you acknowledge him as you do not Mr Ramsay?'

'The cases are hardly parallel,' he drawled. 'Warburton is no child of the mist. I own m'father would have been a deal happier had he been.'

'Better to have no father than one from the stables?' Her voice was vibrant with scorn. 'Is that what you would say, my lord?'

'I would say,' he smiled down upon her, 'that our dance is about to end and if we would procure chairs and some of the nauseous concoctions offered for our delectation, we'd best quit the floor before there is a general exodus.'

Taking her acquiescence for granted, he guided her into an adjoining chamber where the meagre refreshments considered adequate by Mr Almack for his distinguished patrons awaited them. Here his lordship obtained for her a glass of orgeat and seated himself by her side.

'Have you seen—is Mr Ramsay still in England?' she asked hesitantly.

The Earl peeled off his white kid gloves and laid them neatly across his knee. 'Mr Ramsay has prudently withdrawn to Paris,' he told her. Her eyes, following the movements of his hands, widened and she caught her breath in a quick gasp as she saw the bruised and scored knuckles.

'But you did see him, and you came to cuffs?' she persisted.

'I could hardly call him out,' he said mildly. 'I met up with him at Dover, awaiting the turn of the tide.'

'But he is taller—of a heavier figure than you!' Her hand shook so that the orgeat all but overspilled upon her frock.

'I believe I gave a good account of myself,' he said, amused. 'I have been to see John Jackson since my return and he is well enough pleased with me. I doubt they have his equal in France.'

'John—oh, the prizefighter who has a boxing saloon in Bond Street,' nodded Miss Middleton, dismissing the pretensions of the Champion of England in a brief sentence.

'The same,' he agreed gravely. 'At all events, to judge from the letter I received from his mother before I left Beauregard this morning, Mr Ramsay's—er, battle scars have not passed unnoticed. As the Fancy would have it, I blackened his ogles for him.'

Miss Middleton, her concern quite dissipated by his obvious delight in his brutal behaviour, sniffed disapprovingly. 'You received a letter from his mother? Protesting her son's innocence, no doubt?'

'On the contrary, she made no mention of his part in the affair and, from the tone of the letter, I doubt she had had prior knowledge of his intentions.'

'Then what—'

'She merely stated in admirably lucid terms that she was at no time married to my father, and any certificate of marriage produced in support of such a claim must be false. This very gratifying letter I have put into the hands of my lawyer to be locked away with my other documents. A rarely honest lady.'

'So that ghost is laid,' she said, half to herself.

'Yes,' he said softly, leaning forward and covering her

hand with his. 'Now that I know I am indisputably the Earl of Wonersh I can feel free to ask whatever lady I choose to share that position with me.'

Startled by the intensity of his regard, she drew her hand away so quickly that his fell upon her knee. A gentle 'Ahem!' and clearing of the throat brought them to the realisation that Lady Daventry was standing before them, her pretty face creased into a disapproving frown.

'My lord! Verity! To be withdrawn here together in so particular a way is not at all the thing!'

At once the Earl was on his feet, all contrition and begging forgiveness, but her ladyship was not be readily mollified. Miss Middleton hastily tried to pour oil on these troubled waters.

'Pray excuse us, dear aunt, but Wonersh and I had —had things of moment to discuss.'

'Then such things had best be discussed under my roof, not here where every eye is on the watch for the slightest indiscretion!' reproved her ladyship who, despite her easy manners, was a stickler for the proprieties. Wonersh bowed, very straight-faced, but with a hint of derision in his level voice.

'Then, ma'am, if I may pay you a call tomorrow, I will take my leave now.'

'But you have only just come!' objected Miss Middleton.

'And have achieved all I came for, a dance with you, ma'am!'

Thereupon he kissed both ladies' hands and withdrew in good order as the cessation of the music released a horde of flushed and excited young women and their partners upon them.

'I warn you, Verity, it is a beguiling rogue!'

Though clearly beginning to relent of her severity, Lady Daventry was not relinquishing her stand. Her niece was saved the trouble of replying by reason of the descent upon them of Lady Sefton who, having been out of town for some little time, had not yet had the opportunity to renew her acquaintanceship with Lady Daventry and, in the ensuing exchange of confidences, Wonersh's lack of decorum was forgotten.

Miss Middleton, however, was left a little bewildered at the turn things had taken. For a moment it had seemed to her as if the Earl was endeavouring to establish himself as a suitor to her hand, yet surely she had made it very clear that any such advance on his part would be utterly repugnant to her? Oh, yes, she allowed, he knew very well how to fix his interest with the opposite sex. But who was the object of his attentions, she or Eustacia? If she could be sure that he was laying a trap for her then she would know how to deal with him, but if he was genuinely making a play for Eustacia then what a fool she would look! Her soft lips tightened. To be made look a fool for a second time by his lordship was not to be borne.

Her partners for the remainder of the evening found the beautiful Miss Middleton to be a little distrait, even distant, in her manner, and were understandably mortified when their efforts to arouse her interest fell dismally flat.

The Earl, who had elected to walk back to Berkeley Square, the night being a fine mild one, was also deeply preoccupied, not because of what he had said to Miss Middleton, but rather because of what he had not told her. The letter from Mrs Ramsay had contained a final sentence.

'Be warned by me, my lord, there is someone very close to you who bears you great ill-will.'

No doubt but that Roger Percival was the person intended, mused the Earl, letting himself into his house quietly as he had forbidden his staff to wait up for his return, for who else was very close to him save Deborah? And to think of Deborah playing him false was too ludicrous to contemplate. But then, neither had he ever had cause to doubt Roger's loyalty.

Lighting the candle that stood ready for him on the hall table, he made his way upstairs to his bedchamber, there to fall quickly asleep, untroubled by any fears of treachery.

CHAPTER ELEVEN

'No, Mr Warburton, I am persuaded you quite mistake the matter.' Eustacia reined in her lively mare and drew nearer to her companion so that their conversation might not be overheard by the two grooms properly in attendance upon them. 'Verity is going to be as mad as fire when she learns of your Percival connections and, depend upon it, will hold his lordship to blame for not having informed her. He, I take it, is perfectly agreeable to acknowledge you as his cousin?'

'Indeed, he is everything that is amiable.' Mr Warburton's tone was warm with enthusiasm. 'He has paid a call upon mama, and quite stolen her heart. She declares him to have not the slightest height in his manners and to be a man of admirable commonsense.'

Eustacia dimpled at him. 'And, no doubt, his attractive and elegant appearance also played a part in winning her approval?'

Mr Warburton regarded her a shade anxiously. 'He is a very personable gentleman,' he allowed, 'but, although modish in his apparel, there is nothing of the dandy about him.'

'All of which, allied to his rank and fortune, make him well-nigh irresistible,' she concluded. 'Yet my sister will, I do believe, stand out against him to her last breath. Oh, yes,' she went on, seeing her escort's bewildered expression, 'she plans to entrap him for me, that much I gleaned from mama, but what I cannot understand is why he is dancing to her tune when it is very plain he does not care the snap of his fingers for me. No, I am not fishing for compliments, I am well aware I have no hope of making a conquest *there*!'

'Why not?' asked the incredulous but relieved Mr Warburton, who could not conceive of any gentleman being so utterly insensitive as not to fall victim to the lady's charms.

'Because I am convinced that my lord's interest is centred upon my sister, and yet—oh, if only I knew the whole truth! One thing is sure, she holds him to be in some way culpable, and I do believe thinks to get her own again by pairing him off with me. Did he desert her? Did she read more into his attentions than he had intended? Mama cannot answer this either. She will only say he went away to rejoin the army when Bonaparte broke free.'

Mr Warburton cleared his throat tentatively. 'That is not precisely the story as I have heard it,' he ventured. 'His lordship left this country before the Corsican escaped, nor did he go alone.'

'What? You mean he went off with one of the muslin company?' Eustacia's eyes almost jumped out of her head with excitement. 'You make him sound a very Byron! That would never do for Verity!'

'My mother is of the opinion that his rakish days are over, and in this I am at one with her,' asserted Mr Warburton handsomely.

'If only we could bring Verity to see that what an admirable countess she would make,' sighed Eustacia. 'But the whole situation is as delicate as—as that dew-drop glistening upon a spider's web.'

Mr Warburton was prepared to grant the delicacy of the affair but his attention was so taken by his lady's striking appearance in her blue riding habit, frogged and ornamented in black and gold and clinging closely to the curves of her trim figure, that he could think of little else. Despite her presenting so enchanting a picture, he was quick to observe that his loved one was looking a trifle pensive, and wondered hopefully if the same emotions that had kept him wakeful for several nights were disturbing her rest.

The day was a brilliant one after the night's rain, with a brisk little breeze to stir the air, and he had had no difficulty in persuading Lady Middleton to allow him escort her younger daughter on an excursion along the course of the River Chelt, past the Mill and the original chalybeate spa, onwards towards Cirencester. Each of the grooms had strapped behind him a basket filled with sufficient provisions to assuage any pangs of hunger that might assail them and, as it was already past noon, Mr Warburton declared they would be well advised to call a halt and plan their picnic, so together they rode on to survey the terrain, bidding the grooms await their summons when they had found a suitable spot.

The beauty of the surrounding landscape, the cattle grazing peacefully in the meadows by the gently-flowing river, the fresh verdure of the trees and the delight in his companion, all combined so to gratify Mr Warburton's senses that, when Eustacia drew rein at the top of a small eminence crowned by several handsome oaks, declaring with an imperious wave of her hand that this must be the place to spread their feast, he felt himself to be the humble acolyte of some fair goddess—Diana, perhaps, or Venus herself.

Slipping from his arms as he helped her from the saddle, she stood with her back to him, surveying the countryside with as much satisfaction as would any explorer observing for the first time some rare vista unfolded before him. Reminding himself that this could well be the only moment of the day they would have to themselves, Mr Warburton stepped up behind her and, placing his hands on her shoulders, gently turned her to face him.

'Miss—Eustacia, the depth of my feelings towards

you cannot but be apparent. It has been my proudest dream since first I saw you that one day you might consent to be my wife. Is there any hope for me or is my situation in life too lowly for you to contemplate such a possibility?'

'Don't be absurd, Theodore, you know perfectly well it is not!' replied she with a lack of sentimentality that took him aback though, to be truthful, beneath her matter-of-fact demeanour, her heart and emotions were no less disturbed than his. 'And, of course, when your Percival connections are generally known there will be no question of our not residing in Cheltenham.'

'I had every hope that we would reside at least near to Cheltenham,' said he, perplexed. 'In fact, that is why I—but, perhaps, I should not be telling you this.' Eustacia, much relieved at not having to explain that the fact of his mother being a Percival would more than compensate for his father's lowly origin, demanded to be told what he meant. 'I had intended to give you your old home as a wedding present,' he confessed.

'Shurdington Hall? But—the Cloudesley-Abbotts?'

'Are renting it from me and will cease to do so whenever I should require it.'

'Then they are making all those alterations at your behest?'

'I felt Miss Middleton would be more at ease did she not know my money was paying for them,' said he demurely.

'So that is how you chanced upon her that day when you rescued her?'

He grinned at the memory. 'Yes, I was going to see if the wall had been mended and there she was, on top of it!'

She clapped her hands together in delight. 'But if you give me the Hall as a wedding present, she has nothing to say! Theodore, did you buy it for me or for my sister?'

He laughed aloud at that. 'For you, of course, my darling!'

'But you must know that I cannot be wed before Verity.' His face fell and she hastened to reassure him. 'I promise you that is not an insurmountable obstacle.'

'No?' he asked doubtfully, seeing his visions of connubial bliss fade away into an indefinite future.

'No!' she said firmly. 'I have hit upon a capital notion!' He eyed her in some apprehension and begged to be enlightened. 'We must elope! Then, you being the Earl's cousin and I being Verity's sister, they must come in pursuit of us. Is it not a famous plan?'

Mr Warburton could not agree with her. 'I hope I am not so lost to every sense of what is right and proper that I should contemplate such a course!' he said in a very shocked way.

'Oh, we shan't really elope,' she explained airily. 'Only just pretend to and when they are fairly upon our track, I can return home and you can lead them on or something of that sort—I have not thought out the details yet.'

'But what if Miss Middleton does not accompany the Earl?' he protested, quaking a little at the possible consequences of his beloved's harebrained proposal. 'Even if she does, I cannot see that—'

'She will,' Eustacia promised him. 'Her first instinct will be to protect my reputation by adding her presence to that of Wonersh.' She chuckled naughtily. 'A couple of nights spent on the road in his company might turn her thoughts towards her own reputation. It might also encourage her in the belief that I have eloped with you rather than accept him for husband.'

'And would you?' he asked, very low. 'Oh, not elope, of course, but would you marry me?'

Eustacia hung her head prettily. 'Once this business of my sister and Wonersh is resolved—' she intimated.

Mr Warburton's smile broke out again. 'You're a

wicked little puss,' he chided her fondly, 'but I adore you and if that is the price I must pay for winning you I count it of little consequence.'

'I knew you would!' Eustacia raised a face glowing with delight to his and, inevitably, the sight of those rosy lips half-parted in a smile, quite overcame his determination not to take advantage of a helpless girl, entrusted by her mother to his care. 'Mmmm!' she murmured when he relaxed his attentions, 'that was nice—dear Theodore!'

Stifling the last stirrings of conscience, Mr Warburton took her strongly into his embrace and went on kissing her. The lady appeared to take no exception to such familiarity until the voices of the approaching grooms caused them to draw apart and stand, hands clasped, smiling upon each other.

'My little love!' he murmured thickly. She leaned forward to lay a finger on his lips.

'It is our secret—remember!' she warned him. 'Until both Verity and Wonersh are returned to Cheltenham there is nothing to be done. And that may not be for several weeks if my aunt still wishes for my sister's company.'

In this assumption, however, Eustacia was soon found to be at fault. Some few hours earlier on that same morning Miss Middleton, seated at her aunt's secretary reading a letter from her mother which touched upon every subject without giving any real information about any one of them, was disturbed by the entry of Lady Daventry's butler to inform her that a young lady had called to see her.

'To see me?' Miss Middleton laid down her letter and frowned in perplexity. 'But, surely, her ladyship—'

'Her ladyship never leaves her room before noon, miss,' the butler reminded her. 'In any case, it is you who is asked for. By her way of speech, a foreign young lady,' he added helpfully. 'She said her name would mean little to you but she wished to speak to you on a matter of some urgency.'

'I see,' said Miss Middleton, excusably intrigued. 'Well, you had best show her in here, I suppose.'

He bowed and withdrew. Folding up her letter she placed it in her reticule for perusal at a more convenient time, then stood for a moment in front of a pier-glass to approve her appearance. In palest green sprig muslin with a dainty mob-cap of the same trimmed with fine lace set on her golden head, she looked as fresh as the morning itself and was feeling comfortably gratified when the door opened behind her and she was afforded the first sight of her visitor reflected in the mirror. So striking was the impression received that she remained momentarily as if rooted to the spot.

The appearance of the young woman whose entry had prompted this reaction was something quite out of the ordinary way. Neither too tall nor too short, her slender person was attired with a tasteful elegance that won Miss Middleton's immediate approval. A short French pelisse of white satin edged with swansdown was worn over a robe of worked jaconet and a petticoat of the same, flounced with deeply-ruched trimming. Her narrow brimmed bonnet, just showing the frilled edges of a cornette, had depending from it a veil of figured gauze, now thrown back to reveal a flowerlike visage, framed by hair as palely gold as Miss Middleton's own. In short she was a Beauty and Miss Middleton's mild satisfaction in her own get-out suffered a sad reverse.

Observing her chastened expression, the visitor laughed, a clear tinkling sound that sent particles of ice trickling down her hostess' spine.

'Is it not strange that we are both unfashionably fair?' The blue eyes, tip-tilted at the corners to give a faintly Oriental cast to her countenance, danced at some inner source of amusement. 'But that could explain, perhaps

—' She stopped and made a supremely Gallic gesture with her small gloved hands. Her voice, too, held a strong French intonation though her command of English was faultless. Miss Middleton decided it was time she asserted some authority over the situation before this dominant young woman quite snatched it from her.

'Forgive me, ma'am, but I don't believe I have had the pleasure—?'

'To be sure you have not, though I think you have made my brother's acquaintance on one occasion—Mr James Ramsay?' Miss Middleton checked a start of surprise. Anything less like the dark-visaged Mr Ramsay could scarcely be imagined. Great Heavens! Was this lovely creature half-sister to Wonersh? The amusement deepened in the slanting eyes. 'I resemble my father, I believe. My brother resembles his.'

'Oh! I—will you not be seated?' Miss Middleton, belatedly remembering her duties as a hostess, indicated a chair. 'I have reason to be grateful to your brother. His presence of mind saved me from a possibly fatal accident.'

She thought it best not to add that his plotting might well have led her into a more serious scrape and waited for Miss Ramsay to explain the reasons for her visit. That young lady seated herself composedly and drew off her long silk gloves. Miss Middleton was fascinated to observe that her fingernails were painted silver, while any scent emanating from the bunch of violets pinned to her pelisse was surely absorbed in the cloud of perfume that wafted about her person like an invisible veil.

'I am glad James was of service. No doubt he had his reasons.' The near-contempt in her tone aroused Miss Middleton's curiosity.

'What reasons should he have other than that of saving me from injury?'

The perfect mouth twisted sardonically. 'My brother

is a devious man,' was all the reply offered.

'Devious, indeed,' retorted Miss Middleton, spurred into plain speaking, 'if one day he saves my life and a little later puts me in danger of losing it!'

The slim shoulders were raised in a deprecating shrug. 'Of that I know nothing. But I have not travelled from Paris to speak of dear James.'

'Then may I be told the object of this visit?'

'I am informed you are contemplating an alliance between a member of your family and my lord of Wonersh.'

Miss Middleton was strongly inclined to summon the butler and have the lady shown out. Repressing this ignoble desire by reminding herself that she would learn nothing that way, she replied with admirable disregard for the truth.

'Your informant is at fault, ma'am. I have no such intention.'

'It is rumoured that he has been paying court to your sister.' The vivid blue eyes were very intent.

'If that rumour has reached Paris, Miss Ramsay, then it can only have been conveyed there by your brother.'

'What matter how it came?' The silver-tipped fingers dipped into a velvet reticule, half as big as a post-bag, and drew from it a small, silk-wrapped parcel. 'This may help to convince you that I have only your good and that of your sister at heart.'

Though doubting the veracity of this statement, Miss Middleton received the parcel into her hand and, unfolding it, revealed a miniature set in a plain boxwood frame of a very young boy. Dressed in the style of an earlier age, the infant gazed out upon the world with a confident serenity that was hauntingly familiar and, in spite of her determination to remain unmoved by any disclosure, she could not refrain from uttering a gasp of recognition.

'The speaking likeness of his father, would you not

say?' Miss Ramsay was as watchful as a cat with a mouse.

'Who is the boy?' Miss Middleton's voice was scarce above a whisper.

'My son. He died some few months since. Some childish complaint the doctors said but—he died.' The still voice held no trace of emotion but Miss Middleton was horrified to see tears overspill and pour down the powdered cheeks. 'His father would never acknowledge him, never set eyes upon him. He was a beautiful, sweet-natured child.' Her hand touched her face as if to assure herself of her own distress, then sought a handkerchief. 'Forgive me.' The words came muffled from behind the wisp of lawn. 'I had not thought this to be so difficult in the telling.'

Miss Middleton was not unmoved by this sad revelation but felt herself to be standing aloof from it as might a spectator at a play. Somewhere a small voice was hinting that so measured a display of grief could not be spontaneous. Her eyes reverted to the miniature and, as she scrutinised it again, there was that about it that held her attention, something she could not put her finger on yet knew to be of significance. Reminding herself that this was the unhappy child's mother, she forced herself to utter laboured expressions of condolence which were received in total silence. Then, almost without intending to, she blurted out:

'Does his lordship know of your son's death?'

'He would not care if he did. Oh, this is no Banbury tale I am spinning you, ma'am, of that you may be sure.'

'It—it is excessively civil of you to—to—'

'To confess my folly, would you say?' A heavy sigh underlined the words. 'I thought myself to be in love with him then and he with me. I doubt not you can understand that.'

Her meaning was very plain and, beneath her stunned stupefaction, Miss Middleton's temper began to stir.

'For my sister, of course, all this is—you will forgive me—old history,' she said coldly. 'To throw away the hope of so eligible a union on the evidence of a chance likeness—'

She gestured towards the miniature lying on the table beside her, hoping she had struck the right note of polite incredulity.

'You mean, no price is too high to pay for a title?' Miss Ramsay sounded admiring of one who would go her length to attain her object. 'But you know as well as I how little faith you can put in his promises and I would not have your sister tread the path I did.'

'Your sentiments do you credit, ma'am.' Briskly, Miss Middleton wrapped up the miniature and, rising, handed it back to its owner. 'If I may, I will acquaint my sister with all you have told me. Then it will be for her to decide what course to follow.' She raised a hand to the bell-pull. 'My thanks, Miss Ramsay, and my sympathy in your loss.'

The other stood, head to one side, as if for the first time unsure of her ground. 'You'll not confront Wonersh with this?'

'That also I must discuss with my sister.' Dear God, thought Miss Middleton, will she never go and leave me to suffer my misery alone?

'He'll deny it, of course.'

At that moment the butler, who must have been hovering outside in the hall so promptly did he appear, came to end Miss Middleton's torment. With mutually insincere expressions of esteem, the ladies parted and, as the door closed behind Miss Ramsay, Verity tottered to a chair and sat shaking, all colour drained from her cheeks, her hands clenched together as if they had her visitor's slender throat between them and were pressing the life out of it.

'Why should she tell me such a story if it were not true? It cannot benefit her. And the likeness is too striking to be mere chance.' She did not know she was speaking aloud in an anguished whisper, as if the words were being torn from her. 'Dear God, what to do for the best?' She rose and went to the window in time to see Miss Ramsay step into a carriage and drive off. 'She has played her part and can now leave the stage.' Why was she so certain that Miss Ramsay had indeed been playing a part? Was it because she had no wish to believe Wonersh guilty of such perfidy? Presumably it had taken place when he had left her to go to France, yet that would mean, if the child had died some months before, that he could not have been above two years of age when the miniature had been painted, but to her eyes he had seemed to be older than that. Perhaps it was because of the rather old-fashioned and adult apparel in which it was all the crack for doting parents to rig out their young hopefuls when presenting them to posterity. Or could it be possible that the child had been conceived at an earlier date, when Wonersh had been paying court to her? 'Oh, no!' she cried out involuntarily. 'Leave me that at least!'

For a time she remained by the window, gazing unseeingly at the passers-by and the carriages rattling busily up and down the street, before becoming aware that one of those carriages had stopped outside and, if she was bent on taxing the Earl of Wonersh with his despicable behaviour, then Fate had put it into her power to do so without loss of time for he was walking up the steps to the street-door.

She flattered herself that her greeting of him was as gracious as civility demanded but, from the moment he had set foot in the room, Wonersh had sensed something was amiss.

'What is it? Have you had ill-tidings from Cheltenham? Your mother—'

'Enjoys her normal good-health, I thank you,' she cut in. 'But whether she will continue to do so when she hears what I have to tell her is a matter for conjecture.'

'You are talking in riddles,' he said curtly. 'What is this unpalatable intelligence you feel obliged to disclose?'

'A pity you were not here some ten minutes since, my lord, to meet my earlier caller.'

It was plain to the Earl that she was labouring under some strong sense of injustice or calamity, and he came towards her, hand outstretched.

'You are troubled, Verity. How may I be of assistance?'

At that Miss Middleton's iron resolve utterly deserted her. 'You—of assistance?' she cried out wildly. 'That notion is so ludicrous as to be quite diverting!'

He stood, as if transfixed, in mid-stride. 'You'd best be more explicit, ma'am.'

'My visitor was Miss Ramsay, sister to Mr James Ramsay,' she flung at him.

'Half-sister,' he corrected her, his mind more occupied with the realisation of what such a visit might portend than of what he was saying.

'Oh, to be sure, half-sister!' Her laugh had a hysterical edge to it. 'I doubt that even you would—'

'That will do!' The peremptory command shocked her into silence. 'I'll not have you ring a peal over me on that head! She's a gazetted Cyprian—could you not guess it?'

Miss Middleton had guessed it, but she was not going to tell his lordship that. 'Maybe she is now,' she flashed back, 'but was she when first you—you seduced her and left her to bear your child?'

'My child?' He stared at her, incredulous. 'What the devil are you talking about?'

'Oh, she said you'd not acknowledge him.' Miss Middleton was now fairly embarked upon her disastrous tirade. 'Can you be less of a gentleman than your father, my lord? He, at least, took responsibility for his lapses!'

'What would you have me do? Pay 'em all on quarter-day like old "Q"?'

She should have been warned by the quiver of rage in his voice but she plunged heedlessly on. 'And now he's dead and she has nothing! Cyprian she may be but she is also a mother!'

'Who is dead?'

He caught her wrists in a hurtful clasp and she stepped back only to find her further retreat blocked by a fine break-front bookcase which housed Lord Daventry's outstanding collection of first editions.

'The—the boy,' she faltered, all at once aware of the intensity of his anger. 'She showed me his likeness—a miniature—it could be your very self.' Her eyes dropped from the cold fury of his regard to the single pearl in his neckcloth. 'Why, that pin! He was shown as wearing it in the portrait! But how—'

'How, you ask, could he be wearing it unless I had bequeathed it to him?' His tone was so harsh she longed to put her hands to her ears to shut out the sound, but he held them fast. 'This is one of the Percival pearls. My father had it made into a pin for me when I was born, nor has it ever left my possession. There is also a miniature of me at Beauregard, done when I was some four years old, wearing that very pin.'

It took a few seconds for his meaning to penetrate her dazed consciousness. 'How could such a portrait fall into her hands?' she asked at last.

'I do not know nor do I propose to trouble myself with so trivial a matter at this moment. My immediate concern is your willingness to believe the worst of me, to accept every other person's account of my misdeeds before ever hearing my side of the story. There was no child, be assured of that.'

Blind to all else save her catastrophic pursuit of the truth, Miss Middleton pressed on. 'But there could have been?'

'Aye.' His hard eyes never left her face. 'I grant you there could have been.'

She resolved to know it all, cost her what it might. 'Wh—when?' she got out through trembling lips. He looked at her in blank incomprehension then began silently to laugh in a way she could not like.

'So that's it! Doubting to the last! Well, you can go on doubting, ma'am, for damme if I'll tell you!' He released her so violently that she was thrown back against the bookcase and grateful for its support.

'I—I believe we have no more to say to each other, my lord,' she whispered, clutching at a last shred of dignity.

'What? No apology for having blackened my character once again?' The taunt had effect.

'You did not need me to blacken your character!' she retorted with a small flash of spirit.

'Oh, yes, I did, believe me, I did! I loved you, Verity, as I had never thought to love anyone. I needed but to assure myself there was no basis for concern over the Ramsay claim before offering for you. Then you spurned me, condemned me unheard. Would you have married me, I wonder, had the path of true love run smooth? Was it true love on your part or just a sweet girlish fancy to be a countess?'

'How dare you!' she choked. 'The Middletons were a county family before ever the Percivals—'

'Produced a lovely lightskirt to gladden the Merrie Monarch's eye and got an earldom for it? Disreputable lot, ain't we?' The depth of his bitterness touched her.

'I suffered, too.' Her voice was so low as to be almost inaudible.

'Did you, Verity? How much did you suffer, I wonder?' He reached out and pulled her into the circle of his arms. 'Let us put it to the test.'

Unresisting, she was crushed in his embrace. Her mob-cap was swept off and her neatly-coiled hair fell in a shimmer of gold about her shoulders. His mouth hurt and devoured her with a hungry passion that, far from disgusting her, merely induced a sad acceptance of her unworthiness and his right to reparation for her ill-judgment of him. His fury soon abated, he loosed her, a very different expression on his face, his hands stroking the shining mantle of her hair as if to beg forgiveness.

'Verity!' he cried out. 'Verity, listen to me!'

She did not wait to hear what he had to say but tore herself from him and fled from the room, all but knocking down her aunt who was on the point of entering.

'My lord—' began that affronted lady then, seeing how things were, she closed the door firmly behind her niece's distraught figure. The Earl picked up the mob-cap and stood, turning it over in his hands as if he did not quite understand how it came to be there. 'My lord,' said Lady Daventry again, but in a soothing way. 'Pray be seated.' She took him by the arm and led him to the sofa then, gently detaching the mob-cap from his twisting fingers, she sat down beside him. 'I collect that you and Verity have had a turn-up?'

'Yes,' he said. 'I thought I would teach her a lesson. It was foolish of me, I allow, to think I could teach the perfect Miss Middleton anything.'

'Perhaps you did not go about it the right way,' suggested the perfect Miss Middleton's aunt. 'The gentle approach is not for Verity.'

'I was hardly gentle,' he interpolated wryly.

'I am not speaking of love-play,' said Lady Daventry in a large way. 'What my niece needs is to be shown who is master.'

'I'd never raise a finger to her!'

'No one ever has, more's the pity!' she sighed. 'My brother worshipped his beloved daughter and my dear sister-in-law had not the spirit to administer a beating. But leave that for the moment. A message has just arrived from Sir Godfrey to inform us that his lady has reached her time and would his sister make all haste to take over charge of his household until the happy event has resolved itself.'

'And that's a foretaste of her future life, is it not? My lovely Verity!' His resentment encouraged Lady Daventry in the belief that all was not yet lost. 'Looking after a growing horde of little Middletons—aye, and her sister's children, too, I don't doubt! Her looks fading with each passing year, her ripeness desiccated into spinsterhood.'

She patted his hand briskly. 'It is for you to see that does not happen, my lord. Now, do you think you could convey her to Albemarle Street because Daventry is reading a paper to the Royal Society this afternoon and is lunching with them, so has taken the carriage. Something abstruse about early Roman remains in Portugal,' she added doubtfully. 'I am sure I cannot understand the half of it.'

He shook his head decisively. 'She'd not entrust herself to my charge after this. No, I'd best keep out of her way for a time.'

'Out of sight, perhaps, but not out of mind,' her ladyship advised him. 'Flowers and a graceful apology might not come amiss?'

'I'll warrant you they would arrive back on my doorstep!'

Lady Daventry rose and shook out her skirts. 'I'll go to her now. If you would be so good, call up a hackney for me when you leave.'

Miss Middleton had just finished re-pleating her hair about her head when her aunt asked to enter her bedchamber and gave her news of her sister-in-law's condition. Taking scant notice of her niece's wan face and general air of distraction, she bustled about, enquiring how long a stay at Albemarle Street Verity had in mind and what gowns she wished to take with her.

'I have a valise packed and ready.' Miss Middleton spoke as one not fully cognisant of what she was about. 'There are just a few small necessities to be put in—I'll need a hack carriage, will I not?'

'Wonersh is calling one up,' said Lady Daventry with the air of one who was in the habit of using earls to do the work of lackeys. 'He'd have taken you himself but he thought you would not wish for it. What did you quarrel about this time?'

'One of his—his straw damsels!' burst out her niece.

'Really, Verity!' Her ladyship sounded mildly amused. 'For a nobleman of his consequence and looks not to have irregular connections would be something quite out of the way. Nor do I remember your being so censorious about Godfrey's little actresses.'

'He stopped all that when he married Annabelle,' Miss Middleton defended her brother.

'Have you any reason to suppose that Wonersh won't do the same?' enquired her aunt. 'Now, what about this warm robe-de-chambre? You could need that.'

Discussing her immediate arrangements occupied Miss Midldeton's attention and served to compose her agitated thoughts so that, by the time she stepped into the waiting hackney, she had contrived to thrust her worries deep to the back of her mind and concentrate upon the task in hand.

CHAPTER TWELVE

'THERE's a clever baby then!' cooed young Lady Middleton to her gurgling offspring placed in her arms by Nurse. 'See how well he knows just what to do!'

The baby's aunt, seated by the bedside, thought rather cynically that it would be a very odd infant indeed who did not know where his next meal was coming from, but realised that to express any such opinion would be quite unacceptable to her present audience. Babies she considered to be astonishingly disruptive little creatures, nor did the fact that this particular small sprig was her brother's child and destined to carry on the name of Middleton cause her to think more kindly of him. Her sister-in-law's next remark alerted her to hitherto unforeseen dangers.

'And when you are older, my precious, think of the treats in store for you when your Aunt Verity shows you how to put the map of Europe together or takes you to view the animals in the Tower!'

Aunt Verity decided that a halt must be called to this sort of idiocy before it took firm hold of Annabelle's imagination.

'Now that you are so comfortably established,' she said, 'I feel it only right that I should return to Cheltenham and acquaint mama with all the details of these past two weeks. She will be longing to hear everything I have to tell her about her first grandchild.'

Annabelle pouted. 'Such a very obliging letter as I

have had from her. I cannot feel that she would grudge my keeping you by me for a little longer.'

'Much though I would like to remain here and support you,' explained Miss Middleton, quite untruthfully, for she was bored to death by her pampered sister-in-law's whims and fancies, 'I feel that my duty at this moment lies in seeing how Eustacia goes on.'

Annabelle's eyes lit up. 'Oh, yes! Mama Middleton did mention that Wonersh was paying her some distinguishing attention. Now, that would be a famous match for her!'

Meeting her sister-in-law's speculative regard, Miss Middleton wondered how much she knew or guessed about her own earlier association with the Earl, but concluded it could be little, if anything, since Annabelle had not entered upon the London scene from her native Yorkshire until the following year.

'I doubt we can entertain any great hope of Wonersh making her an offer,' she began, but Annabelle was already embarked upon future plans that envisaged, among other things, having the Earl stand godfather to her son.

'Or perhaps you could persuade your unknown admirer,' she suggested archly, waving a hand to embrace the floral offerings with which the big room was overfull. 'So generous of you to insist that I should have the pleasure of them. Who can he be? Come, Verity, you must have a suspicion!'

Miss Middleton knew very well from whom the flowers came, but as no card or message ever accompanied them it would have been a great presumption on her part to have returned them to Berkeley Square. In any case, Miss Liddell, who had called a few days before, had informed them of her and the Earl's imminent departure for Beauregard, after which she had expected the daily tributes would cease, but still they came. She roused herself from her reverie to listen to what her sister-in-law was saying.

'I do understand your concern for Eustacia. Dear Mama Middleton so dotes upon her that a touch of your firm hand is very necessary to induce her to keep the line. So prestigious a gentleman as Wonersh must have every unattached young lady of his acquaintance on the catch for him. You will know just what to do, dear Verity, without making it seem too odiously matchmaking. I fear, in this instance, I must agree that Eustacia's need of you should take precedence over mine.'

Being all too well aware of Annabelle's vacillating temperament, Miss Middleton lost no time in removing herself back to Park Place before her sister-in-law should change her mind. Lady Davenport put no obstacle in the way of her departure but sent her off armed with a cordial invitation to the Dowager to join her at Brighton in June.

'I have signed the lease for the best possible house to be had on the Steyne—far too large for just Daventry and I to rattle about in—so do come, all of you.'

Miss Middleton, taking farewell of her aunt with genuine regret, gave it as her opinion that the project would find great favour with her mama, and set off in a reasonably confident frame of mind. She had resolutely put behind her all recollection of her last meeting with the Earl, though the very thought of having to face him again, as she surely must if he was continuing to wait upon Eustacia, aroused sentiments of a nature difficult to disregard. He had loved her, or so he had avowed, but now, surely, that love was dead, so what had she to fear in meeting him? Nonetheless, because she knew in her heart there was a deal of truth in his bitter accusation of her, she did not relish a meeting.

Upon returning to Cheltenham, however, she found the situation to be other than she had expected. His lordship had not called at Royal Crescent and Mr Warburton's star was very strongly in the ascendant, a state of affairs which the Dowager, in her delight at becoming a grandmother, had done nothing to curb, while any protest to Eustacia on the impropriety of her conduct met with a cool defiance that bordered on the impertinent. Mr Warburton, too, though unfailingly courteous, exuded a confidence that defied any efforts to depress his pretensions and, while Lady Middleton declared he had not formally applied to her to address Eustacia, her sister greatly feared that an understanding existed between them.

It was with a sense of foreknowledge therefore that, having returned unexpectedly early from accompanying Lady Middleton to the Pump Room at Montpellier, she found propped up against her dressing-table mirror, a letter addressed to her in Eustacia's handwriting. Tearing off the wafer that sealed it, she had only to glance through the carefully worded epistle to discover that her worst fears had been realised.

'Verity, dear sister,' the younger Miss Middleton had written, 'never had I thought to have to pen such lines to you and the very impropriety of my action so sinks my spirits that I hardly dare beg for your understanding let alone forgiveness. Theodore and I are persuaded that the only way to convince you of our unalterable determination to be wed is to present you with a *fait accompli*, thus absolving you and dear mama from all blame in the matter. Believe me, we have not reached this decision without agonising deliberation and can only pray that, in time, you may find it in your heart to receive again two people who hold you in the most sincere and respectful affection . . .'

For several minutes Miss Middleton found her normally agile brain to be quite incapable of coherent thought. Then she sat down and forced herself to consider the matter rationally. Eustacia had declined to accompany them that morning, giving as her excuse that she had the headache. Doubtless within minutes of their departure Mr Warburton had presented himself to take her for what was establishing itself as an almost daily drive. None of the staff, not even the vigilant Griffiths, would suspect anything was amiss in so common an occurrence.

'And then?' cried out Miss Middleton in despair. 'On to Gretna Green?' Where else could they go? Eustacia was under age, no churchman would perform the ceremony, so Gretna Green it must be. 'It will *not* be!' she muttered fiercely. 'I'll stop them!' But how? To follow with Wilkes in her mother's carriage would be to announce to the whole world what had taken place. The fancy to saddle up Marigold and set off in pursuit took hold of her imagination. Her sister and Mr Warburton could not know that Lady Middleton had paid only a brief visit to the Pump Room that morning and had excused herself and Verity from joining an old friend from luncheon because of wishing to rest before attending Lady Gower's soirée later in the day. They must have counted on having at least another two hours before a pursuit was mounted. She sat a moment longer, deep in thought, then holding Eustacia's letter folded in her hand, she got up and went to knock upon her mother's door.

'A letter from dear Deborah, mama, to say she called to find Eustacia very much in the dismals so has borne her off to Beauregard and begs that I follow at my leisure and take dinner with them.'

'How kind she is!' The Dowager was resting comfortably with the latest romance from the subscription library lying open upon her knee and a box of sugar plums at her elbow.

Thanking whatever gods there were that Eustacia had had the wit not to acquaint her mother with her situation, Miss Middleton went on smoothly. 'You will be requiring Wilkes and the carriage as you are staying on to dine with Lady Gower so, as I have not been on her back since my return, I will ride Marigold over to Beauregard.'

Lady Middleton regarded her with a horrified stare. 'But, Verity, you cannot go to dinner in a riding habit!'

Her daughter laughed with well assumed light-heartedness. 'To be sure I cannot so I must suspend my smallest valise containing gown and slippers from the pommel of my saddle. Deborah assures me there will only be we three ladies for dinner, no need for an elaborate toilette. And I will ask for a lad from the stables to escort me,' she added quickly lest the Dowager should take it into her head to require to see Miss Liddell's letter. 'It is no great distance after all and he can take Marigold back with him. As to my return, if Deborah must sweep Eustacia off in so high-handed a fashion she must be prepared to send her home in her chaise and can scarce refuse to do the same service for me. No, mama, I would not dream of depriving you of your carriage.'

With a nice show of reluctance, Lady Middleton allowed herself to be persuaded and her much relieved daughter hurried away to change into her riding-habit.

It was not yet two o'clock and a bright, warm day when she rode away from Cheltenham, accompanied by a willing if surprised stableboy. A casual enquiry had elicited the information from Griffiths that Mr Warburton had called for Eustacia a little before noon. That gave them a scant two hours' start and the late May evening would provide ample daylight in which to overtake them did she make haste. Miss Liddell, she was confident, would have no hesitation in joining her and in fabricating some story to cover the occasion. Wonersh, of course, would be the better choice, but she was resolved that he should know nothing of the escapade nor could she bring herself to ask him for assistance.

As they entered the gates of Beauregard, opened for them by a bowing lodge-keeper, her heart sank into her boots when she perceived a horseman cantering towards them along the grass verge of the drive. A closer glance confirmed that it was not the Earl but Mr Roger Percival, and she at once drew rein to exchange greetings with him.

Mr Percival, who had not set eyes upon the lady since the interesting happenings at the tower, was vastly curious to know the object of her visit. Though Miss Ramsay had reported to him that, in her opinion, Miss Middleton had taken the news of the Earl's deplorable behaviour very coolly, yet he was reasonably confident that she must regard the whole unsavoury business with disgust, however good a face she might put on it for Miss Ramsay's benefit. The Earl, too, had been in a very strange temper since his return from London, and there had been no social exchanges between Beauregard and Royal Crescent which seemed to postulate that Miss Middleton had spoken her mind and dismissed her—or her sister's—noble suitor.

'Why, this is an unexpected pleasure, ma'am!' He swept off his beaver and bowed low from the saddle. 'I trust you are in good health—but I need not ask! You are ever in such looks it is difficult to conceive of your being out of sorts!'

'You are too kind, sir,' returned Miss Middleton in the most friendly way. Truth to tell, she was feeling a little guilty about Mr Percival. Though Miss Liddell was at one with her in her suspicions of him, yet there was no sort of proof that he had been involved in their recent misadventures and the Earl was clearly disinclined to think ill of him. Nonetheless, she could not feel at ease with him and sought to curtail their meeting by enquiring if Miss Liddell was at home.

'Why, no, ma'am. She left yesterday for a short visit to her cousins at Oswestry. His lordship rode with her and will be returning at any time now. May I be of assistance?'

Miss Middleton found herself at Point Non-Plus, but the threat of the Earl's imminent return urged her to a quick decision. 'No, I thank you, it is of little importance. I thought as I was riding nearby to call upon her. We will go back now, Samuel,' she informed the stable-boy, who expressed his gratification by a gap-toothed grin. Escorting young ladies was all very well, but there was a cocking at Bayshill that evening and he had no mind to miss it.

Politely declining Mr Percival's offers of hospitality, Miss Middleton made her adieux and turned the ever-willing Marigold for home. This set-back to her plans called for careful deliberation and once they were well clear of Beauregard she drew rein and instructed Samuel to precede her.

'I wish to call upon some acquaintance who live not half-a-mile from here,' she said, marvelling anew at her own gift for invention, 'but you had best be gone lest your master should have need of you. Do not be concerned if I do not return Marigold tonight. I may well leave her here and come back by carriage.'

Samuel, well-pleased with the turn things had taken, made token protest, volunteering to accompany the lady to the house of her friends lest they should be from home.

'No fear of that,' replied she, wishing the tiresome boy a thousand miles away, 'the lady has been in poor health of late and has only just risen from her bed.'

His conscience appeased, Samuel rode off and Miss Middleton was left to her own devices. If their destination was Gretna Green the fleeing couple would have had to pass this way, so that calling at Beauregard had not set her back in their pursuit, but now a choice of routes presented itself and all depended on where they aimed to join the Great North Road. She recalled to mind that Godfrey, on the occasions when he had journeyed to visit Annabelle's home, had always contended that Grantham was the place best suited to this purpose. She herself had never been further north than Stratford-upon-Avon, where Godfrey had deposited her on one occasion with some friends and taken her up again on his return from York. If a fleeting doubt crossed her mind that she was being ill-advised to chase the runaways single-handed, she firmly suppressed it. They would be travelling in the happy assumption that no one, as yet, knew of their flight, since they would not have expected her to have returned to Royal Crescent so soon after leaving it. To squander that precious advantage might be to lose them altogether so, whipping up the reluctant Marigold, she rode on a short way into Winchcombe.

Here at the George, to her vast relief, the old ostler who came hurrying to attend upon her, described the gentleman who had got down from the driving-seat of his phaeton to procure refreshment for his lady in such detail that she had no doubt of his being Mr Warburton.

'Headin' for Grantham, his groom gave me to understand,' went on this garrulous ancient, 'an' wishful o' keepin' his own team for the first stages—as neat a set o' sweet-steppers as ever I saw.'

Once again Miss Middleton felt the stirrings of doubt. Surely one did not take one's groom along on an elopement? She had had sufficient proof of Mr Warburton's ingenuity, however, to be assured that he would find good reason to dispense with the man's services before the day was out. She then became aware that the ostler was regarding her with covert curiosity and realised what an odd appearance she must give, quite unattended and with a valise suspended from her saddle.

'I had thought to stop them before they set out,' she hastened to explain. 'It is my sister and brother, you see. Our mother has—has met with an accident and I must recall them. I had no notion they would have got so far on their way.' Great Heavens, into what a morass of untruths had she plunged herself!

'Well, miss,' the ostler cast a disparaging glance over Marigold. 'If y'don't mind my sayin' so, y'll not overtake 'em afore dark on that slug. I've a prime bit o' blood, left here t'other day, not yet claimed. So be it y'can get him back to me tomorrow, he's yours.'

Miss Middleton was too thankful for any assistance to be resentful of this criticism of her faithful steed and waited impatiently while the ostler, whistling softly to himself, led Marigold away. A lady and a gentleman he had been warned to expect and hoped he was doing the right thing in encouraging this pretty young thing to continue on her way alone. He consoled himself with the thought that, could she handle Rufus, she would have the heels of the pair in the phaeton and his hand closed over the guinea in his pocket bestowed upon him earlier that day as he recalled the gentleman's words.

'Just say sufficient to set them on our track without doubt of our destination.'

At first he had wondered if he was aiding an elopement but why, if that was so, should the eloping pair be so anxious to set their pursuers on their trail? Shaking his head at the strange ways of the quality, he set to removing the saddle from Marigold's back and harnessing up her successor.

Miss Middleton's new mount was a lively bay, a shade impetuous but well-mannered enough and clearly not unused to carrying a lady's saddle. In a very little while they came to terms with each other and the ostler watched them trot briskly off, his qualms partially appeased and his pocket considerably heavier.

On his advice, Miss Middleton had decreed that her

next stop should be at Broadway. Not that she really expected the phaeton to have called there for Mr Warburton's team would be capable of a much greater stretch before requiring to be baited, but she wished to be on the safe side of chance. She gave her mount his head and so nobly did he respond that she was pulling him to a stand before the Lygon Arms little more than half-an-hour after leaving Winchcombe.

As she awaited someone to help her dismount, a light travelling carriage moved smartly past her out of the yard and, glancing at its occupant, she was dismayed to meet the level gaze of Lady Castlereagh, wife to the Foreign Secretary. A slight inclination of her ladyship's elegant chip straw bonnet which set a-quivering the tall ostrich feathers with which it was adorned, confirmed that she had been recognised. Mentally bewailing the ill-fortune that had caused her path to cross with that of one of the most formidable patronesses of Almack's, Miss Middleton slid down from her saddle. No doubt but that that cool intelligence had observed every detail of her dusty and solitary condition, nor that it would be reported upon in the highest quarters.

'Well, I don't care for Almack's above half after all,' she consoled herself philosophically as she watched Rufus being led away for a rub-down and a drink. 'So I shan't go into a decline if I never set foot in the place again!'

Nonetheless the encounter had greatly dashed her spirits, since the whole object of her journey had been to ensure that no breath of scandal should attach to Eustacia's name. Stifling her apprehensions, she began to make enquiries of the stableyard staff and was gratified to learn that Eustacia and her escort had called at the Lygon Arms, apparently having had some difficulty with the sway-bar of the phaeton, which had necessitated a lengthy halt. Spinning her tale of misfortune once more, she was assured that their lead on her had been cut by half and she could expect to catch them up no later on the road than Stratford-upon-Avon. Thus encouraged, she remounted and pressed stoically onwards, once again leaving mixed feelings in the breasts of her informants.

At Stratford, which she well remembered from her former visit, her luck seemed to desert her. None of the better-known inns had anything to tell her, it was getting on for evening, both she and her mount were weary and, for a moment, she toyed with the idea of calling upon the friends with whom she had lodged previously and taking them into her confidence. Upon reflection over a cup of coffee, however, she soon put this notion out of her head. There were still at least three hours of daylight, the runaways must now be pressing forward to make up for time lost at Broadway and could well deem it advisable to avoid the more renowned hostelries and put up at some lesser known place for the night.

'They must stop somewhere soon,' she argued. 'If I don't meet up with them in the next hour I must return here and seek assistance.'

The decision made, she finished her coffee, paid her shot and, suppressing any craven pangs of hunger, set off once more. Now the road was a very much busier highway and she became aware that her progress was arousing a greal deal of interest, in particular among the male members of her fellow-travellers. This concerned her less than the fact that Rufus was visibly tiring, the sky was clouding over, and she would very soon have to turn back, her mission unaccomplished. A sudden violent downpour of rain cut short her ruminations and, looking about for some shelter, she perceived set back a little from the road a small and unpretentious tavern.

'Well, at least they can give me some food and Rufus can rest awhile,' she told herself hopefully. 'Maybe they have word of the phaeton for I vow I have passed no other inn since leaving Stratford.'

But the surly individual who looked her up and down in obvious disbelief of her story had nothing to add to her knowledge and, for the first time, Miss Middleton began to fear that she had lost the trail. The rain had now set in steadily and there was no question of her going on for the moment so, rather doubtfully, she entrusted Rufus to the care of a loutish oaf who looked not to be in possession of more than half his wits, and asked if she could partake of a meal, hopefully to resume her journey when the weather had improved.

The interior of the building was, if anything, less agreeable than its outward appearance. The coffee-room, into which she was shown, looked to be rarely used and was, she thought at first, unoccupied until a movement in the corner warned her she was not alone. Conscious of a pair of eyes peering furtively at her from the shadows, she seated herself as far distant from this dubious companion as possible and forced herself to partake of the unappetising food slapped down before her by a slattern of a maid, who she at once antagonised by requiring her to take away the eating utensils and wash them thoroughly.

As the outraged damsel flounced off, she thought she heard a chuckle coming from the corner of the room then, to her alarm, a long lean figure dressed in ill-fitting homespuns got to its feet and shambled across to sit at the table nearest to her.

'Ain't a deal of use having the utensils clean, the food is filthy anyway,' he informed her. Then, taking a long pull at his tankard, he rested his feet upon a chair and settled down to bear her company. Repressing a strong desire to take her leave of him without ceremony, Miss Middleton made some civil reply and sipped her glass of indifferent wine. 'Nice bit of blood you've got out there.' Her new acquaintance jerked his head in what was presumably the direction of the stables. Miss Middleton felt the stirrings of panic and was obliged to school her expression lest it should betray her alarm. What if Rufus was stolen and she left in this terrible place? His next words were more reassuring. 'The boy is simple but he has a way with animals, as is often the case. You need not fear for your beast's welfare.'

Well, at least, he spoke with the accent of a gentleman, though there was little gentlemanlike about his appearance. Miss Middleton, eyeing the continuing rain, felt she ought to be glad of any company in so dismal a situation.

'What place is this? I do not recollect seeing an inn-sign?' she asked.

'That got blown down in last year's gales and no one has thought to put it up again,' he told her. 'You're a winsome young lady to be riding on your own on such a highway.'

The return of the maid with the cleansed cutlery checked Miss Middleton from giving him a very sharp set-down and, upon reflection, she concluded it was best to ignore the implications of his last remark and give some account of herself.

'I am staying with friends at Stratford-upon-Avon,' she informed him icily. 'Not being familiar with this district, I got a little lost and thought the highway to be the most likely means of finding my way home. Then, of course, the rain came on and I was forced to take shelter.'

He was watching her, head to one side and leering in a way that she found far from pleasant. 'Your friends will be anxious for you, no doubt?'

'Yes, indeed they will,' she agreed, sampling the muddy-looking stew on her plate with a grimace of distaste. 'So the moment the weather improves, I must be off.'

'Could have set in for the evening,' he said helpfully. Miss Middleton had her fears on that count, too, but concentrated on getting on with her meal when, to her alarm, he leaned forward and laid a hand on her wrist. 'So be it does, there's no call for you to be lonesome, my pretty puss!' he whispered, sliding his hand up her arm. 'Oh, come now, don't play the innocent with me! I know you fine ladies—in between the sheets with any likely buck who takes your fancy!'

'You—you're no likely buck!' Miss Middleton heard herself retorting indignantly. His fingers tightened on her arm.

'Maybe not, but I'm your only choice. There's not many travellers call here.'

As he spoke, he moved quickly to the chair beside her and his other arm encircled her waist. With great presence of mind, Miss Middleton picked up her plate of stew and emptied it over his head then obeyed her first instincts and fled from the room.

Outside in the dark passage she had no idea of her direction, but the stream of imprecations following in her wake drove her forward and up a steep flight of stairs. Once at the top, she opened the first door she came to and found herself in a drab and scantily-furnished bedroom. She was less interested in the furnishings, or lack of them, than in the fact that the door had a key in the lock and a stout bolt which she lost no time in securing. Presently the noise downstairs abated and she crept to the window to see her erstwhile admirer, still plentifully besmeared with stew, emerge from below and walk purposefully to the stables. To her horror, he re-appeared a few minutes later leading Rufus, at the same time as a mud-splashed curricle and four turned into the yard.

'Oh, no, you don't!' Miss Middleton applied herself to the lattice windows and flung them wide. 'Stop, you thief! Sir! Sir!' She appealed to the driver of the curricle. 'That man is stealing my horse! Restrain him if you—oh, good God !'

The words died on her lips for the gentleman who had sprung so lightly down from the curricle and stood, looking up at her, apparently oblivious of the driving rain, was none other than my lord of Wonersh.

CHAPTER THIRTEEN

'How could you be so utterly bantam-witted as to expose your person to the rigours of such a journey? A lone female subject to the attentions of every sharp and rake-hell on the road—'

His lordship paused to draw breath before embarking on further pungent criticism of her behaviour while Miss Middleton sat with eyes closed, letting the wave of his anger sweep over her and wondering that she should feel so strangely comforted by it.

'I did call at Beauregard and found no one at home,' she put forward in her own defence.

'You found Roger!' he flung at her. 'Why did you not ask him to accompany you?'

'I—I could not ask him to witness Eustacia's shame.' Her voice trembled in spite of her determination to carry things off with a high hand.

'Had it not been for my arrival you, too, could have been quite discredited,' he told her. Miss Middleton, remembering Lady Castlereagh and the incident in the coffee-room, hung her head to conceal her rising colour.

'How did you find me?' she asked.

'Warburton had written me a letter in much the same style as did your sister to you which I found awaiting me on my return. Then Roger came to inform me that you had called at Beauregard and were on your way back to Cheltenham. I at once went after you to acquaint you with my intention of pursuing the tiresome couple. When I did not meet up with you I went on to Royal Crescent where I was informed that you and Miss Eustacia were dining at Beauregard at Deborah's invitation. From that I deduced the whole story.'

'Oh, Heavens, you did not tell mama?'

'I spoke to Griffiths only. It was already coming on to rain in Cheltenham so I thought it advisable to hint that if the weather should prove too inclement you might well be detained overnight.'

She sighed her relief. 'That was well done of you, my lord.'

'That was mere commonsense!' he rasped. 'How could you have supposed, even if you had overtaken them, that you could have got back to Cheltenham by nightfall?'

'I had not really planned as far as that,' she admitted. 'But what are we to do now?'

'Go on, of course. The rain has nearly stopped. Have you eaten?'

'A little,' she said quickly, unwilling to tell him of the use to which she had put her dinner. Her unwelcome gallant had not waited to make his lordship's acquaintance but had departed in haste, leaving a mildly surprised Rufus standing in the middle of the yard.

'Then, if you please, we will waste no more time.' The Earl rose and shook out the capes of his wet driving-coat.

'But—' She hesitated. 'Did you have word of them at Stratford?'

'I had no need to ask for them,' he returned with some asperity. 'You were my lodestone, ma'am, no one who spoke with you was likely to forget it.'

'But they did not call at Stratford!' she almost wailed. 'That is why I pressed on in the sure conviction that they must stop at some little-known place like this!'

She then told him of the intelligence she had gleaned on her way and of the mishap to the phaeton at Broadway. He regarded her frowningly.

'Grantham, eh? Then I'll warrant Warburton is resolved to rest snug in the Angel this night. He must know that I will follow him, but he cannot know how close.'

'He must also know that the Angel is the first place you will think to look for him,' she pointed out with some truth, but he scarce heard her.

'So very free with information—could it be a ruse to lead us astray?' he murmured. 'Yet, after all, where else can they go?'

'You mean—they could have taken another road?'

'And have holed up in some unlikely spot where no one would think to seek them.'

'But they must come to Grantham!'

'Not of necessity. It is where they would expect me to head for. They could take a more roundabout way.' The Earl was pulling at the lobe of his ear and at sight of the familiar gesture her heart seemed to stop beating for a moment, leaving her oddly breathless. 'But now we are left with no alternative but to continue to Grantham.'

'Then let us begone from this place—oh!'

'What is it?'

'Rufus. I could no more leave him here than stay myself.' A fleeting smile crossed his face.

'I'll saddle him and secure him behind us. I know of a reputable inn at Warwick where I can leave him—and you.'

'Me?' She glared at him, affronted. 'I am coming with you, my lord!'

'Loath though I am to contradict a lady, you are not coming with me. This will be a breakneck chase if I am to discover them tonight and I have no wish to be hampered by a wilting female.'

Words failed Miss Middleton at this unhandsome epithet. When she considered the effort she had put forth and her strength of purpose, to be dubbed 'wilting' was the outside of enough! She was forced to allow that she was a little tired and in need of her dinner, but that was all. However, she followed his lordship out to the curricle submissively enough and watched while he secured Rufus to the rail.

'He is going to slow us down, is he not? Would it not be better if I rode him?' she offered.

'You are not riding any more, you are quite done-up,' he said curtly. 'It is but a few miles to Warwick, he'll not hinder us for long.'

She made no further demur and in a shorter period of time than she had believed possible they were drawing in to a well-kept inn and the Earl, relinquishing the reins, sprang down to free Rufus.

'You are my cousin,' he instructed her. 'I dare not claim closer relationship for these people know me well. You are not feeling up to snuff and we are bound for Melton Mowbray to stay with others of our family. I will leave you here while I go on to allay any anxiety at our tardy arrival and return for you tomorrow.'

'What is supposed to be the matter with me?' she asked.

'Oh, Lord knows!' he replied impatiently. 'You ate something that sat ill on your stomach—will that do?'

Near enough to the truth, she supposed, gathering the reins into her hands. 'But I am not remaining here, my lord. Should we find Eustacia and Mr Warburton my presence is very necessary to protect her reputation. Yours,' she added witheringly, 'would have quite the reverse effect!'

'And if we do not find them, what of *your* reputation?' he taunted her.

'All I have to say on that head is that we must find them,' she returned stubbornly. 'And I am not getting down from this seat!'

'Then, by God, when I've seen to this beast, I'll drag you from it!' he promised her, his quick temper flaring.

'And carry me, kicking and screaming, into the house?' she said sweetly. 'For I warrant you I will kick and scream and bring about the very situation we are both so anxious to avoid.'

'You would suffer more by it than I,' he reminded her. 'My reputation is not so tender that it could not survive so small a shock.'

'Then you must take thought for me, my lord,' she charged him.

He stood, glaring up at her, before turning on his heel with an explosive 'Damn you, Verity!' and applying himself to releasing Rufus. Miss Middleton permitted herself a self-satisfied smile. The smile quickly faded when the Earl, having disposed of Rufus, rejoined her. 'You do realise,' he said in a more measured way, 'that even with two changes of cattle, we cannot reach Grantham before midnight?' Having no knowledge of the distance involved, she had not realised it, and her spirits suffered another reverse. 'And I am going to drive each team to the limit of its endurance,' he went on relentlessly, whipping up his horses to prove his point, 'for, as you rightly observed, when we get to Grantham there is no knowing where those two young fools may be lodged.'

Miss Middleton felt she ought to protest against her sister being referred to in such terms but decided against it, finding it necessary to devote all her attention to retaining her seat. Once or twice she was obliged to close her eyes when a collision with an approaching vehicle seemed imminent, or they scraped past some lumbering coach ahead of them with inches to spare, but each time they came off safe, thanks to the Earl's skill and good judgment.

'We will change teams at Coventry,' he said suddenly. 'These beasts of mine have borne us well but I'll not spring 'em further. While that is being done I will enquire at other inns in the place on the off-chance that our prey may have chosen to call a halt there. You might care for some refreshment while I am so engaged,' he added, stealing a glance at her wan face. Miss Middleton forbore to tell him that, as she was not in the habit of taking breakfast and had not paused in her hasty departure from Royal Crescent to indulge in even a light luncheon, the mere mention of food caused such an agitation of her gastric juices she scarce knew what to do with herself. He took her air of constraint to mean something quite other and laughed shortly. 'Don't be thinking that I'll go off and desert you in a strange town. Whatever your opinion of my morals, I am not entirely lacking in common courtesy.'

'You were ready to leave me at Warwick!' she accused him.

'I know the innkeeper there and his wife. He was once in my father's employ at Beauregard. They would have kept you safe.'

The lights and bustle of the posting-house at Coventry made such a slight impression upon Miss Middleton that she could not have put a name to the place. All she was conscious of was the comfort of being able to sit in a chair without having to cling on for dear life. With a brief word to the deferentially bowing landlord to serve the lady with whatever she fancied, Wonersh left her, and she at once confessed to her need for sustenance. The landlord readily entered into her requirements and in no time she was installed in a private parlour, eating her fill of an uncommonly good beefsteak pie, supported by a variety of vegetables, a pulled chicken and a Nottingham pudding. So absorbed was she in gratifying her hunger that she all but choked when the Earl's amused voice sounded from the doorway.

'Do you mind if I join you? I must admit to feeling remarkably sharp-set.'

'P—please do,' she gulped. 'This pie is quite out of the ordinary way.'

Still smiling, he sat down opposite her and poured himself some wine. 'As was your need of it?' he suggested, his eyes mocking her over the rim of the glass. Miss Middleton did not feel obliged to enlarge upon the requirements of her appetite.

'What have you discovered?' she demanded to know. 'Have they passed through Coventry?'

He shook his head. 'No, of that I am certain. If they changed horses here no one recalls having seen them. The more I think on't the more I am convinced we have been lured away on a fool's errand.'

She sat as one stricken, a spoonful of pudding arrested in mid-air. 'What can you mean, my lord?'

'That, at the first, things fell into place too neatly. Grantham, you were told, and then how you were gaining ground upon them until—pouff!' He snapped his fingers. 'They disappeared into thin air. Warburton is no fool, d'you think he would tell the world his destination? Unless, of course, he had second thoughts about the whole business and was hoping that I should overtake him.'

'In which case, why disappear?' she countered. 'And why should it be your cousin who had second thoughts? Why should not my sister have repented of her foolish impulse?'

He shrugged and helped himself to what was left of the pie. 'Have it whichever way you please. All my concern is that the scent is cold.'

'But if they took another road we could still meet up with them at Grantham, could we not?' she persisted.

'Having gone so far there is little object in turning back now,' he allowed, but in so disinterested a fashion she could have shaken him.

Of the rest of their interminable journey Miss Middleton had only the haziest recollection. The effect of a substantial meal on her overwrought mind and overtired body soon became evident. The new team were well-matched, willing beasts, the threat of rain had quite receded—indeed, the further North they progressed the more tranquil became the weather—and, despite the rocking and swaying of the fast-moving curricle, she found herself dozing off until aroused by a shout and a hand grasping her shoulder.

'Verity, for God's sake! You were all but out on your head!' He drew the vehicle off the road and proceeded to make her more secure by wrapping a rug about her and tying the ends behind the seat. 'It will only check you,' he warned her, 'so you must stay wakeful if you'd save your neck.'

'If you would drive a shade less perilously, my lord, it would be more to the purpose!' she ripped up at him.

'I warned you how it would be,' he said coldly, easing the curricle back on to the road. 'If we are to catch them, then we must make what speed we can.'

'We'll not catch them by ending up in the ditch!' she flared back, her weariness very apparent.

'You chose to come with me and you must abide by my conditions.'

There seemed to be no answer to that, none at least that her flagging wits could unravel, and presently her head began to nod again so she sat up very straight and directed all her energies to staying awake. Nonetheless she was only half-aware that they had reached their destination when they turned in under an arch, surmounted by an angel bearing a crown, and came to a stand in the yard of Grantham's famous hostelry.

'Now, remember,' his lordship reminded her. 'You are my cousin, we are bound for Melton Mowbray but you were taken ill on the journey, delaying us some hours. Do you think you could manage to stagger a little and lean heavily on my arm as if quite done up?'

Miss Middleton was of the opinion that such behaviour would be no trouble at all in her present condition. In fact, she all but fell when descending from the curricle and he had to clasp her close to steady her. Then she was being half-carried rather than escorted into the building and deposited upon a settle in a secluded corner while his lordship went to secure beds for what remained of the night. In spite of the lateness of the hour, the inn was as busy as if it was full day, with so many persons coming and going she was tempted to wonder what their business could possibly be. Presently the Earl was with her again, all solicitude and begging to know how she did. Under the pretext of arranging a shawl about her shoulders, he spoke low in her ear.

'I am not using my title but have announced myself as plain Mr Percival. In order to account for our travelling together unattended you had best be my wife rather than my cousin. Oh, have no fear!' The satirical twist to his mouth effectively stilled her protestations at so sudden a transition to the married state. 'Due to your delicate—ah, condition, you will have a bedchamber on the first floor which has fallen unexpectedly vacant, while I climb heavenwards to a garret under the eaves! I have also asked for a serving-woman to attend upon you, since your own maid together with my valet and the luggage, have gone on ahead of us to Melton Mowbray.'

'That's all very well,' she said when she had found her voice. 'But what did you mean by my "delicate condition"?'

'Perhaps I should have said "interesting condition"?' he murmured, gently malicious. 'We have not been married many months and this is the first—'

'What?' Her voice escalated to a shriek and his hand, drawing the shawl close about her face, closed like a caress over her mouth.

'Be brave, my dear!' he adjured her in the most loverlike way imaginable. 'I know how tired you are but a night's sleep will set you up amazingly. Ah, here is the good creature who will take you in her charge.'

'Aye, and she looks as if she could do with a bit of cossetting, poor lamb!' Miss Middleton looked up to see a large, rotund personage bobbing before her, who inspected her out of shrewd bright blue eyes that glittered like pieces of coloured glass in the plumpness of her pink cheeks. 'I am Mrs Dawes, the under-housekeeper, ma'am. If you'll come with me I'll soon have you comfortable.'

Miss Middleton felt her head spinning and instinctively clutched at the Earl's arm. 'You—you'll not leave me?' she whispered urgently.

A curious expression crossed his face, so transient as to be difficult of interpretation. 'No,' he said very softly. 'I'll not leave you.'

The housekeeper observed this tender exchange with tolerant understanding and soon had her bewildered charge upstairs and into her bedchamber. Apart from an enquiry as to when the happy event might be expected to which Miss Middleton was able to reply truthfully that she hardly knew as this was the first time she had felt at all conscious of her condition, the good woman asked no questions. To be sure, when she opened the valise and drew out the simple muslin gown with its deep-flounced neckline and long full sleeves she did look a little surprised, and Miss Middleton found herself talking almost at random in order to explain her lack of night attire.

'I—I call it my double-duty gown—how fortunate I thought to take it with me for our valises are all gone before us to Melton Mowbray! It is so simple it can as easily be worn by night as day,' she prattled wildly as she pulled it on and scrambled under the covers.

'Well, here's one garment you'll not be needing for a few months, ma'am.' Mrs Dawes held up her dusty riding-habit. 'I'll just take it away and freshen it up. I'll call your husband—ah, there you are, sir. Just five minutes, if you please, your lady needs her rest. Sleep well, ma'am.'

She held the door for Wonersh to enter, then closed

it smartly behind her and her footsteps could be heard echoing down the passage.

'They are not at the Angel.' Of the two the Earl seemed more ill-at-ease. 'I pretended we had expected to find your sister lodged here as she is on her way from London to Melton Mowbray and described her in detail, but no one admitted to having seen her.'

'They'd not be likely to forget her if they had.' Miss Middleton was sitting bolt upright in the big four-poster, her hair loosely confined by a blue ribbon flowing over her shoulders, her hands clasped tightly before her on the coverlet. 'You—you are tolerably well lodged, my lord?'

'Hardly in this style,' said he, looking round the handsomely appointed room as if grateful for an excuse to wrest his gaze from the delightful picture she presented. 'But I'll do well enough for the hours left to me. It is too late to do more tonight so I have asked to be roused at six o'clock tomorrow when I will go to enquire for our fugitives elsewhere.' A stifled sound, half-sob, half-moan, came from the bed. 'Tomorrow, you are thinking, will be too late? No, I take Warburton to be an honourable man. This sort of thing is not at all in his style. I cannot but feel that Miss Eustacia, with her love of the dramatic, has over-persuaded him.'

'She is scarce eighteen and you make her sound an—an unprincipled jade!'

'A very few years younger than you were when—' he began sharply and left her to read what meaning she chose into his words. 'If I do not find them I will continue on the road tomorrow while you rest here. Your—ah, condition, will serve as an excuse for my leaving you another day.'

'And if you don't find them?'

A muscle quivered beside his mouth. 'Then the only thing we can do is go on to Gretna Green and give them our blessing at the anvil! Oh, depend upon it, it will only be a nine-day wonder and at least they will be wed. Which brings me to our less happy situation.'

As he spoke, he walked over to the bed and stood, hands on hips, looking down on her. For the first time Miss Middleton's concern for her sister was forgotten in the realisation that she was alone in her bedchamber with a gentleman who was in no way related to her.

'I—I do not understand you, sir,' she said in a small voice and slid down deeper under the covers.

'Oh, yes, I think you do. You, of all people, must be sensible of the impropriety of our case. Another night spent with me in the pursuit of that wretched pair would be more than even your reputation could withstand. There's no help for it, ma'am you'll have to marry me.'

The resigned acceptance implicit in this outrageous statement went far to bolster up Miss Middleton's flagging spirits.

'I am obliged to you, my lord, for your very civil offer,' she returned in a passable imitation of his detached manner. 'But I am persuaded we would not suit.'

'That is nothing to the point,' he informed her. 'When you think on't you will see the good sense of my suggestion. I wish you a peaceful day tomorrow, ma'am, when you will have ample time to consider what I have proposed. If you will be advised by me, you will turn the key in the lock when I have gone. This inn is full to bursting with all manner of folk, some of them more than a little on the go. Good-night, ma'am.'

'Good-night, my lord,' she said as the door closed behind him, leaving her to mull over all that had passed. His proposal, she knew, was no more than the gallant gesture expected of any gentleman in a like situation and could be dismissed as such. With startling clarity it came home to Miss Middleton that she did not wish to dismiss it, that life could hold no greater joy for her than to be his wife, be he plain Mr Percival or the Earl of Wonersh. A small sob escaped her at the hopelessness of her case. He no longer held her in affection, she had forfeited all claim to his esteem and must bow herself out of his life. The tears were now flowing freely and she started out of bed in search of a handkerchief when a light tap sounded upon the door.

Believing it to be the housekeeper coming to assure herself that all was well, she got into bed again, dabbing at her wet cheeks with the corner of the sheet, and called out: 'Enter, if you please,' before she remembered the Earl's injunction to her to lock her door. It opened at once in response to her call and Mr Roger Percival stepped into the room.

So dumbfounded was she that she could only stare at him, speechless, as if he was some apparition from another world. He, on the other hand, was far from tongue-tied.

'Why so taken aback, ma'am? After all, I am Mr Percival, and you, I understand, are Mrs Percival! What can be more natural than that we share a connubial bedchamber? I am truly sorry to disrupt your plans, I confess it was a capital notion to lead Wonersh on this wild-goose chase. You contrived it very skilfully, you and Miss Eustacia.'

'I—I don't know what you are talking about,' she gasped. 'How dare you—how did you know anything of this?'

'Simple, my dear lady.' The predatory glint in his eye caused her to shrink back as far as her pillows would allow. 'In his haste to catch up with you, Leo left Warburton's missive lying upon his desk. In order to shield it from prying eyes, I took it into my care.'

'So you know all about it,' she said despairingly. 'My poor Eustacia!'

'Do you take me for a fool, ma'am? I'll warrant Miss Eustacia is abed at Royal Crescent this very moment, secure in the knowledge that you are now so completely compromised his lordship can do no less than offer for you! But why so desperate a plan? I find it difficult to believe that Leo was proving so dilatory a lover!'

'Eustacia at home?' Her voice was trembling on the verge of hysteria. 'How can this be? She would know I would follow her, she would not permit me to go on if—if she turned back.'

' 'Pon my word, you act your part well!' he congratulated her. 'Had I not chanced upon your sister and Warburton returning to Cheltenham this afternoon I might be tempted to believe you.'

'Returning to Cheltenham?' she repeated as one in a dream. 'But how could I not have encountered them if this was so?'

His lip curled scornfully. 'Because, as you well know, they did not continue their supposed flight beyond Broadway, but came back by Stow-in-the-Wold where they were conveniently detained by the downpour. By a happy chance, I had business in Stow this afternoon and—need I say more?'

'I cannot understand—oh, what am I to do?' she cried out, quite cast down at what seemed to her to be her sister's treachery.

'I can tell you that at least, ma'am,' said he, throwing his coat upon a chair and sitting down to ease off his boots. 'You can make room in your bed to accept your husband and hold yourself ready for him to exercise his marital rights!'

If the ceiling had crashed upon Miss Middleton, she could not have been more astonished. 'Good God! Are you mad? The Earl—'

'The Earl has no more use than most men for the leavings of others. And why should he have everything —Beauregard, the title, the most lovely of women? That last I can deny him!' He kicked his second boot across the floor and threw his neckcloth after it. 'So now, my pretty, my very pretty Miss Verity Middleton!'

As he advanced upon her, she sprang from the bed and took refuge behind a tall ladder-backed chair. 'Mr Percival, sir, I beg of you, consider what you do!'

He looked her over in a way that made her feel doubly conscious of her flimsy attire. 'So, you would have me chase you? Well, it all adds to the pleasure of conquest!'

On stockinged feet he padded after her and she looked wildly about her for some weapon with which to defend herself.

'Dear God, help me!' she breathed. 'Send Leo—send someone!'

As if in answer to her prayer, the door swung slowly open to reveal a gentleman of full habit and obvious insobriety who swayed upon uncertain feet before stumbling forward to fall flat upon his face into the room. Behind him from the darkness of the passage peered a circle of vacuous, grinning faces.

Miss Middleton, looking from these unlikely saviours to the glowering Mr Percival, felt most strongly that to be standing in a diaphanous muslin robe under the interested gaze of several perfectly strange gentlemen was not at all the thing. She felt this with even greater certainty when the onlookers were thrust aside and the Earl, a murderous expression on his face, stepped over the insensible body.

One sweeping glance around the room took in the shrinking girl and the deflated, partly unclothed Mr Percival, before he rapped out a command.

'Take this fellow out of here!'

It said much for his authority that his besotted audience obeyed him without question. The unfortunate gentleman was removed with more haste than dignity and, with a flick of his heel, the Earl kicked the door shut behind the bearers and advanced upon his cousin.

'Now, Roger,' he said very softly and the knuckles of

his clenched fists showed white by his sides, 'perhaps you will tell me just what precisely you are doing here?'

At this point Miss Middleton formed the opinion that to have to witness a set-to in her bedchamber would be beyond anything disagreeable so, very sensibly and for the first time in her life, she fainted quietly away.

CHAPTER FOURTEEN

'BUT, Miss Eustacia, I was given to understand you was dining at Beauregard. Miss Verity has gone to join you there.'

'But how should this be, Griffiths? I have not—'

Eustacia felt a warning pressure of the hand she had extended in farewell to Mr Warburton and, to borrow a favoured phrase of his, took a tuck in her lip.

'Miss Verity had a note from Miss Liddell, though when it was delivered I'm sure I can't say,' grumbled Griffiths, 'and she set off on horseback at once.'

'On horseback?' echoed Eustacia and Mr Warburton in unison.

'Aye,' corroborated Griffiths, plainly gratified at the effect of this disclosure. 'She would have it that your mama must have the carriage tonight and that Miss Liddell would see you both got home safe. Then his lordship called and he didn't know nothing about your dining at Beauregard either,' she added with mordant satisfaction.

The other two exchanged startled glances then Mr Warburton stepped into the hall and took up the story. 'I can explain about the note from Miss Liddell,' he said, deceptively off-hand. 'I encountered her in Cheltenham this morning and, learning that I was on my way here, she asked me to deliver it.'

'I put it in her room,' supplemented Eustacia helpfully, marvelling at her swain's inventiveness.

'That's all very well, miss,' Griffiths was like a dog

that refuses to be parted from its bone. 'But if you wasn't at Beauregard where have you been, if you please? 'Tis past four o'clock, miss.'

Eustacia, well-accustomed to such strictures from one who had known her since childhood, had a ready reply. 'The rain, Griffiths! We were obliged to shelter for hours! Was it not so?' She appealed to Mr Warburton.

'Then 'twas your duty to have sent your groom back with a message, sir!' Griffiths reproved him. 'Did she not believe that miss was safe at Beauregard then my lady would have been in a rare taking.'

Mr Warburton was preparing to defend himself with some glib story of his groom having just recovered from the influenza and he not wishful of having the fellow's possible demise upon his conscience, when Eustacia interrupted the inquisition.

'Griffiths, is mama home?'

'No, miss. She left not ten minutes since for Lady Gower's soirée.'

'Oh, it's too provoking!' Eustacia spoke as if she had not been perfectly aware of the Dowager's departure, having witnessed it from a discreet distance. 'I can only think that Verity must have misunderstood Miss Liddell's letter. Ask Bowles to bring up some wine, if you please. Mr Warburton and I must discuss this puzzle.'

Griffiths, her rigid back oozing disapprobation, reluctantly obeyed her young mistress's request. 'Nothing to discuss,' she flung over her shoulder. 'Miss Verity had a lad from the stables to escort her, said he could bring Marigold back and she'd ride with you in the carriage.'

'She never went to dine in a riding-habit?' squeaked Eustacia in unconscious imitation of her mother.

'Took a change of clothes with her,' submitted her redoubtable henchwoman as the door to the kitchen quarters closed behind her. Eustacia seized Mr Warburton by the sleeve and hustled him into the saloon.

'It has all fallen into place!' she cried triumphantly. 'Verity went to Beauregard to consult Wonersh, making this excuse to cover her absence and mine!'

Mr Warburton was not so sanguine. 'Why then did the Earl come here?' he asked.

She waved aside the objection. 'He must have been in town and came to pay us a call. Depend upon it, when he learned that Verity had ridden to Beauregard he would waste no time in following her.'

'One can only hope he did meet up with her.'

Eustacia had been pacing the room, all eager excitement, but his sombre tone brought her up short.

'Why should he not? What can you mean, Theodore?'

'I mean that I have the greatest respect for your sister's strength of purpose, my darling,' he said gravely. 'If she saw it to be her duty to follow us she might not have waited for him.'

'Followed us by herself—alone, d'you mean? And on horseback? Oh, never, Theodore! She would have enlisted Miss Liddell's aid.'

'My love, Miss Liddell is not at home. My mother had the felicity of receiving an invitation from her to visit at Beauregard when she returned next week from Oswestry where she is staying for a short time. That is how I knew the story of your sister having received a note from her was all a hum.'

'Oh!' said his love, a shade limply, then the entry of Bowles with the wine put a period to the conversation.

'May I ask,' said Mr Warburton when the door had closed behind the old servant, 'what tale you had in mind to tell your mother to explain Miss Middleton's absence tonight?'

'Why, nothing,' she said. 'Mama is staying on to dine at Lady Gower's and, after that, the card-table will be set up. She'll not return before the small hours and will sleep late to-morrow, by which time if Verity and the Earl have not returned—well! This business of dining at Beauregard was a capital notion of Verity's to account for my absence. Now it must suffice to cover her own.'

Mr Warburton, in the act of raising his glass to his lips, lowered it again. 'Have you considered the consequences if his lordship does not offer for her?'

'Oh, but he must!' Eustacia was all outraged horror. 'No gentleman could do otherwise!'

'If he believed himself to have been tricked into this affair—'

'But Verity is innocent of any deception, she is as much a victim of our design as he, he cannot hold her to blame.'

'She may well take the blame for our conniving however,' pursued Mr Warburton.

'And refuse to marry him? Oh, la!' Eustacia clapped hands to cheeks in dismay. 'I had not thought of that!'

'I believe I must go to Beauregard.' Mr Warburton drained his glass and set it down carefully. 'If I find Wonersh there and not Miss Middleton then I must make a clean breast of the whole thing and enlist his aid to discover her before nightfall.'

'You are not going without me! I am the one at fault in all this and so I shall make clear.' The younger Miss Middleton when put to it, could display as much tenacity as her sister.

Mr Warburton hesitated. There was no doubt that the Earl would listen to Eustacia's confession with a deal more complaisance than to any excuses of his. 'Very well,' he agreed, 'my man can drive you home later if it becomes necessary for us to embark upon a search.'

Eustacia did not agree with this high-handed disposal of her person but she let it pass. 'There is no need to confess to the whole,' she pointed out. 'We need only say that we hoped by this means to convince Verity of our determination and—and then my heart misgave me and I could not carry it through.' Mr Warburton nodded agreement and allowed himself to be hurried out to his waiting carriage. 'We are going to Beauregard, Bowles,' said Eustacia with convincing aplomb. 'It would seem that Miss Liddell expects me for dinner.'

'Yes, miss. Will you be returning tonight, miss?'

'Oh, I hadn't thought of that. I'd best take some night attire, had I not?'

'Should you be detained I am sure Miss Liddell is amply provided with whatever should be necessary to your comfort,' said Mr Warburton repressively.

She giggled. 'Amply, indeed! One of her nightrobes would quite envelop me!'

He thought it a delightful idea and smiled upon his exuberant little lady, but when they arrived at their destination to be informed by Threadgold that his lordship had no sooner returned from Oswestry than he had set out again, saying he was not to be looked for again that day, his expression became very serious indeed.

'I will not conceal from you that I do not feel at all easy in my mind,' he told his jubilant intended as they drove back to Cheltenham, 'and can only hope they find they have been duped before they are advanced too great a distance on their journey.'

She gave a little trill of laughter. 'I declare that it is the most diverting thing that ever I knew—our dear, staid Verity galloping *ventre á terre* all over the country in search of us with Wonersh hot upon her heels!'

There were times, considered Mr Warburton, when his beloved's innocent sense of fun went beyond what was quite pleasing, and he was trying to find words to convey his dissatisfaction as they turned into Royal Crescent.

'Why, there's mama's carriage and Wilkes, I do believe! What can have brought her home so soon, do you suppose?'

Mr Warburton could not enlighten her, but he felt a sense of impending disaster which was in no way mitigated as they entered the house to be greeted by a smell of burnt feathers and a deeply shocked Bowles.

'Thank Heaven you are here, miss! Her ladyship is all to pieces—near to hysterics, I'd say!'

In the saloon, where Griffiths was ministering to her mistress, they discovered he spoke no less than the truth. The sight of her younger daughter temporarily restored the distracted Dowager and gave her strength to utter a few coherent sentences.

'It was Lady Castlereagh, you see, she is Lady Gower's house-guest. She said she saw Verity at Broadway, quite alone at the Lygon Arms! And she told me she was going to dine with Miss Liddell! What can she be about?' Eustacia, disentangling the 'shes', tried to interpolate a question but her ladyship was in full spate. 'And to be seen by Lady Castlereagh, of all people! I was obliged to leave, I could not support the stares and conjectures I had to endure.'

'You should have outfaced them, mama! You could have said Verity was in the company of friends who were following behind her in their carriage—anything to supply a reason for her being at Broadway!'

'What reason could there be for her to go there alone, without even the stableboy?' The Dowager was too distraught to take in what was being said to her.

'Well, she won't be alone for long, Wonersh is close after her!'

This misguided attempt at consolation penetrated her ladyship's bemused understanding. She sat up, fixing her daughter with so accusing a stare that even that young lady began to experience some twinges of guilt at her share in the business.

'Wonersh? A single gentleman! And she unattended!

Griffiths, my bonnet and pelisse at once, if you please, and bid Wilkes have the horses put to again.'

'Mama, what are you proposing to do?'

'Rescue my unhappy daughter from the consequences of her own foolishness!' said her ladyship with rare authority. 'You and Mr Warburton will be so good as to come with me and claim to have been in Verity's company for all of the afternoon.'

'But, mama!' Eustacia saw all her carefully laid plans crumble to nothing in the face of such fierce maternal protectiveness. 'She may not be there, she—they will most likely have gone on to Grantham.'

'Wherever she may be, I am not resting in my bed tonight until I have found her,' said the Dowager in so inflexible a manner that, for once, Eustacia was over-awed. 'And while we are on the way you will please enlighten me as to what you know about all this.'

'Yes, mama,' said Eustacia, with a meaningful glance at Mr Warburton, and they meekly took their places in her ladyship's carriage.

Miss Middleton blinked sleepily in the gloom, a little astonished to find herself tucked up in bed while, on the other side of the close-drawn drapes a low-voiced conversation was being conducted. At first she was only aware of an almost irresistible desire to be left alone, then an equally irresistible urge to know what had taken place seized hold of her and she called out. At once the hangings were parted, letting in a flood of candlelight, and Wonersh and a gentleman quite unknown to her stepped up to the bedside.

'My—sir—'

He caught the hand she held out to him in both of his. 'My dearest,' he said so fervently she could nearly believe he meant it. 'How is it with you? Why did you not lock your door as I bade you?'

'I—I was about to,' she began, casting a doubtful eye upon the stranger.

'This is Dr Goodenough who is lodging here at the Angel,' explained the Earl quickly.

Miss Middleton sternly repressed the temptation to commiserate with the doctor upon so equivocal a choice of name.

'So milkish of me to have fainted,' she murmured. 'It was all so—so unexpected and I was so tired.'

'Indeed, ma'am, the shock of seeing a drunken bully lurch into her bedchamber would be enough to render insensible any lady of delicate breeding, let alone one in your condition,' declared the doctor roundly.

She closed her eyes while her thoughts buzzed around in her head like a swarm of angry bees. It would appear that the fact of Mr Percival's having been in her room was not generally known and, for the time being, she was well content to leave it so.

'I do thank you, sir, for your kind attentions,' she said, 'but I am persuaded I need not trouble you further.'

'You are a brave young lady,' said he, patting avuncularly the hand which Wonersh had just released. Miss Middleton thought him a pompous ass but summoned up her sweetest smile. Thus encouraged, he went on. 'I have arranged for a truckle-bed to be set up and one of the maids to sleep here with you. Should you need me in the night my room is just down the passage and she will fetch me.'

'I cannot believe that to be necessary—' she protested, but he was insistent.

'If you prefer it, of course,' he quizzed her archly, 'your husband can take the truckle-bed. Would that make you easier in your mind, ma'am?'

Miss Middleton thanked Providence for the indifferent light that concealed her blushes and for the Earl's intervention, explaining that, as he had to rise at a very early hour, it would be best if he remained in his own room and did not disturb her.

'Six o'clock, eh?' Dr Goodenough consulted his pocket watch. 'Then I shall leave you to get what little rest you can.'

His patient's earnest wish that the Earl would accompany the doctor and give her time to sort out her disordered thoughts was not to be fulfilled. No sooner had the door closed than his lordship was at her side.

'What the devil was Roger doing here?' he began without preamble, tossing a piece of crumpled muslin on to the coverlet. 'He forgot his neckcloth in his haste to begone! And why did you faint? You are no vapourish female. Come, I want no Banbury tale, the plain truth, if you please.'

Miss Middleton felt that if ever she had need to swoon, now was the moment. 'He—he followed us here,' she said, as steadily as she could. 'He came in before I had time to lock the door and—and—' She found herself to be unable to tell the Earl of Mr Percival's intention and hid her face in her hands.

'And what?' He grasped her wrists and pulled them apart so that she was forced to meet his regard.

'He—he began to disrobe,' she faltered.

'Indeed? I had not thought my cousin to be a man to put himself forward in such a way without encouragement,' he drawled, his grey eyes as hard as flint.

'So little did I encourage him,' she flashed, stung to retort by the insinuation, 'that I got out of bed in search of a weapon with which to defend myself.'

'Did it not occur to you to scream—to call for help? There were plenty of people about to hear you.'

'How could I? Your cousin—the scandal—' Her voice faded to a piteous murmur.

'I see. You preferred to be ravished rather than offend the sensibilities of the polite world? Most commendable, ma'am, I congratulate you!'

'Yes—no! Oh, cannot you understand? I did not believe he would do it!'

He released her wrists and stepped back. 'Roger to throw himself upon you like a wild beast?' he mused. 'No, I must say I find it hard to envisage such a scene.'

'He said something about you having everything, Beauregard, the title, and—and you'd not have me as well,' she enlarged miserably.

'He said that? Can it be that he has a tendre for you, ma'am?' The Earl sounded mildly incredulous which did nothing to support her wilting self-esteem.

'I doubt that,' she told him sharply, 'but he has a very great envy of you and means you nothing but ill-will. My lord, where is he now?'

'I could hardly challenge his intentions in front of so large an audience. He slipped away while I was seeing to your disposal,' he added casually.

A tap on the door and the housekeeper's voice addressing her saved Miss Middleton further mortification. 'If you please, ma'am, I have a lady here who claims to be your mother.'

'Mama!' Miss Middleton slid up from under the covers then, remembering her muslin nightrobe, slid back again. 'It cannot be!'

'Well, we'll soon see that!' The Earl strode to the door and flung it wide to reveal Mrs Dawes, imposing in dressing-robe and beribboned nightcap. Over her shoulder were to be seen Lady Middleton and Eustacia, while a shadowy figure in the background hinted at the presence of Mr Warburton.

'Good-evening, mama,' said Miss Middleton, after the fashion of one who was experiencing a particularly unpleasant nightmare, which indeed she was. The Dowager, taking in the cosily domestic scene before her, uttered a strangled croak and would have sunk to the ground had not the Earl stepped forward to support her.

'We had given up all hope of seeing you tonight,

ma'am,' said he briskly. 'You must be burned to the socket after such a journey. Miss Eustacia—your servant. And—can it be Warburton, too? Pray come in and satisfy yourselves as to Miss—to Verity's well-being.'

'Sir,' protested Mrs Dawes, all concern for her charge. ' 'Tis gone two o'clock in the morning, your lady must rest! Her condition demands it.'

Lady Midldeton, allowing herself to be handed to a chair, sat as one transfixed. 'Her condition?' she queried faintly.

'Yes, yes, of course!' Hastily the Earl urged Mrs Dawes out of the room, muttering under his breath. 'Her ladyship don't know about that yet!'

'I don't know about what?' For one who had been near to collapse a moment before, the Dowager was reviving fast.

'Why, that you are going to be a grandmama, your ladyship!' announced the housekeeper before Wonersh had time to close the door upon her beaming face.

'Wh—what?' almost shrieked Lady Middleton, her eyes in imminent danger of starting from their sockets. 'Oh, Verity, never say so! You'll marry her, my lord, if I have to—have to stand over you with a horsewhip!'

The mental image conjured up of so unusual a situation brought a fleeting grin to his lordship's rather tight mouth.

'Have no fear on that score, ma'am,' he assured her then, rounding on Eustacia, he demanded, 'what the devil have you two been about?'

'Pretending to elope so as to convince Verity of our unshakeable resolve to be married,' confessed that young woman glibly. 'Only it all went wrong because she set off on her own instead of—' She bit back the words as she saw a dawning comprehension on the Earl's face.

'Instead of calling upon me to help her? But she did

call at Beauregard and I would not even have known had she not met up with Roger—Roger!' He slapped hand to thigh. 'I'd all but forgotten him!'

'Yes, what is Mr Percival doing here? Did he come with you?' asked Eustacia with bright interest. 'He was leaving as we were talking to the porter in the hall and was in such haste he took no notice of our party.'

'You will forgive me, ma'am,' Wonersh sketched a bow in Lady Middleton's direction. 'But I must have a word with my cousin.'

His hand was on the door-knob when Miss Middleton's voice arrested him. 'My lord, I beg you, be careful.' For a moment their eyes met across the room, then he nodded and was gone. 'Mr Warburton, of your kindness, please go with his lordship. He—he could do something irrevocable.'

Her anxiety communicated itself to her listeners and, without question, Mr Warburton obeyed her and followed the Earl. It was left to Eustacia to break the ensuing silence.

'Verity, you're not with child?'

'Of course I am not!' said Miss Middleton crossly. 'But Wonersh had named us man and wife and there was only this room and one other to be had, so some excuse had to be made to account for his not—mama, you'll have to sleep here with me and Eustacia on the truckle-bed.'

Her sister began to gurgle with irrepressible laughter. 'I must say he is the most complete hand! But why the green sickness, of all things?'

An expression of profound exasperation passed over Miss Middleton's lovely face. 'To pay me out, I suspect,' she said tartly, 'for—for—'

'Planning to marry him off to me? Well, if you will try to arrange other peoples' lives without their consent,' sighed Eustacia virtuously.

'And what about you?' her sister accused her. 'What

were you and Mr Warburton doing if not trying to arrange other peoples' lives?'

A low moan from the Dowager drew their attention to that afflicted lady.

'I am, of course, gratified to learn,' she said in suitably feeble accents, 'that my daughter is not about to bear a child out of wedlock but, nonetheless, your association with his lordship, his being here in your bedchamber—he must offer to marry you, Verity.'

'He has already done so,' replied Miss Middleton with devastating finality, 'and I have declined the honour.'

'Then you *are* ruined,' said her ladyship with the calmness of despair.

'I think not,' returned her daughter coolly. 'If we continue to act out this charade no one here will guess the truth and we can all leave, ostensibly for Melton Mowbray, in the morning.'

'Why Melton Mowbray?' Eustacia wanted to know and listened to the explanation with an outward semblance of approval that was not shared by the Dowager, who deplored such a web of deceit and wished to be told what the world was coming to.

Thereafter, there being nothing else left for them to do, the three ladies composed themselves for sleep, but for Miss Middleton the passing hours brought no rest.

If Wonersh caught up with Roger Percival and forced the truth from him, the result could be disastrous. Whether he cared for her or not, his anger at such an attempt upon a lady in his charge might well lead him into an indiscretion that could prove fatal. If he killed Roger Percival he would be forced to flee the country, the stigma of having slain his cousin would never be wiped away. If, on the other hand, Roger was the victor—but that she dared not contemplate and lay, with wide-open eyes and heavy heart, watching the dawn light slant into the corners of the darkened room.

CHAPTER FIFTEEN

'A WORD with you, if you please, Roger.' Mr Percival, his foot in the stirrup, reluctantly lowered it to the ground. 'This, I believe to be your property.'

The Earl was holding out a neckcloth between his finger and thumb as if it were something extremely distasteful to him, nor was his cousin deceived by his seeming affability.

'Oh? Oh, indeed, I wondered where I could have mislaid it,' said he, endeavouring to emulate his lordship's easy civility.

'You know perfectly well where you left it.' The Earl was still courteous, but there was the suggestion of menace being held in check. Mr Percival, however, took courage. If, after all, his lordship did not intend to offer for Miss Middleton, then perhaps no irreparable harm had been done.

'Careless of me, I allow,' he admitted. 'But to be so interrupted at the very pinnacle of—er, one's wildest aspirations—'

'Excessively frustrating, I have no doubt,' murmured the Earl.

'Indeed I could scarce believe my good fortune. I owe you an apology, Leo,' said Mr Percival, warming to his theme. 'I feared you had designs upon the lady's virtue, hence my following you. Conceive of my delight when I discovered that I, and not my noble cousin, was the object of her affections!'

'You are a liar, Roger,' said Wonersh pleasantly.

'More than that, you are a villain who has attempted my life before now or caused others to do so.'

'Do you dare suggest that I—I am a common cut-throat?' spluttered Mr Percival with a fine show of indignation.

'Perhaps not common but a cut-throat certainly, and not a very efficient one, I fear,' deplored his lordship, dropping the neckcloth and grinding it into the mud with his heel. 'You choose your tools with less care than your firearms. Yes, when I thought on't, I did recognise those pistols. Foolish of you to have lent them to such a clumsy fellow. It was a nice touch, I agree, to have sent Miss Ramsay to call upon Miss Middleton.'

Mr Percival, who felt the interview was not going just as he had hoped, tried a softer approach.

'That,' he said sadly, 'was as much for my sake as any other. My aim was to convince Miss Middleton of your perfidy so that she would look upon my suit in a more favourable light.'

'And did not tonight's happenings prove that you had achieved that aim?'

'Indeed,' declared Mr Percival eagerly, 'I scarce knew how to contain myself when she greeted me so warmly!'

'That,' said his lordship levelly, 'must have afforded you much gratification.'

'How lovely a creature she is! How deliciously immodest in her conduct!' rhapsodised Mr Percival.

He got no further. The Earl's left hand snaked out and it was a full minute before his cousin picked himself up, tenderly fingering his bruised jaw. To Mr Warburton, watching from the shadow of the nearby archway, it was as if Wonersh had not moved.

'The ties of blood forbid that I should kill you, Roger, or even take my whip to you as you well deserve. I will, however, do that which will pain you a great deal more. I will send you away from Beauregard, never to return—hey! Whoa, my beauty!'

This last was addressed to Mr Percival's horse which had taken understandable exception to seeing its master laid low. The Earl caught at the trailing reins but the nervous creature shied away from him, the whites of its rolling eyes clearly visible, its hoofs striking sparks from the slippery cobbles.

'Have a care, my lord!' The warning was wrung from Mr Warburton as Mr Percival's hand slid under his coat and emerged holding something that gleamed wickedly in the moonlight.

The encounter was taking place in a small yard, hemmed in by high walls, at the back of a snug tavern, for Mr Percival had been prudent enough not to lodge at the Angel. To Mr Warburton's fascinated gaze, the enclosure was overfull of hostile gentlemen and agitated horse.

Even as he called out, the Earl was forced to turn his back upon his cousin in an effort to control the excited beast and Mr Percival raised his knife on high.

'This time I will deal with you myself, dear Leo!' he hissed, a maniac gleam in his eye, and pivoted upon one foot in order to get a sharper angle to strike.

While knowing he was too far away to be of practical use, yet Mr Warburton threw himself forward, praying that some miracle might occur to deflect the descending blade. At the same moment the Earl slipped upon the muddy surface of the cobbles and, as he fell, one of the horse's outflung hoofs struck him on the shoulder with sufficient force to toss him aside like a truss of straw.

Mouthing an oath, Mr Percival sprang after him, in his determination not to lose his prey quite oblivious to the danger presented by the frantic beast. Mr Warburton's shout of horror choked in his throat and he flattened himself against the wall as the horse bolted past him and away, leaving a motionless heap in its wake.

For a time nothing disturbed the quiet save the diminishing clatter of hoofbeats down the street. Then the Earl dragged himself painfully to his feet, one arm hanging useless by his side.

'Roger!' he gasped, stumbling over to the inert body. Mr Warburton came to full realisation of what had happened and as he stepped forward his foot kicked something on the ground that winked evilly at him. The Earl was on one knee by Mr Percival. 'He's dead,' he said in a dazed voice. 'His neck's broken.'

A period was put to further discussion by the arrival on the scene of several interested parties from the direction of the tavern, led by a nightcapped personage, clutching a lethal-looking musket.

'I—there has been an accident.' Mr Warburton felt it incumbent upon him to offer some explanation as the Earl was clearly in no condition to do so.

'Aye, I saw't all through m'window. Horse took fright and lashed out. What's th'damage?'

'One dead and one injured,' said Mr Warburton with commendable brevity, surreptitiously sliding the knife into his pocket.

'Can't do aught for the first,' said his questioner, plainly a man of sound commonsense. 'Here, sir, you don't look too peart. You shoulder, is't? Best come wi' me and we'll see t'it,' and, taking the Earl by his sound arm, he led him away.

Mr Warburton could not help but wonder just how much the good fellow had witnessed of those dramatic few moments, but applied himself to directing the inn servants to remove Mr Percival's lifeless person and to place it in a less conspicuous place until arrangements could be made for its disposal.

* * *

'But what exactly *happened*?' Miss Middleton ceased her restless pacing of the room to repeat her question.'

'Theodore won't say precisely, except that it was all an accident and only the horse to blame.' Eustacia flung her arms wide in a gesture of exasperation. 'He is keeping a guard on his tongue, of that I am perfectly certain, but why I cannot discover.'

Miss Middleton walked to the window and looked out upon the sweep of Royal Crescent bathed in warm June sunshine. It was all so utterly peaceful and commonplace, she could scarce believe that but two nights since Mr Percival had burst into her bedchamber and offered her violence.

'My lord—' she began again.

'Wonersh has taken little harm,' Eustacia assured her. 'A dislocated shoulder and a knock on the head. He will be back at Beauregard in a day or so after —after he has attended to the necessary sad arrangements.'

The Middleton ladies had returned from Grantham on the day of Mr Percival's unhappy demise. They had spoken only briefly with the Earl, who had looked pale and drawn, and scarcely at all with Mr Warburton, who had remained with his lordship for one more day. Both gentlemen seemed bent on getting them out of Grantham as speedily as possible and, for her part, Miss Middleton was only too pleased to leave a town where so much that was unfortunate had happened. Lady Middleton was, mercifully, too overcome by her exertions of the previous day to do other than sleep for the greater part of the journey, her head lolling against the squabs, her mouth slightly open, emitting a gentle snore. She had, however, lost none of her resolve to ensure that Wonersh did just as he ought in making reparation for any wrong he might have done Miss Middleton. This she made perfectly clear when she entered her salon to interrupt the discussion between her daughters.

'Was that not Mr Warburton's carriage I saw outside?'

'Yes, indeed, mama. He came to enquire how we go on and to inform us that the—interment will be at Beauregard on the day following tomorrow. I understand Miss Liddell is being summoned home.'

'His cousin's demise will lay a deal more work on the Earl's shoulders. He will not,' said her ladyship with some satisfaction, settling herself in her favourite chair, 'be quite so free to leave Beauregard as hitherto. I must stress, Verity, that your association with him bears all the marks of an established understanding and that, if you wish to hold your head up in society, you can do no other than accept his offer of marriage.'

Miss Middleton, who was finding the effort of holding her head up at all a very difficult one that afternoon due to the combined effects of lack of sleep, constant anxiety and a thundering headache, summoned up the shreds of her sorely-tried patience to make reply.

'Wonersh has suffered a bereavement, mama, as painful as it was unexpected, and which must, I believe, overshadow all other considerations for the moment.'

'I wouldn't be too sure of that,' said the Dowager with surprising percipience. 'I doubt there was much love lost between the cousins. They were useful to each other, that was all.'

Miss Liddell confirmed this opinion when she called at Royal Crescent on her way back to Beauregard the next day.

'Roger was an uncommonly good steward and Wonersh will find it no easy task to replace him,' she said bluntly. 'For myself, though it may sound unkind of me to say so, I feel a certain lifting of the spirits at the knowledge that his critical presence will not be forever at my elbow.'

That consideration of his cousin's replacement was in the forefront of the Earl's mind was made plain when he and Mr Warburton returned to Beauregard after consigning Roger Percival's remains to the family mausoleum.

'It has occurred to me, Warburton, that you will be in need of an establishment of your own if you propose taking a wife.'

'Does that mean, my lord,' said Mr Warburton cautiously, 'that you approve my suit?'

'Who am I,' said the Earl in a tone of bland astonishment, 'to approve or disapprove?'

'As the head of the family or—as an elder brother-in-law, perhaps?' ventured Mr Warburton, greatly daring.

Wonersh picked up one of the many letters of condolence that littered his desk and appeared to be absorbed in its contents.

'There is another head of family to be won over,' he murmured.

'I cannot feel that Lady Middleton would throw a rub in the way,' demurred Mr Warburton, all innocence.

The Earl laughed at that and put down his letter. 'Nor I, to be plain with you. But what I had in mind for you and Miss Eustacia was the Eridge holding. The house has lain vacant since my Aunt Amelia died and is a shade run-down, but there's nothing that cannot be put readily to rights.' Mr Warburton began to stammer his thanks but the Earl waved them away. 'This, I warn you, is not an entirely disinterested proposal. Now that Roger is no longer with us, I need someone to assist me in the running of the entire estate. Would that be to your liking?'

Mr Warburton gulped. 'The thing is, my lord,' he confessed. 'I had in mind to give Eustacia Shurdington Hall for a bridal gift.'

'No reason why you should not,' said the Earl, helping himself to snuff with a graceful turn of the wrist. 'It is no great distance from Eridge, after all, and there is Lady Middleton to be thought on. I am sure both her daughters would be happy to see her re-established in her old home.'

Mr Warburton did not look as if he shared in so felicitous a prospect. 'And—Miss Verity?' he asked doubtfully.

'Leave Miss Verity to me,' advised his lordship.

Mr Warburton was well satisfied to leave Verity to the Earl. He had the uncomfortable feeling that she held him largely to blame for what must have been a mortifying experience for her, and was of the opinion she would be more likely to lend a forgiving ear to the Earl's representations on his behalf than did he attempt to plead his own case.

So it was that the next morning his lordship, resplendent in dove-coloured pantaloons and coat of blue Bath cloth, presented himself at Royal Crescent. Bowles, who opened the door to this vision of sartorial perfection, was heard to murmur that her ladyship was still abed and Miss Eustacia gone riding. The Earl, who knew very well that Eustacia was riding since he had detailed Mr Warburton to see to it, was not in the least put out by these revelations.

'Then a word with Miss Middleton, if you please,' he said with easy authority, handing over his gloves and curly-brimmed beaver.

The old butler was at something of a loss. While he knew the Dowager would not approve of her daughter receiving a gentleman alone, yet the Earl was such a regular visitor to the household—who all entertained the highest hopes of his intentions—that he could not feel obliged to deny Miss Verity to his lordship. The rustle of paper as it passed from the Earl's hand to his went far to convince him of the rightness of his decision. His confidence, however, was sorely shaken when he announced the caller to his young mistress, who was sitting before her mirror while Griffiths tried the effect of a delicate arrangement of rosebuds in her bright hair.

'No, Bowles, I am not at home this morning. Pray make my excuses to his lordship.'

Griffiths, who had not failed to observe that Miss Middleton's cheeks were as softly pink as her pretty jaconet gown, darted a minatory glance at the butler who responded nobly.

'His lordship did say he had something of importance to impart to you, miss, and would be humbly grateful for a few minutes of your time.'

Wonersh—humbly grateful? Miss Middleton all but laughed. But perhaps he did have something to tell her, perhaps she could get the full story of what had happened at Grantham from him. Thus she argued silently, while knowing in her heart that the only reason she would accede to his request was because she longed to see him again, to have him touch her hand, to hear him speak, to see him smile.

'Very well,' she said briskly. 'Tell his lordship I will join him presently. 'You'd best take all this nonsense off my head, Griffiths, it's scarce suitable for morning wear.'

'Oh, leave it, miss,' advised her dresser craftily. 'You'll be but a few minutes. I've her ladyship to see to and I'll be wanting her opinion on it, so if I take it off it will all be to do again.'

Miss Middleton hesitated. There was no doubt that the dainty artificial spray was excessively becoming and she felt that any assistance, however trivial, would be welcome to support her confidence. That the effect was all she had hoped for was evident from the glow of approval in the Earl's eyes as she entered the salon.

'My lord,' she said, giving him her hand. 'I—that is, my mother, sister and I, have scarce had time to offer you our heartfelt condolences on your sad bereavement.'

'Are you honestly commiserating with me, Verity?' he said, as if unable to believe his ears. 'After what passed between you and Roger at Grantham?' She snatched her hand away.

'To taunt me with reminder of an episode that covers me with shame, my lord, is beyond anything unkind!'

'My intention was not to taunt you. It is charitable to suppose that my kinsman was quite bereft of reason. His later actions were certainly those of a man deranged. I came to offer apology for his ill behaviour and to repeat my intention to do all in my power to make reparation for any hint of impropriety that may attach to your name because of our association in the business.'

'Hint of impropriety?' she cried, a little wildly. 'Mama declares I am ruined!'

'Then marry me, Verity.'

'My lord, while having the greatest respect for my parent's scruples, I do not believe I am ruined, that is unless you or Mr Warburton choose to disclose what you know. My family never will.'

'We—ell, of course,' he pondered, deliberately tantalising. 'If Mr Warburton is to wed Miss Eustacia, that will include him in your family.'

'Oh!' she gasped. 'So that is to be the price of his silence?'

'And what of me?' he went on. 'How do you propose to put a curb on my tongue if you don't marry me? If I may misquote, Hell hath no fury like a suitor scorned!'

At that, Miss Middleton who had entered the room prepared to be all sweet reasonableness, quite lost her temper.

'I have told you before, my lord, I'll not be bullocked into marrying you to save my reputation!'

' 'Fore God, Verity,' he said, as sharp as she, 'you'd try the patience of a saint!'

'And that you are not!' she flashed back. 'Once the marriage vows were made and your duty done, you'd be off with the first lightskirt that took your fancy and—oooh!'

In one swift movement he had set his foot upon an adjacent chair and, clipping both hands about her waist, had laid her across his knee. His hand rose to strike the tempting target thus presented then, with a stifled groan, he cried out: 'No, I cannot! Oh, Verity, Verity!' Setting her back on her feet, he clasped her to him so closely that her face was buried in the folds of his neckcloth. 'Your aunt told me the only way to prove who was master was to beat you!'

Receiving no reply to this provocative statement, he put a finger under her chin and gently raised it. She stood passive in his embrace, her arms by her side, the tears streaming silently down her cheeks.

'Y—your p—pearl p—pin scratched my n—nose!' she stammered.

For answer, he kissed the tip of the injured feature, her eyes, her trembling parted lips. 'Oh, my darling girl, don't cry!'

'I—I am not crying,' she informed him, with flat disregard for her wet cheeks. 'And please release me, my lord.'

Contrary to obeying this politely worded demand, the Earl kissed her again, long and tenderly. To her utter dismay, Miss Middleton felt her defences crumble under this determined assault, and accepted with shocked resignation the fact that she desired nothing so much as that the present deplorable situation should continue indefinitely.

When at last he left off kissing her, he tucked her head into his shoulder and addressed himself to her left ear.

'To revert to this question of marriage, I think you will agree that your harebrained scheme of having me for a brother-in-law won't fadge.' A slight movement of the rosebuds in her hair he took to be a nod of assent. 'Warburton will do very well for that rôle, I believe. But what to do with me? If I cannot wed Miss Eustacia and you won't have me, my case is desperate indeed. Does the idea of marrying me so disgust you, Verity? Cannot you entertain some little affection for me?'

Miss Middleton had been brought up, in common with most other young women of her social standing, to believe that never should a lady reveal her feelings until the gentleman of her choice had declared himself, and even then sweet womanly complaisance was all that he had a right to expect. So it was with a sort of bewildered disbelief, as if she was standing apart watching two other persons enact the scene, that she drew herself free of his arms and spoke steadily and with dignity.

'My lord, I think I have held you in affection since the day when first we met. I was gathering blackberries at Shurdington and you were riding by with my father. You were not the Earl then,' she added wistfully. 'Just Lord Leo.'

'How well I remember,' he said huskily. 'And how I have longed to hear you speak those words for I have adored you ever since that moment. After you cast me off, I cared little for what happened to me or what I did. That accounted for Miss Ramsay and her like. There'll be no more of them, I promise you. If you'll have me, I'll engage to be a truly conformable husband.'

Miss Middleton knew herself to be defeated and never did the vanquished rejoice more in losing a battle.

'And I undertake to be an obedient and tractable wife,' she whispered.

'That I'll not believe!' The laughter was back in his

voice. 'You'll browbeat me, defy me, read me a curtain-lecture every night on the follies I have committed during the day, while I—' He stopped to kiss her again.

'Oh, Leo, Leo!' she breathed, looking up at him mistily.

'My darling, what have I said now to make you weep?'

'It—it's just that I'm so happy and I don't deserve to be!'

The Earl came to the sensible conclusion that further discussion was clearly unprofitable and set himself the agreeable task of convincing the lady of his utter devotion. In which object, be it said, he succeeded so admirably that Miss Middleton was quite lost to all sense of decorum and reciprocated his sentiments with heartfelt enthusiasm.